P9-CLD-994

TAKING CARE OF CLEO

TAKING CARE OF CLEO

A NOVEL BY BILL BRODER

HANDSEL BOOKS

an imprint of
Other Press • New York

Top photo by Bob Miles, courtesy of the Charlevoix Historical Society, Charlevoix, Michigan.

Production Editor: Mira S. Park

Book design by Natalya Balnova

This book was set in Caslon 540 by Alpha Graphics of Pittsfield, NH.

10 9 8 7 6 5 4 3 2 1

 Printed in the United States of America on acid-free paper. For information write to Other Press LLC, 307 Seventh Avenue, Suite 1807, New York, NY 10001. Or visit our Web site: www.otherpress.com.

Library of Congress Cataloging-in-Publication Data

Broder, Bill, 1931-
Taking care of Cleo : a novel / by Bill Broder.
p. cm.
ISBN 1-59051-213-8 (978-1-59051-213-5) (alk. paper)
1. Young women—Fiction. 2. Yachts—Maintenance and repair—Fiction. 3. Michigan, Lake, Region—Fiction. 4. Autism—Patients—Fiction. 5. Jewish criminals—Fiction. 6. Summer resorts—Fiction. 7. Prohibition—Fiction. 8. Michigan—Fiction. I. Title.
PS3552.R619T35 2006
813'.54—dc22

2005006933

To Gloria

ACKNOWLEDGMENTS

I would like to thank Robert Mezey who suggested this work to Handsel Books; my children, Tanya and Adam, who, with good humor, have borne my addiction to writing; Eleanor and Bill Ratigan, whose love of tales inspired me while writing this book; and Martin Billik, who provided the seed of my plot. I am very grateful to my editor Harry Thomas and my publisher Judith Feher-Gurewich for their excellent suggestions and support and to the staff of Other Press for their enthusiastic aid in bringing this book to publication. I must also acknowledge the glorious landscape surrounding Charlevoix, Michigan.

AUTHOR'S NOTE:

The Purple Gang was an actual gang of Jewish bootleggers, who dominated Detroit crime in the 1920s and early 1930s. They were responsible for a number of murders during this time; many gang members were arrested in the 1930s and sent to prison. The elementary school they attended—the Bishop School—was made up largely of Jewish immigrant children. As adolescents, the gang wore purple jackets to identify themselves—hence their name. They played basketball at the Hannah Schloss Community Center for Jewish immigrants in Detroit. They turned to petty crime while still in high school and during Prohibition they became major criminals. After the Second World War, the survivors of the Purple Gang ended up operating casinos in Las Vegas. One of their reputed early associates came to be a part owner of the Beverly Hills Hotel.

TO BEGIN:

A Few Words by Rebecca Bearwald to Her Family on Her Ninety-fifth Birthday

On my ninety-fifth birthday, I want my children and my grandchildren to understand me a little better than they do. For their sake, I've decided to recount my departure from home at the age of eighteen. That year my family experienced a crisis that exploded the careful order of our affections and left each of us scrambling to find an acceptable way of life.

In my wonder and guilt at the swiftness of my flight from the home and town I loved, I became obsessed with the events leading up to my departure. For the next ten years, every time I visited my parents, I relentlessly questioned them about what had happened during the last winter, spring, and summer I lived in Charlevoix. At first they were reluctant to confide in me—especially my father, a reticent man by nature. My mother was always willing to talk, but she embroidered her account so romantically that I had to torture her to get at the truth. Finally, they became so exasperated by my frantic search that they revealed as much as they knew of their motives and of the suspicions they had nurtured about others. After each interrogation, I took extensive notes and later revised them in an attempt to reconstruct the entire experience. It was as if I had been afflicted with an unnatural growth deep within and could not rid myself of it and move on with my life unless I understood the full dimensions of that family crisis.

When my mother died, I was stunned to find that she had left me a complete diary of that time—an intimate day-by-day report of her feelings about the situation. She was not an accomplished writer, but she had a good eye and she knew her own excesses much better than I had guessed.

So here is my reconstruction of those absurd, comic, and terrifying days. I'm sure my mother and my father would accuse me of distorting our story. But because both were intelligent and loving human beings, they would have read the following pages with interest. I wonder how it all would have worked out if the 18th Amendment prohibiting the sale and consumption of alcohol had not been passed and the country had not chosen to disobey it.

PART ONE

ONE

MY FATHER OWNED THE dry goods store in the small resort and farm town of Charlevoix, Michigan. Charlevoix lay on three lakes: Lake Michigan to the west, Lake Charlevoix to the east, with Round Lake linking them by dredged channels. Prosperous dairy farms and orchards spread out over the surrounding countryside, alternating with forests of birch and pine and hardwood. Elms, oaks, and horse chestnuts lined the streets of the town. The houses were of white clapboard. More than half of them, belonging to summer residents, were shuttered during the fall, winter, and spring.

As Christmas of 1927 approached, the occupied houses of the town sported colorful Christmas lights strung over evergreens on generous front lawns. In living rooms, Christmas trees spread their branches, hung with angels and stars and balls and candles and lights. At the top of Park Avenue, the street just south of the Lake Michigan Channel, our tall Victorian house had no lights on the lawn and no tree in the living room. Instead, in the front bay window, an elaborate electric candlestick with eight high candles topped with frosty, twisted gold lightbulbs, shone out on the world.

At 7:30 in the morning, when my father opened the front door, the frozen lake air blasted in. I clenched my teeth and tightened my stomach for the coming ordeal. The family leaned forward and strode out onto the porch to confront the winter morning darkness. Snow covered the ground; snow rested in clumps upon the limbs of trees; piles of snow to the height of two and a half feet lined the street; and fresh snow came driving in from Lake Michigan, sweeping past the dim street lights which barely cast a small circle of illumination below. Bracing a foot against the storm door, my father pulled the front door closed. After the storm door slammed shut, he offered his arm to my mother and the two led the way down the freshly shoveled front walk. I came next, carrying my school books clasped to my chest. My older sister, Cleo, followed, half a step behind me, clinging to a fold of my coat. At the sidewalk the family paused and turned as one to look at our new golden candlestick in the window.

I had always found warmth and comfort in the image of my family marching through town together every morning. The Bearwalds knew who they were, the town knew the Bearwalds, and I knew who I was. My grandfather had settled here to open Charlevoix's only dry goods store, my father had been born here, and so had my sister and I. Along the street, the houses that belonged to summer people loomed dark and forbidding. From the windows of the occupied houses, warm light streamed out upon the snow as their residents prepared for work and school. The Christmas lights would not be turned on until evening. We were always among the first out on the streets. This morning I felt as if my family resembled the remnants of Napoleon's defeated army fleeing through Russia's cold winter. For the last month, I had been breathlessly reading *War and Peace* late at night after I finished my boring homework. I had recently discovered Tolstoy at the town library where I worked in the afternoons.

As we continued down the street in the dark winter morning, the sight of the boarded-up houses provoked my mother. They were handsome houses—no handsomer than hers of course—belonging to well-to-do, Jewish Detroiters. Several of them would be available for summer-rentals, she knew, but these houses were not good enough for her brother and sister-in-law, who had always stayed in rented rooms before. Perfectly adequate houses, she thought. Not that she wanted her brother and his family so close by. She knew why Maureen preferred Michigan Avenue. Maureen was jealous because Henry was a Bearwald and the Bearwalds were an important family in Detroit—German-Jews, like the Michigan Avenue crowd, some of whom were even distant cousins of Henry.

Absorbed in her thoughts, my mother did not notice the pharmacist, Jim Morris, fiddling with the key in the lock of his store door. The door was already open, but he lingered outside waiting for us. Jim Morris prided himself upon the most up-to-date knowledge on every subject from vitamins to politics. He specialized in the private lives of our fellow townspeople. He liked to begin each day by imparting a tidbit of information to my parents.

He tipped his hat to us.

"Morning, Jim," said my father.

"Morning, Hank, Belle, kids," said Jim. "Right on time." He patted his stomach where his watch lay securely in his watch pocket. "You know what they say about regular habits—"

My mother smiled briefly and hurried us along. Anyone who paused for a moment beside the pharmacist became engaged in an interminable, jocular conversation full of references to natural functions.

Jim Morris took a step out onto the pavement so that we had to detour around him. "Mrs. Thrush and her—" his eyebrows darted up and down, "'sister,' appear not to know the difference between night and day."

At this mention of my study hall counselor and her sister, I hesitated. Cleo ran into me and uttered a short cry.

"Rebecca! Cleo!" Mother was fond of the pharmacist's thick eyebrows, the way the blinking of his large round eyes punctuated his lectures. But on this cold morning she had no desire to dawdle outside—not even to hear his latest sly musings about Mrs. Thrush. Before we reached the store, the family was greeted by Tom Tolliver, the president of the bank, Vernon Hayes, the sheriff, and the mayor, Dwayne Snow, the town's only realtor. My father was "Hank" to all of them, my mother was "Belle," and Cleo and I were "the kids."

My father returned the greetings enthusiastically. Although he often made fun of the unvarying rituals of our small town, he needed continuous assurance that he belonged in this improbable place where he had been born. I found it difficult to understand his insecurity—to believe he had any doubts. He was, after all, a member of the Rotary, the Elks, the Knights of Pythias, the Chamber of Commerce, and a number of other town organizations. Many of the dignitaries of the town or their fathers had known his father before there had been a Bearwald store—known him when he had traveled through these parts with a horse and a wagon and sold his dry goods off the tailgate.

Tom Tolliver opened the morning newspaper and showed the headlines to my father: GANGLAND WAR; TRUCKS COLLIDE NEAR GRAYLING; EXECUTION STYLE MURDER IN FORESTVILLE. "Bootleggers again," said Mr. Tolliver, with a grin.

My father nodded sympathetically. I had the sense he did not quite know how to respond. "If they'd only stay down in the big cities."

The banker laughed. "Well, even us hicks up here need our booze."

"With this weather," replied my father, "you can't blame us."

Tolliver clapped my father on the back and we went on. At the store, my father paused, as he always did, to look up at the front of the building that he owned. "BEARWALD" announced handsome Gothic letters chiseled in stone across the front. In similar script a sign at the base of the window repeated: "Bearwald's, Clothing for the Entire Family." The prominent display of his family name disconcerted my father. At the same time, he took a secret and wry pride in this proof of his existence.

As we did every day, the family examined the two broad window displays. The display to the left of the door featured winter work scenes with Men's sheep-lined genuine horsehide leather coats, $15 and $18 values for only $11.98; Boys' moleskin coats with wide sheep-lined collars for $5.57; Men's sweaters at $3.89; and Men's 12-pound union suits, ecru-ribbed, long sleeves, ankle-length, at the low price of 89 cents. The display to the right offered dressier Sunday clothes, clothes for the town and city. Suits for young men, with two and three buttons including two pairs of trousers on sale for $24.75—suits in semi-English modes, pure cashmere in various shades of gray with fancy stripes and herringbone weaves. The window also featured silk frocks, economically priced; novelty hose for Misses and Women; and heavier hose for outdoors wear.

In the right window display, my father allowed my mother to offer a few items that would interest only the wealthiest clients: Women's winter coats, for example, in modish styles, trimmed in fur. Mother had worked late the night before to complete a new display with newspaper advertisements that she had composed mounted in front of the models. "*Women everywhere are wearing these wraparound and side-closing styles. The flattery of furs makes these coats most attractive and youthfully charming. Elaborately furred borders and tab treatments of fur are distinctive details of these new coats.*" A few expensive dresses completed the display. "*Charming new frocks for daytime and evening wear,*" my mother wrote. "*Here Milady will find the smartest Paris-sponsored models for every winter occasion featuring newest fashion trends and coloring. Developed of crepe satin, flat crepe, crepe romaine velvet, and combinations in colors proclaimed ultrasmart for the season's wear.*"

My father looked at my mother, looked at me to make sure I appreciated her talent, and then back at the window. All the clothes were arranged cleverly as if invisible people were enjoying their work and leisure. A truly creative woman, he thought with satisfaction, and then frowned. He knew his wife was not happy with her lot.

Cleo and I waited patiently to receive the embraces which would send us off alone into the world. Mother hugged us first with a theatrical clutch and wet smack of the lips. Then Father leaned over us, restrained and dry, but concentrated. I returned the kisses with fervor, guilty for my disloyal thoughts about our family's isolated situation in town; Cleo, as always, cringed, turned, and lowered her head so that our parents' lips landed low on the back of her head. She found it painful to be touched by anyone other than me.

"Your cheek, Cleo, your cheek!" Mother demanded.

"Every day, Momma?" I protested, catching my father's eye. We shared a certain exasperation with Mother's excesses.

"Come into the store, Arabella!" commanded my father.

Not to be deterred, my mother grasped my older sister's chin and held her head upright while she planted a wet kiss on the cheek near the mouth. Cleo's brilliant black eyes fastened, stricken, on the storefront. "Now you must kiss me back, Cleo."

"Let the girls go," said my father, annoyed.

I turned away, unwilling to witness the scene.

"Cleo!" Mother pulled Cleo's chin forward and inclined her cheek, until Cleo's lips touched her skin. Cleo flinched. When Mother released her, she leaped away to her habitual position half a step behind me, holding onto my coat. As Cleo and I marched down the street, my mother watched, brooding. Only when we crossed to the park did she enter the store to join my father for the day's work.

The park was bounded by the town's main street on one side and by Round Lake on the other. For most of the year, the small lake served as a harbor for pleasure and fishing boats, for larger ships seeking refuge from storms, and for a ferry boat that took passengers and cars to Beaver Island, some thirty miles out in Lake Michigan. Round Lake's shores were lined with wharves and boathouses. Today a sheet of blue-gray ice covered the lake. The wind had cleared the lake of snow. The docks were empty of boats. I paused for a moment to take in the scene to the east—all whites and blacks and grays: delicate pencil lines, deep pen slashes, broad brush strokes, smudges, and blobs on a white canvas. The black frame of the railroad trestle bridge, across the channel to Lake Charlevoix, stood out boldly against the brilliant white backdrop of the frozen lake. Delicate mantles of snow decorated the dark needled canopies of the pines near the shore and the finely etched branches of hardwood forests that clothed the rising land on either side of the lake. The beauty of the landscape in which I had been born filled me with uneasy remorse. How could I yearn to flee such a place?

Cleo broke away and raced down the hillside toward a park bench on which two friends of ours sat—John and Ruth Clover.

I marveled at my sister's grace. As she leaped through the deep snow in great, sure-footed strides, her odd voice trilled out a wild, happy sound which ceased as she arrived at the bench. There she turned, sat down without the slightest greeting to the couple, and put out her hands, her eyes staring straight forward. Ruth Clover set a bun in one hand and John placed a full cup of coffee in the other. Steam from the cup rose in slow wisps into the air. Cleo dipped the bun into the coffee and chewed on it, her face expressionless.

Ruth and John Clover were full-blooded Ottawa Indians, members of a dwindling local Indian colony. John had been one of the two town postmen. But one day three months ago he had handed his keys, key chain, and leather bag to the postmaster without a word and had come to this bench. Now, every morning, he arrived at the bench before dawn and remained until dark. His wife Ruth, a teller at the Charlevoix National Bank, brought breakfast and lunch every day and ate with him. Their eight children visited John whenever they passed through town. No one could understand why John, with only a year and a half left before retirement, had quit. The townspeople were too diffident to ask him face to face—he was such a private man—but they did question Ruth. "He has his reasons," she replied, smiling, "good reasons."

As I approached the bench, I thought how much my sister resembled the Clovers—shining black hair and eyes, vividly etched eyebrows, high cheekbones, burnished dark skin, and a calm, patient expression that revealed nothing. My mother, too, resembled the Clovers. I looked like my father's side of the family—fair skin, soft, reddish hair, freckles, gray-green eyes, and small, fine features. "Redheaded Jews!" Mother always said, with some pride. "A lost tribe of converts, I'll bet."

"Morning, Clovers," I said. The Clovers offered me a cup of coffee and a bun. I refused politely. "Have to get to school."

And Cleo has to get to work, I thought, but my sister continued to dip her bun and to munch very slowly.

"Come on Cleo, Mr. Weyrich is counting on you."

Cleo stared deeply into her coffee cup.

"Please."

John Clover leaned over and took hold of Cleo's coffee cup. Cleo gripped the cup tighter. "Now Cleo," said John in a low voice, "you listen to your sister." Slowly Cleo's fingers released the cup.

"You have to get to work, Cleo," said Ruth Clover, putting her hand under Cleo's elbow. Reluctantly, Cleo rose and marched along the wharf ahead of me. I followed, shouting back over my shoulder, "Thanks, Clovers."

"Study hard, Rebecca!" Ruth called out.

"Smart girl," said John.

"Good girls, both of them," said Ruth.

Just beyond the park stood a pair of large yellow clapboard boat-houses with the name, "WEYRICH BOATYARD," printed in bold letters on the side facing the lake. At the end of a working dock complete with chain pulleys, cleats', capstans, bollards, and davits stood a bright red gasoline pump. Cleo reached a small door in the largest of the yellow buildings and turned around, jumping up and down impatiently. I hurried to her side. She thrust out a hand and I placed a large key in it. Holding the key high in the air, she approached the door and unlocked it. She placed it back in my hand with a grand gesture. I put the key into my pocket and remained waiting in front of my sister. Solemnly, Cleo placed her hands upon my shoulders and kissed me on the cheek. I tried to return the kiss, but before my lips touched my sister's cheek Cleo leaped back and darted into the boathouse, uttering her strange cry of delight.

Smiling, I marched up the hill to the corner where two of my girlfriends, Sandy Murphy and Barbara Sneavely, waited. Sandy and I had founded the French Club the year before and spent hours together dreaming of how we would live in Paris. Barbara, who had been going with the same boy since the eighth grade, thought our talk racy and tantalizing. My friends and I linked arms and the three of us crossed the main street in step with one another. I could hardly keep from dancing, so relieved was I to leave my sister behind for the day. No one suspected my feelings. If anyone had guessed, I would have been ashamed.

Before we reached school, Sandy told us that Jim Morris had reported to her father that he had seen Mrs. Thrush chasing her sister down South Point Road in the snow at midnight the night before. Both were wearing fur coats over their night clothes and seemed more than a little drunk. As always, Jim Morris insisted that the woman Mrs. Thrush lived with was not her sister.

TWO

ONE AFTERNOON SHORTLY BEFORE winter vacation, as I walked down the hall on my way out of school, Mrs. Thrush stepped out of her office and fell in step with me.

"Rebecca," Mrs. Thrush said, "have you given any thought to which college you're going to apply?"

I walked several paces before I realized what Mrs. Thrush had said. Even though I allowed myself to dream of a life of my own in some large city far away, like the heroes and heroines of my novels, I dismissed these yearnings as even less real than the fiction within the covers of my books. I assumed that I would spend the rest of my life in Charlevoix, close to my family.

"But I hadn't even thought of going to college."

"I'm not surprised," she replied. "You have no idea who you are." She reached into her briefcase, removed an envelope, and handed it to me. It was labeled, "Application, University of Michigan." I looked up in surprise at the small, fierce, sharp-faced lady. Mrs. Thrush turned and walked on.

I hurried after her, down the steps and to the street where her car was parked. "Do you think I should go to college, Mrs. Thrush?"

The teacher stared at me, her gray eyes flat disks, her thin mouth clenched. Without replying, she slid into the car and drove off, leaving me standing there, my hand to my hot cheek.

No one at school liked Mrs. Thrush. She was harsh and distant. She had worked at the school for only two years as a counselor. She was so smart and sarcastic that she terrified even the teachers. There were all sorts of rumors about her past, but Mr. Scott, the principal, said only that she was more than qualified to counsel the students. Jim Morris gossiped that her credentials were too good and that she had left her last job under a cloud of suspicion. She lived with her sister out in Boulder Park in one of the new stone cottages Dwayne Snow had built for summer visitors. Mrs. Tolliver, the banker's wife who was on the school board, said that the district was lucky to have her on the staff.

I walked home in a daze, my thoughts scrambled. Mrs. Thrush's words continued to resound in my mind: "You have no idea who you are." The image of Mrs. Thrush drunkenly chasing her "supposed" sister down the snowy road—both of them in fur coats over night clothes—added an unsettling excitement to my mood.

A few of my classmates planned to go on with their schooling after graduation. I thought of college as a luxury which only the wealthy could afford. I had been working since the age of ten—first at our store and then as a babysitter, a house-cleaner, and a waitress. Before I discovered Tolstoy, I had been reading Lincoln Steffens and Upton Sinclair who revealed to me the terrible injustices suffered under capitalism. In fact, I had pretty much cast my lot with the working class. College implied privilege, a grasping at power over others which, as a socialist, I rejected. And there was my family to consider. What would happen to them if I left home?

During supper, I looked around the table, wondering if my family had any better idea of my identity than I had. I excused myself as soon as I finished my dessert and left the house. Slowly I made my way out to the end of the pier. The black waves dashed themselves upon the concrete footing, sweeping down the channel toward the highway bridge and Round Lake. I held onto the trestle of the lighthouse pyramid, leaned out to feel the wind and the spray. Above me, the beacon sent its message in an arc, encompassing our house at the top of the hill, the town, North and South Points, and the dark expanse of the western horizon. That intermittent brilliance seemed to promise me a rich adventurous life, far away.

The next day I went to see Mrs. Thrush for help in filling out my application.

*

On the last night of Chanukah, my mother left work at three to begin preparations for a festive meal. Father closed the store an hour early so that he could say his afternoon and evening prayers before lighting the candles. Even though he lived miles from a proper Jewish community, he observed the rituals of Judaism. He donned the phylacteries every morning, just as his father had; said his afternoon, evening, and Sabbath prayers; kept the Sabbath as well as he could; and studied the Talmud.

Only my mother and I understood the spirit in which he practiced his religion. Even as he repeated the many required prayers in praise of God, he watched and judged his Lord with the same irony with which he watched and judged himself and his fellow man. When he thanked God for the blessing of life, he demanded an accounting for injustice and human suffering. To my father, God's liabilities appeared to be balanced perfectly with his assets: God's malicious, wanton willfulness with his generosity. The more strictly my father observed, the more severely he judged his God. Because he lived so far from a kosher butcher, he did not demand that Mother keep a kosher house. Nonetheless, we used separate sets of meat and milk dishes and silverware and ate no pork. Of course, he had to open the store on Saturday, because Saturday was the big shopping day for farmers. In keeping with the Sabbath laws, though, on Saturdays hired help turned the lights on and off and handled the money.

My mother, who took religious matters casually, cooperated. She claimed it was my father's isolation that inspired him to resist the laxity of his cousins to the south. When she felt annoyed with him, she called his religious practice simple stubbornness.

Father's greatest regret was that he could not attend a regular Jewish service. He believed that a constant communion with fellow worshippers might have taken the edge off the bitter humor with which he viewed God's works. He yearned for a few moments of simple joy in the blessings of life so that occasionally he could sing God's praises without equivocation.

Father never discussed these matters with me, nor did he suspect that I understood his attitude toward God. He didn't talk much and never about himself. Mother often complained that the men in her life had little to say—her father, her brother, her husband—all silent men. She needed conversation as much as she needed food or even air to breathe. She, of course, talked a great deal about everything. From my earliest years, I remember her long disquisitions upon my father's character and his attitudes. I was very young when she first told me how sad my father felt that he had no son to whom he could impart his love of the Torah and Jewish ritual, to whom he could pass on his store and his standing in the town of Charlevoix, and with whom he might possibly share his ironic judgment of life. As I grew older, I didn't need my mother's conversation to teach me this bitter lesson. I, too, wanted to put on the phylacteries, to pray, and study the Talmud. But my father would not yield to my pleading. When I pressed him for an explanation, he would repeat the simple observation that men and women played different roles in Judaism. If I spoke of taking over the store, he only laughed and remarked that he could not wait to teach my future husband his trade. My father was always loving, generous, and kind to my sister and to me, but it was obvious that we had been born the wrong gender.

In the darkened living room, Father lit the *shammas* candle and held it in the air. Together, the family intoned their prayers, first in Hebrew and then in English:

"Blessed art Thou, O Lord our God, King of the Universe,

Who has sanctified us with Thy commandments and has commanded us to light the Chanukah candles.

"Blessed art Thou, O Lord our God, King of the Universe, Who has done miracles for our fathers in bygone days at this time of year."

Now Father lit the first of eight orange candles set in a shapely antique silver candlestick. Intently, the family watched the flame transfer its power from the wick of the *shammas* candle to the first candle. My father handed the *shammas* to my mother, who lit the next two candles. She then handed the *shammas* to Cleo. A low sound of distress came from deep within Cleo's throat. Her mouth clenched, her brows beetled down over her eyes, and her hand began to tremble. My parents hunched as if they were about to receive a blow. My hand shot out to clasp Cleo's hand so that the candle would not fall. My parents relaxed. They knew that if the candle had fallen from Cleo's hand, she would have gone into one of her frenzied tantrums.

My father bitterly resented the tyranny of his eldest daughter's fits: the piercing howl, the twitching limbs, rolling eyes, frothing mouth, and then the deliberate smashing of that lovely head against wall, floor, table. It seemed as if some primal, filthy aspect of life were being revealed—just for us—a terrible indictment of the family.

With my fingers around hers, Cleo touched the flame to the rest of the candles, one by one. My parents glanced at one another and shrugged: they could never predict when a simple task might intimidate their eldest daughter. Usually, she was more skillful and confident with her hands than anyone else in the family. As each successive candle added its light to the brightness of the room, Cleo's mouth spread with pleasure, her eyes widened with awe. Eight flickering arrows of light were mirrored in her great dark pupils. In the faces of the family, Cleo's delight found an answering reflection of joy.

"Thank you, Lord," said my father silently, "for giving us this strange, miraculous child."

This gratitude cost him great effort, for Cleo had been an overwhelming burden on the family from her earliest years. Physically, she was a wonder of beauty and agility. But mentally, emotionally—the mystery of Cleo's anguished mind took us to the limits of endurance. Often in the last twenty years my father had reviled God, demanding to know why he tortured poor Cleo and her family. At this moment of ritual, however, my father abandoned his irony for a moment. He basked in Cleo's awe and delight and forced himself to thank the Lord.

"Well, let's get on with the meal," said Mother with an impatient snort.

I glanced irritably at her. Cleo put her hands over her ears.

"No," replied Father. "For at least an hour, we should take joy in the light of the candles and do no work. That's what the first letters of Chanukah mean—'and they rested,' rejoicing in the miracle of the light of God's teaching."

"I'll rest after dinner," said Mother.

"*Pirsum hanes*," Father let the Hebrew words roll off his tongue, grinning at his wife's discomfort, "by lighting the candles we publish God's miracle—you shouldn't hurry off now when we are all taken by delight."

Perhaps, thought Father, it added up to this: by granting an instant of peace and worship to the troubled souls of Cleo and her family, God displayed His mystery and His glory. A small miracle, he reasoned, to remind us how the Lord kept the sacred lamp burning for eight days in the Temple when there had been only one day's worth of oil left after the heathen's defilement.

"Come on, girls," urged Mother, who could sense her husband's mind working away behind his cover of amused silence. "We'll let the man of the house rest with his menorah and his deep thoughts."

"And the presents?" I asked, glancing slyly at my father.

Father nodded and coughed to signify that he appreciated my stratagem.

"The presents!" Mother stopped in mid-stride, registering the look of complicity between her daughter and her husband. "How on earth could I have forgotten the most important thing?" She rolled her eyes and made a face, mocking herself. My father and Cleo laughed. I watched Mother, exasperated by her performance even though I had deliberately provoked it. "You know how much I love giving gifts," Mother hugged herself, "and, even better, receiving them!" My father and Cleo applauded.

Everyone went off to closets and drawers where the gifts had been hidden and came back into the living room. Before the first gift could be opened, the telephone rang. Mother warned the family that they better not open one gift before she returned. Then she went to the pantry to answer.

Father, Cleo, and I contemplated the candles. We were grateful for the quiet moment. Cleo smiled, lost in the life of the flickering flames. A distant look of contentment settled upon my father's face as he pictured the eternal lamp—God's metaphor for His Word, the Torah, the Five Books of Moses, The Law.

The lamp mounted over the Torah's ark had burned for seven days in the wasted Temple in spite of the absence of oil. For Father that lamp burned just as improbably in Charlevoix. His one article of absolute faith consisted in his belief in the rule of law. His pride in Judaism rested upon the Jewish invention of the concept of written law; his pride in the United States lay in the fact that it was a country ruled by written laws.

I watched my father and sister and wished that I too could lose myself in the candles. Instead, I saw only the image of Mother's pantomime of greed. Annoyed by her voracious appetite, I tried to argue myself into a better mood. The magnanimous spirit of the warm candles rebuked me. I should be grateful for Mother's liveliness. Without her vivacious moods and extravagant gestures, life would be very solemn and dull.

In the pantry, Mother answered the phone. It was Uncle Sy calling long distance to wish us a happy holiday. Mother rendered this conversation and the following ones with Sy and his wife almost word for word in her diary, commenting guiltily how sad she felt at the wreckage her "white lies" later wrought.

At first their talk proceeded normally with good-natured sparring. Uncle Sy called my mother "Bella," though she had changed her name to "Arabella" at the age of six. Mother bragged about my father's prominent German-Jewish family. Uncle Sy retaliated by reminding her that her husband had settled her in a small town three hundred miles north of Detroit where we were the only year-round Jewish residents. Mother replied that Detroit, where Uncle Sy lived, was a very ordinary city. She concluded her case by remarking that Sy's wife had not even been born in the United States and that her true name was Malkeh, not Maureen.

Uncle Sy then asked a curious question: "Say Bella, you didn't happen to hear about an accident involving a couple of trucks over near Grayling, did you?"

"Why are you asking?"

"Some friends of mine were interested. I told them you wouldn't have any information."

"Oh, you think your sister doesn't know anything, is that it?"

"I'm sorry I asked."

"Well I know a lot more than you think about what's going on. And I know who your friends are, Sy Lefkowitz."

"You got a big mouth, Bella. Here's Maureen."

Uncle Sy turned the phone over to Aunt Maureen, who surprised Mother with the news that they were calling from Florida. "Every day the sun is shining, the palm trees are waving, and there's a dock with a cabin cruiser right at the house of Sy's client who invited us—all of us—down for the holiday."

Mother replied gamely, "I know all about Sy's clients—you think I didn't go to the Bishop School too? I used to watch him play basketball at the Hannah Schloss with them—the Purples, the Sugar House Gang. And I know where their money comes from too."

"Shuuushshshsh!" Maureen's voice dropped to a whisper. "You shouldn't talk like that on the phone, Bella. You never know who's listening in. It's not our phone."

"So! I've never been afraid to speak my mind." Mother grinned as though she had regained the upper hand.

"Sy is a legitimate businessman. We're getting to know the better crowd in Detroit."

"A better crowd of bootleggers?"

"We've been asked to join the Great Lakes Club. Our Seymour—he's almost a lawyer—is dating the Weintraub girl. Her father's the president of the Jewish Community Center. And just so you won't be lonely up there in the North Woods, we're coming to your beautiful little resort for five weeks this summer—all of us—and I want a house."

"You already told me. What's wrong with the rooms you've been taking all these years?"

"And not just any house. Like I said, I want one on the north end of town where all those fancy German Jews from Cincinnati, Chicago, St. Louis have their summer homes—on Michigan Avenue, by the big lake."

"Did Sy discover a gold mine or something?"

"He's doing very well. We'll be entertaining. Sy's clients will be up in your neck of the woods and they want him nearby."

"If you think for one moment that those fine folks on Michigan Avenue from St. Louis, Chicago, and Cincinnati will have anything to do with you Detroiters—besides, those houses don't come cheap."

"We'll pay whatever we have to. We plan to show you a lively time this summer. After all, life with Henry—"

"I don't need any favors, Maureen. We have plenty of connections of our own. Henry's no slouch."

"Studious is the way I'd put it, and careful."

"Careful? That's a laugh."

"He lets his fancy Detroit family step all over him."

"Henry's more adventurous than you think. He's got a lot of irons in the fire, and fires under boilers."

"Boilers? What are you talking about?"

"I'm talking about territory"—Mother hesitated and then plunged ahead—"Michigan, Wisconsin, Minnesota, the Dakotas —the whole Northwest Territory. If you want to know what I mean, ask your husband what happened to his friends' trucks over near Grayling."

"Henry's a decent guy, but—"

"He's an *éminence grise*—"

"I suppose you got that from one of your correspondence courses."

"What's wrong with trying to improve oneself?"

"So say it in English."

"Henry's a gray eminence—he works behind the scenes. His operations—"

"I don't know what you're talking about, but if it's what I think it is, I don't believe it, and you shouldn't be talking about it over this telephone. I'm going to hang up now."

As a little girl, I admired Mother's invention. Often, when she read to my sister and me at bedtime, she would lay down the book, gaze out the window toward the lighthouse and the lake beyond, and embroider a tale in which we were the main characters. She took us to Paris, Moscow, Constantinople, and the Orient. She sent us up high mountains and across vast deserts. We always began in hovels and ended in grand palaces. Only when I grew old enough to read novels did I begin to understand the desperation of my mother's romantic yearnings. I was eighteen years old and a senior in high school in December of 1927, when my mother bragged to her brother about her husband's "far-flung empire." Even later in life, I found it difficult to imagine that her innocent fibs could lead us into so much trouble.

THREE

AFTER THE CALL FROM Florida, Mother went into the kitchen to check on the progress of the holiday dinner. My father passed through the kitchen on his way to the basement to stoke the furnace. Mother stood next to the open stove, stirring the matzoh ball soup. An intermittent brightness from the lighthouse flashed across the dark frosted window. Gazing through the strip of clear glass above the frost, she could barely make out the steep white slope that led to the Lake Michigan Channel. Momentarily, the flashing light illuminated the pier, piled high with wind-twisted snow and ice. My mother hated the long torture of these northern winters.

Mother rendered her private thoughts eloquently in her diary. She enjoyed her moments alone in the kitchen, warming herself before the open stove as she cooked and imagined a grander life. Tonight she was troubled by the telephone conversation during which she had misrepresented her husband. Stirring vigorously, she frowned and her lower lip puffed with discontent at the thought of her sister-in-law's bragging and her own response.

Catching her reflection in the frosted glass, she thought, Almost forty years old and still not bad looking. With pleasure she examined her unblemished olive skin, black hair, shining black eyes, vividly etched brows cocked at a mocking angle, and wide mouth turned up with humor. A dark beauty, her husband declared. Holding the wooden spatula in the air, Mother placed her other hand on her hip and twirled around, tapping her heels like a Spanish dancer. An impulsive woman, she thought, eager for experience, with a full bosom, slender waist, and long, slim legs. How had she ended up here in this dull northern resort town that came to life for only two summer months a year?

Outside, the snow absorbed all sound. To Mother, it seemed as if each house existed in sad isolation from the other houses of the town, from the stores and schools and small county buildings, from the surrounding farms, and from highways that led to the Straits of Mackinac fifty miles north and to Detroit, two hundred and eighty miles south.

My father appeared from the basement, meticulous in his suit, his white, starched cuffs just visible, and his rimless spectacles gleaming. Pale, slim, scholarly, he wasted no movements as he strode up to the sink and began to scrub his hands. Mother knew he would remain before the sink for exactly sixty seconds, about forty-five seconds longer than necessary. Then he would dry his hands for twenty seconds. She tried to control her annoyance by reminding herself what a good husband he was, a good father, an excellent citizen, and even a very satisfactory lover. Although Henry was twelve years older than she, well into middle age, she still thought him very attractive. Even in her later years, my mother made a point of stressing my father's erotic abilities. This talent of his seemed to puzzle her.

After he had folded the towel precisely and hung it back on the cupboard door, he touched her briefly and gently on her buttocks, an intimacy he allowed himself only when they were alone. Mother leaned in toward his spare body, her discontent evaporating. His orderliness contained within it a comforting power that his secret passion enforced. My parents' eyes met in the window's reflection. My father's right eye squinted, his spare mouth narrowed to the right and lifted in an amused irony with which he judged the world. Mother felt privileged to be allowed a glimpse into this private man's thoughts. She turned her head and nipped his neck slightly with her teeth. After all, her little lie about Henry had not been all that serious—hardly a lie, really, an implication, an enticement for her sister-in-law's imagination. Neither Maureen nor Sy, for that matter, had ever appreciated Henry Bearwald's true qualities.

As Mother basted the chicken, she smiled. She had given Maureen something to chew on for the rest of the winter. And besides, Henry Bearwald was, in fact, no slouch. He could easily have been the brains behind any number of important enterprises, if he had any ambition. Standing in the kitchen, stirring the dinner soup, Mother imagined herself the wife of a prominent gangster, so wealthy and powerful that an entire empire of violent crime awaited the slightest squint of that gray-green eye shielded behind its rimless glass, the slightest downturn of that neat, narrow mouth.

Her lies had done no harm, she reassured herself. But she had gone too far. There had been fear in Maureen's voice just before she had hung up. Maureen's caution made sense. She had called from the house of a man who thought nothing of killing his rivals. My mother had read it all in the newspapers: the Purple Gang machine-gunned men in apartment buildings, they blew up stores, they kidnapped families and assaulted them.

Who could believe that those boys who had played basketball at the community center had turned into gangsters—wealthy gangsters—and clients of her brother?

The phone rang. It was her sister-in-law Maureen again.

"On Michigan Avenue, remember."

"How could I forget?"

"For five weeks. And we'd prefer it on the lake side. Sy's clients like the privacy of their own beach."

"No kidding."

"If your husband is such a big operator as you let on, I shouldn't have to draw pictures."

Mother slammed down the telephone and stalked out into the living room. She stopped in the center of the room and fixed an accusing glare upon her husband and two daughters who sat together on the edge of the sofa, gifts stacked in front of them. "Do you realize," she announced, "that I'm going to be forty years old and I have very little to look forward to. Forty years old, Henry! You'll be fifty-three. And what do we have?"

"Aren't we going to open the gifts?" I asked.

"For years you've been putting our gold away in that safety deposit box—"

"Mother, please don't start on that tonight." I could not bear my mother's campaign to expand the business. She always exaggerated the family's resources.

She ignored me, addressing her remarks to Father. "—gold that could be used to start a chain of Bearwald stores—like your uncles and your cousins. The country is prospering and we're not sharing in that prosperity."

"It won't last," said Father.

"Everybody's richer and more comfortable—"

"That doesn't make them any happier," I said, standing up.

"—traveling to Florida, renting big summer houses, joining fancy clubs. And look at us."

"Wretched, deprived, poverty stricken," I said, embracing my mother.

"Go to Russia, Rebecca, and you'll see that socialism isn't very charming."

"Sit down, Momma." I led her to the large easy chair by the fireplace. "It's time for presents."

Mother let me sit her down. "I'm going to be forty." Mother trembled with frustration.

I smoothed her brow and then put my hands over her eyes. "Now, Daddy! Bring it in."

"Henry," said Mother, her eyes still covered, "I want you to talk to Uncle Adolf and Cousin Rudy about opening a branch in Palm Beach next year."

My father peered at my mother. His sardonic gaze met mine. I turned my head. I did not want to know what he was thinking. The more I understood about my family, the more I felt obliged to resolve their discords. At the same time, I had my own argument with each of them.

Father left the room and returned wheeling an object the size of a small table, wrapped in colorful wrapping paper. He placed the object in front of my mother who resumed her speech. "The summer people will be impressed—we'll have all the latest styles—and the folks around here will benefit too. We'll hire someone to run this store in the winter, while we—"

"Happy Chanukah!" I exclaimed, drowning out her demands. I removed my hands from Mother's eyes and went to stand next to my father. Cleo joined us, her arm just touching mine.

Mother's regarded the large, poorly wrapped package. The paper overlapped itself, the ribbon drooped. My mother's face relaxed. A smile started at the edges of her lips. "Whoever bandaged the patient did the poor thing in."

My resentment faded. I laughed and then felt odd that my mother could still charm me.

Mother peered at one corner and then at another.

"Open it, open it," I said. Cleo picked up the last note of my voice and howled in key. Her body twitched about. My hand crept around Cleo's back, patting it gently. Cleo's voice trailed off; her movements slowed.

"I don't want to spoil the fun," said my mother and slowly began to peel away the wrapping paper, exposing a gleaming new Singer sewing machine.

"The latest model," said my father.

I stepped forward to show the printed manual and the various attachments. “See, it’s got its own cabinet and bench, blond wood, Hollywood style.” I pulled out the bench.

Mother got up and sat upon the bench. Slowly she ran her hands over the machine, studying the mechanism, feeling the gleaming metal plate and the waxed wood.

“Do you like it?” I asked.

“Thank you, Henry,” said Mother, lifting her head toward my father who bent to receive her kiss. “It’s very beautiful.”

“And look what we’ve given you.” I nudged Cleo who turned and picked up three colorfully wrapped packages from the couch. Together, we held the packages toward Mother.

She opened the packages one by one. Each was a different fashion magazine with a colorful card pasted to the cover. “Subscriptions to your three favorite magazines—so you can see the styles and copy them,” I said.

“Styles of the decadent bourgeois?” she asked, with a shrewd smile.

“I didn’t think overalls would suit you.”

She stood up and hugged me. “You’re a generous soul, in spite of your political preaching.”

She turned to Cleo. “Thank you Cleo.” She smiled, but did not try to kiss her. “You worked hard for my gift, I know.” To her astonishment, Cleo leaned her cheek forward toward Mother’s lips. She kissed Cleo’s cheek. Tears came to Mother’s eyes. “Your cheek is the best gift.”

The family milled around the sewing machine, embarrassed. Mother began to leaf through the sample fashion magazines, pointing out costumes that she would make for us and for herself. "This summer we'll be the best dressed women in town, girls, and next fall, too, in Detroit."

"Detroit?" asked Father.

"Next fall?" I asked.

FOUR

"AND NOW FOR MY gift to my husband," announced Mother. "It isn't much," she went to her purse and extracted an ordinary envelope which she handed to my father with a casual flick of the wrist. He opened the envelope. Within, he found family tickets to both the Reform Temple Emmanuel and the Conservative Beth Abraham Synagogue in Detroit for the coming year's High Holy Days.

"Oh," he said, sitting down. Already he could hear the sound of the ram's horn and the glorious tenor of the cantor announcing the New Year. He remained for a moment, entranced. Then he jumped up and threw his arms around Mother, lifting her off her feet. He set her down slowly, without letting go of her. "A truly wonderful gift."

"You see," said Mother, "I knew he'd be happy." He buried his face into her hair, kissing her neck. "Henry!"

He released her, smiling sheepishly around at us. He

examined the tickets. "But why both the temple and the synagogue?"

Mother cast a long, seductive look at me. "Rebecca will graduate this June. This next year will be the most important in her life. I want everyone in Detroit to see what a wonderful daughter we have."

My parents smiled at one another—as if my future were at their disposal.

"Mo—Mother, Father—" They turned, taken aback at being addressed so formally. "The counselor at school said that I might have a good chance at—for a scholarship."

"A scholarship?" Mother looked bewildered.

"To the University of Michigan."

"You want to go to college?" My parents spoke in unison, their voices strained.

Cleo had become very still. She listened intently, her black eyes fixed upon me as if she could see into my mind.

"Yes, I do."

"I thought you were a worker," said Mother. "And besides, college is no place for a girl. Isn't that so Henry?"

"Well, well—" my father mumbled, but did not continue.

"But Daddy, I'd have a scholarship, maybe." My father would not meet my eye.

"Henry!" Mother challenged.

Father bowed his head and obeyed his wife's demand. He stammered as he spoke. "You have to understand, Rebecca, that boys and girls, men and women, that is, have different—different functions in life."

"You will soon be ready for marriage," said Mother.

Appalled, I blurted out, "You mean the clothes, the synagogue, the temple—" Mother had talked about my marriage since I was a little girl. But until this moment, all of her talk had seemed to be just another one of her romantic fairy tales. "Men get married too."

"But they have to earn a living."

"Momma works in the store." I could not think clearly. My plans for the future seemed ludicrous.

"You don't understand. College is very expensive—"

"Of course, if I didn't get the scholarship, well—I wouldn't expect—" I mumbled, my eyes on the dining room windows, waiting for the flash from the beacon at the end of the pier.

"Why haven't you said anything before this?" Mother spoke sharply, but her anger had within it a note of pleading.

Ashamed, I nodded. "I should have—I'm to blame—it's my fault." Of course, I was not all that certain that I ought to go to college. Marriage, however, had not entered my mind.

"But women have children," said my father. "They raise the children, keep the house—they help the needy, volunteer in the community, aid in education—what they do is very important, essential."

I seized upon the issue. "You mean that if I were your son, you would send me to college?"

"Oh Rebecca." He examined me with a searching glance. He too realized that the argument was irrelevant.

"You say you believe in education, Daddy."

"Not that you couldn't take courses, and read on your own—my mother was a very well-educated woman and she never even went through high school." He cast a helpless look at me and then at Mother.

She ended the discussion with an emphatic wave of the hand: "There are other reasons too, dear, why college is out of the question—which we won't go into right now. And anyway, this is no time to carry on about such matters—there's dinner to eat and our presents to enjoy."

"Don't you understand—?" I began. My parents had turned away.

If we had been talking about someone else's life, I would have forced a debate, made a declaration. But tonight I was the subject of our argument. What a laughable dilemma, I thought. I condemned injustice to the working class and yet I did not have the courage to pursue my own interests. I was afraid to abandon the high moral ground from which I proclaimed the rights of others; I was afraid to speak out for myself.

The frosted windows glowed momentarily and then fell into darkness. Once more the light had entered the house, captured me, and flung me out toward the limitless horizon. That beacon had punctuated my nights for my entire life. Since I was a little child, I had lain in my bed watching the moments of brightness on the ceiling, imagining that the brilliant lens cradled so high upon its dull red pyramid contained the promise of my future.

I looked around the carefully furnished living room, with its mohair sofa, its wing armchairs, its Persian carpet, and polished mahogany coffee table. I contemplated my mother and father and sister, the human furnishings of my life and admitted that my departure had been only a dream all along, insubstantial, fleeting, with no possibility of fulfillment. This snowbound house was my permanent place, its front window blazing with eight gold lamps marking my family's difference from all the other houses of the town. The flames of the eight golden candles on the mantelpiece flickered, about to go out. The beacon intermittently illumined the back window, signaling my permanent imprisonment.

From deep within me, a strange disturbance rose up through my stomach, into my lungs, forcing its way to my throat. Before I understood what was happening, I opened my mouth, about to give vent to a full-bodied howl. My limbs twitched, aching to jump up and down, to fling my body about, breaking all those precious furnishings which had surrounded my childhood. I felt invaded by Cleo's mad spirit. It took all of my strength to shut my mouth and restrain myself. Bewildered by my rage, I crumpled into a chair and held myself with all of my strength.

At dinner, I did not speak, kept my eyes on my plate, and avoided my parents' questioning glances. For the first time in my memory, I neglected to kiss my mother and father good night. I was unable to bear the touch of these people who seemed determined to keep me captive, an attendant to this family.

Was it naivete that allowed me to remain subservient to the needs of my parents and my sister? Pride? Or simple blindness? There I was, just discovering Tolstoy and Dostoyevsky—appalled and delighted at the complexities of human character revealed in their novels—and yet I knew little about my own heart. It wasn't simply the question of college or marriage that disturbed me. There were more obscure issues. On the last night of Chanukah, I uncovered within my soul a sullen anger which must have been burning there for many years.

In the bedroom we shared, Cleo opened her new hope chest. When Cleo had first unwrapped it, Mother had displayed the contents, item by item: fine sheets and pillowcases, handsome blankets, table linens, and two sheer nightgowns. "Cleo," she had declared, "you must think about the future." My father and I had cringed at the gift—ill-suited either to Cleo's prospects or her desires. Mother had glared at us. No matter what happened, she was determined not to give up her belief in the recovery of Cleo's sanity.

Now Cleo threw the bedding, linen, and night clothes into a heap on the floor. Intently, she filled the chest with her own treasures: Petoskey stones from the beach, birds' nests, marbles, a collection of birch bark cut in odd shapes, her knives for wood carving, and finally, the precious tools and tool belt she had just received for Chanukah from my father and me.

When she realized I was watching her, Cleo pointed to the collection of Tolstoy's short stories she had given me and gestured imperiously for me to read. I lifted the book up in my right hand, tempted to throw it into her face. Cleo's expression shifted slightly, as if she understood the depth of my anger. Unnerved, I turned to the desk and opened the book. I discovered, tucked inside, a note from the town librarian:

Dear Rebecca,

Your sister Cleo came into the library a month ago with five dollars. She took my hand and led me to the fiction shelves and pointed to our selection of Tolstoy's books. She indicated that she wanted me to pick out one of them as a present for you. I don't know whether she thought she could buy the book from me, but, anyway, I ordered the book from the bookstore in Petoskey. I will return the change to you on Monday. I hope I didn't misunderstand Cleo.

Love and Happy Holidays,

Mrs. Leland.

Even this note did not calm my rage and frustration. I looked out the window. Cleo grunted and once more gestured for me to read a story. I lowered my head and pretended to read, but I could not concentrate. I clenched my eyes shut. Startled by a sound on my desk, I looked down to see that I had gripped the new book so fiercely that its binding had almost begun to break. Quickly, I smoothed the pages, dismayed that I could treat a book in such a fashion.

Of course, I should have expected my parents' reaction to the idea of my departure from home. But now that the issue had been raised, my own feelings remained too confused and troubling to sort out. Instead, I focused upon the question of marriage which, conveniently, deflected my attention. I blamed my mother for this neat arrangement of my life—blamed her the most. My father, I decided, was simply going along with her plan for my future. Why, I asked myself, why couldn't she do anything simply for its own sake? Why had her Chanukah gift to my father contained within it so many other purposes, motives, schemes? The tickets that would carry my father to his beloved services would also allow my mother to escape her isolation for a few days; my wedding would provide her with a fine stage on which to shine.

Worst of all, as angry as I was at my mother, at the same time I sympathized with her. She had received little of what she wanted out of life. I had always been in awe of her beauty and her liveliness. In the fairy tales I had read as a child, I imagined my mother, not myself, as the princess who had been kidnapped from her rightful palace. In Mother's face when we went to the movies or when she read her romances at night, I saw her hunger for a different life. And I agreed. Mother belonged in New York or Paris, in mansions, grand hotels, not behind the counter of a dry goods store in northern Michigan, hoping to fulfill herself with the marriage of her daughter.

Surreptitiously, I slipped the large manila envelope Mrs. Thrush had given me out of my desk drawer and slid out the contents. There before me lay an admission and scholarship application to the University of Michigan. The stiff paper and elegant print impressed me. At the top of the page the University's seal promised great wonders to anyone who was lucky enough to be accepted. With Mrs. Thrush's help, I had already filled out the entire application, including information about the family's income. I knew the figures because I had been helping my parents with the books at the store since I was twelve. In spite of my mother's claims, there was barely enough to sustain the store and our family, with a little left for Cleo's care and my parents' old age.

I had even written the required essay about my goals in education but had not yet copied it out. I had worked on it for many weeks. It had grown to twenty pages before I had cut it down to the required page and a half. I had shown the essay to Mrs. Thrush, who had glanced through it and said, "It's too general, too grandiose—all those phrases about the working class, injustice, equality." Once again I had stared, tongue-tied, at the fierce little teacher. She had added with exasperation: "If you were granted the answer to one question about your life today, what would that question be, Rebecca Bearwald?"

Since that interview, I had been trying to think of that one important question.

What do you ask yourself, Rebecca Bearwald?

I imagined my whole family waiting for the answer to that question. Bitterly I wondered whether my parents had a purpose in mind when they named me Rebecca. In the Bible, when Abraham's servant asked my namesake for water from her pitcher, she replied, "Drink, and I will give thy camels drink also." The servant took this generosity as a sign that God approved of the match between Rebecca and Isaac. Rebecca's helpfulness had won her a husband. I too had grown to be a caretaker. In the Bible, caretaking is applauded, but tonight I was not at all certain that it was wise to take responsibility for other people's lives.

Now I read through the essay once more and as I read I began to understand what it was, above all else, that I wanted to know. Having labored all my life to be a "good" daughter and a "good" sister and a "good" human being, I realized that I didn't understand the word "good" at all. This was particularly true tonight when I bitterly resented the burden of my goodness. At college, then, I hoped to learn what the word "good" meant and why it ruled and confused my life.

I seized a pen and began to scribble notes on scrap paper. I worked for some time before I was satisfied with my revision. Then, carefully, in the space remaining upon the application, I wrote out the essay. To complete the document, there remained only my father's signature. I clenched my teeth until they hurt. Through the frosty window, I could barely see the channel that ran below the back of the house. A crest of snow covered both the breakwater on the far side and the pier leading to the lighthouse on the near side. A small cap of snow rested on the roof of the lighthouse.

Every fifteen seconds, the light flashed across the pane, brightening the room for a moment. It beckoned me to sail out through the channel onto the lake, to sail away from this home and this town I loved so well. First I would go to college and then travel to some great city where I would battle against the wealthy and the powerful and work for a better world. Of course, I would keep a Jewish home, observe the holidays, attend services, write to my parents and to Cleo; I would even visit home on vacation. Never again, however, would I march down the street with my family on dark winter mornings.

But during the last few days the channel had frozen solid. The lake too had frozen out to a hundred yards from the shore. The snow had banked up over the ice in wild shapes, looking as if the waves themselves had been struck suddenly by a commandment of God in mid-motion on their way to the shore.

Out of my drawer, I slipped a blank sheet of paper and a cancelled check signed by my father. Slowly, laboriously, I attempted to copy my father's signature on the blank paper, but I could not duplicate the elaborate Gothic curlicues that he fashioned so perfectly. Tears of frustration coursed down my cheek.

A hand clasped my shoulder. Fearfully, I turned. Cleo leaned over me, looking down at my botched attempts. Her hand still on my shoulder, Cleo picked up the pen and inked out a perfect imitation of our father's signature.

I looked up into my sister's dark eyes. Cleo did not flinch. As I had done many times, I searched into those black depths for some hint of understanding. Unfortunately, I saw too much in Cleo's gaze, as if my troubled sister understood more about life than I would ever know.

Slowly, I drew the university application forms over the scrap paper and pointed to the proper line. I covered my eyes with my hands and waited. I heard the pen scratching across the surface of the paper. Through my fingers, I watched as Cleo inked the name, "Henry Bearwald" in our father's Gothic script on the application.

FIVE

THE WINTER ENDED SUDDENLY with a thaw that melted the snow for two balmy days, leaving a sodden slush along the streets, pockets of white upon the lawns, and the sound of running and dripping water everywhere. A fresh west wind drove glistening, inky blue waves across the lakes. Skipping whitecaps at the crests of the waves seemed almost to be reflections of the small, puffy white clouds skidding through the mild blue atmosphere. People walked about the town with smiles.

My father was particularly happy because of an unexpected windfall in his business. Some months before, one of his jobbers had given him the opportunity to purchase a large lot of expensive English wool at an extremely favorable price. Even before the wool had been delivered, the market price almost doubled and my father sold it. He said nothing of the matter to my mother because he knew she would demand that he invest the profit in expansion. Instead, he directed the money to his brother-in-law's office in Detroit with instructions to purchase an annuity in Cleo's name.

Shortly after the spring thaw began, he called Sy to confirm the transaction. The hysterical response bewildered him. "My God, Henry, how could you do this to me?"

"What do you mean, Sy? I just didn't want Arabella to know. You know I'm not a gambler, but it was such a sure thing."

"I don't want to know anything about it, Henry. I mean, thousands of dollars—no, no, I mean, there are people here who are watching me."

"I'm not asking you to do anything illegal. Just buy the annuity in Cleo's name and put it in your safe. If that's too much trouble—"

"I'll do it this one time. Christ, the damage's already done. But promise me, Henry, never again. Keep your money and your affairs to yourself."

My father promised and said good-bye.

"Wait," said Sy, "wait just a minute." Sy was away from the phone for some time. When he returned his voice was hoarse and a bit shaky. "Before you hang up, Henry, some friends of mine want to know if you know anything about a roadhouse over near Cheboygan."

"I haven't been to Cheboygan in twenty years."

"You're sure? I'm talking about an establishment owned by my clients. Jake's Place."

"The Knights of Pythias had a get-together over there, must have been '08 or '09. Why?"

"It burned down, Henry, to the ground, just last week." Without another word, Sy hung up.

My father concluded that Sy's criminal clientele was warping his judgment. He decided he would counsel his brother-in-law to stop doing business with his childhood friends. Some years later when I questioned him about his responses to Sy's questions, he berated himself for his stupidity.

The conversation continued to trouble Father, in spite of the fine spring sunshine which we thought had brought winter to an end. However, after only two days of balmy weather, the wind shifted. To our dismay, a cold front out of the northwest met a warm, moist stream of air from the southeast and the skies began to fill with towering black storm heads. The light in the sky intensified as if it were cast by a filament in a lightbulb about to explode. The edges and corners of every object, building, and tree in town stood out starkly, straining against the clarity of the atmosphere.

On that day, just as the great March storm was brewing and everyone's nerves were rubbed raw waiting for the tempest to burst, Mother found the perfect house for her brother's family. She called her sister-in-law from the store with the news. The house was located between the Kuhns of St. Louis and the Eisenstadts of Cincinnati and backed upon Lake Michigan.

"At last!" said Maureen. "I don't know why it was so difficult."

"It was so difficult," my mother enunciated each word clearly, "because you made it difficult with your demands. First it was Michigan Avenue, and then for only five weeks—not four, not six, not eight."

"Well, excuse me."

"Then, suddenly it had to back on the lake itself because you wanted privacy, and then—"

"It's not just for us, you know. Sy's business, his clients expect—"

"Look, I'm just Sy's sister, not a real estate agent."

"Well, we are grateful, Bella, you'll see how grateful. We'll show you all a wonderful time."

"We have wonderful times all year long."

"Don't be that way, Bella. We just want to share some of our success with you. Is that so bad?"

"Henry's success is quite sufficient."

"Sy's clients are going to stock our cellar with the finest alcoholic beverages—the real stuff, not bathtub gin. We'll have plenty for your cellar too."

"Henry's far-flung operations keep us well-supplied."

"Are you telling me that Henry Bearwald is a bootlegger?"

"I said he is a gray eminence—an *éminence grise*."

"Why do you keep throwing your correspondence-school French at me?"

"I'm saying that Henry is the brains and that's all I'm willing to say."

Mother replaced the phone firmly on the hook. With angry, swift gestures, she began to exchange the winter window display with spring items from a rolling rack.

When my father returned from the finance committee meeting at City Hall, the wind swirled into the store through the open door. He struggled to close the door behind him. "Wow!" he shouted. "It's going to hit hard."

The wind caught hold of the rolling rack and overturned it.

Mother stood, hands on her hips, regarding the jumble of clothes on the floor. "And I thought winter was over."

While they righted the rack, he spoke with excitement, "You'll never guess what they found on the beach out toward North Point: three bodies. Two men shot in the back of the head—gangland killings, according to Vernon—and a third drowned. No boat or anything. Vernon thinks it was a hijacking—bootleggers carrying liquor from Canada by boat all the way to Chicago."

"Probably some of Sy's clients," said my mother. "Maureen hardly even thanked me for finding that house. All she could talk about was how well they're doing with their gangster friends."

My father thought for some time and then approached my mother and spoke in considered tones. "I wouldn't talk about Sy's clients outside the family."

"You're in the family, aren't you?"

"I've heard you gossiping around town about your brother. There's so much violence going on—one gang against another. You don't want to implicate Sy."

"Maureen is such a braggart!"

"Absurd, isn't it, that gangsters have become celebrities."

Mother flushed and turned away. "Oh Henry, you're so—so righteous!"

"It's not wise of Sy to do business with those people. I think I'll talk to him."

"Everyone in the country does business with those people. How many towns in Michigan have their own elegant speakeasy and gambling tables patronized by the best citizens?"

My father did not answer. They worked in silence until the rack was filled with winter clothes for storage. He rolled it back into the storeroom. When he returned, he declared, "They should have closed Beechams down years ago. They know where I stand on that issue."

"Well you stand alone," Mother challenged. "We're the only people in this town that won't go to Beechams—the one decent dining establishment in northern Michigan."

My father sank into his desk chair. "I wish you were more—satisfied."

"Who could be satisfied after this winter? The girls are impossible." Mother rearranged the spring display with quick, angry gestures. "If Becky were a brilliant student, a prodigy or something, that would be a different matter." She marched to the desk, planted her hands on the top, and leaned toward her husband. "As it is, she's a lovely girl who ought to raise a family, and—and—be close to us—well, you know what we planned."

"And very convenient too." My father got up and walked to the front door. He gazed across the street at Round Lake through the buildings. "If only Cleo weren't so sensitive to Becky's moods."

"Sensitive? She's had more of her fits this winter than she's had in years. People—Dottie Morris, Vernon Hayes, even Roberta Snow—are beginning to suggest again that we send her away." She took my father's arm and turned him toward her. "I'll never let them send Cleo away."

"Poor Becky," sighed my father.

"You think you're the only one who understands Becky? You and Becky, Becky and you—you're always ganging up on me. Cleo too, for that matter. She treats me as if I had the plague."

"Come on Arabella, don't exaggerate."

"Well, it's true."

"If things were only different—"

My parents looked at one another. Father put his arm around Mother's waist. She leaned against him.

At Weyriches, Cleo worked on a thirty foot sloop up on the ways of the boathouse. She had caulked, sanded, and painted the hull. All of the mahogany woodwork gleamed with a new coat of varnish. The coming storm made her nervous. I've thought about these crucial moments Cleo spent in the boathouse and the events that followed, going over them again and again as if it were a recurrent nightmare. The break up of our family began in this unlikely place. Of course, I was never able to interrogate Cleo, but, like my mother, I had inhabited Cleo's mind and body since I became old enough to think. For many years, I led a dual life—mine and Cleo's. When I was away from her, suddenly, in the middle of a conversation, I would imagine what Cleo was doing and feeling. My friends sometimes commented that I got a spooky look in my eyes and they wanted to know whether I was haunted. I usually managed to make up a story about a forthcoming test or a dentist visit, an excuse that satisfied them.

And so, in the boathouse, as Cleo began to varnish the mast that lay stretched out next to the hull on sawhorses, she paused to gaze up through the dusty window into the sky. Several times during the morning, she ran to the door of the large boathouse to look out. She could smell the warm, moist breeze from the land and the hard, cold wind from the lake blowing through the cracks of the building and up the water well where the boathouse extended over the lake.

Even as a small child, Cleo had been fascinated by Weyrich's Boatyard. She had demanded to be taken there instead of to the playground. Soon she became a mascot of the yard. We would leave her there when we were too busy to watch over her. Gradually, she began to help out. At first she swept up and gathered scraps. She learned how to care for tools. Before long she was assisting the craftsmen. We didn't realize how much she had learned until my parents and the school authorities finally admitted that Cleo's problems would make further schooling a burden on everyone. To our surprise, Mr. Weyrich offered her a job, declaring that over the years Cleo had become quite proficient as a boatwright.

In the corner, a small Dutch wood stove glowed with a fire of heavy wood chips which Cleo fed from time to time. Suddenly the gale-force wind of the coming storm backed up the chimney and a puff of smoke leaked out into the boathouse. Cleo, her varnish brush still in hand, ran over to the stove to adjust the flue. She opened the stove to add some wood, but a wild barking and scratching at the door distracted her. She dropped the varnish brush and rushed to open the door. Across the threshold hurtled Mr. Weyrich's three-month-old golden retriever. He jumped onto Cleo's chest, knocking her down. A fresh gust of wind blew in. It caught the unlatched stove door and flung it open. A rain of sparks swirled out of the stove and fell upon the varnish brush. Flames sprouted on the floor.

Cleo threw the affectionate puppy off her and bounded up,

knocking the half-varnished mast off the sawhorses. Flames leaped to the wet varnish of the mast.

Cleo ran to the stove and slammed its door shut. She reached behind the stove, picked up a bucket of sand, and flung the sand over the flames. She picked up a second bucket of sand and threw it over the flaming end of the mast. Then she carried the empty buckets to the boat well, filled them with water, and returned to spread the water over the flickering remnants of the fire.

Smoke billowed through the boathouse and out the door. Cleo stumbled through the door coughing. At that moment, Mr. Weyrich and his oldest son, Richie, appeared. Later, the Weyrichs told me how the three collided outside the door.

"What the hell!" shouted Mr. Weyrich.

"Goddamn it, Cleo!" screamed Richie. "You trying to ruin us?"

The golden retriever came howling out of the boathouse and flung himself on Richie. Richie kicked at him and he ran squealing away. Richie darted into the boathouse.

The red-faced boatyard owner stood over Cleo, shouting: "I told you to keep that damned hound out of the buildings, Cleo."

Cleo cowered against the side of the building, her gaze fixed on the ground.

In a moment, Richie appeared. "It seems to be out, Dad. She threw sand on it. It's a real mess."

Father and son turned toward Cleo, who kept her eyes on the ground. Mr. Weyrich took a step toward her. With a howl, she ran up the muddy road toward the main street.

"It's all right, Cleo!" yelled Mr. Weyrich, running after her. "You did fine, Cleo! Come back, for Christ's sake."

Cleo arrived at the high school a few minutes before class change. Soot covered her hair, face, and clothes. She made her way down the hall, peering through the windows of each classroom door. If the shade was drawn, she opened the door and stuck her head in, searched the room looking for me and ducked out, closing the door behind her. She kept blowing on her right hand which she had burned on the stove door.

I came out of class on the second floor and stopped next to a bank of lockers, talking to Ben Near, the senior class president. We stood very close, looking into one another's eyes. Barbara Sneavely stopped momentarily next to me and whispered in my ear. "Your sister's here again—on the staircase. The kids are tormenting her." She rushed away. I took a step down the hall. Ben put his hand on my arm. I stepped back next to him and continued the conversation.

I heard the rising chant of the ninth graders: "Silly Cleo, silly Cleo! Cleo, Cleo, Cleo, Cleo! Silly Cleo, silly Cleo! Cleo, Cleo, Cleo, Cleo!" I felt Cleo's pain curdling within my stomach. I took Ben Near's arm and turned with him away from the staircase. I had a life of my own, apart from Cleo, apart from my parents. I told Ben I wanted to show him the University of Michigan catalogue I had checked out of the library.

From the staircase came the familiar strange, earsplitting wail that rose and fell without ceasing. I felt like throwing up. Instead, I dropped my books and sprinted down the hall, pushing my way through a crowd of students and teachers who were moving in the same direction. At the top of the stairs, I paused.

On the landing my sister lay on her back, flailing the air with her arms and legs while Mr. Croton, the gym teacher, and Mr. Bono, the assistant principal, tried to get hold of her.

"Leave her alone!" I screamed, plunging down the stairs. "Damn it, don't touch her." Two steps from the landing, I launched myself at the two crouched men. My shoulder crashed into Mr. Croton's head. Mr. Croton fell against Mr. Bono's side, and the two men went sprawling down the staircase. The students who were watching from above and below the landing cheered as if they were at a football game.

I flung myself on my flailing sister, receiving blows all over my face and body. "Stupid idiot, it's me, Becky!" The heel of Cleo's boot crashed against my nose which began to bleed. Dazed, I shouted, "Stupid, stupid, it's Becky." Suddenly Cleo became still. I gathered her into my arms. Cleo thrust her head against my breast and began to whimper. I caressed her back and head. Blood ran down my face onto Cleo's back.

My head resounded with the blow of Cleo's boot to my head. Her kick had not been accidental. She had heard me clearly. I, too, had meant to injure her—with my words. We were enslaved to one another and could do nothing about it. In the years since, whenever I have thought of the corrosive power of the word "good," the memory of Cleo and me clutched together on the high school landing—my blood staining her—comes to my mind. This was the bondage in which I had pledged to live out my life.

Teachers appeared from everywhere to herd the students back into the classrooms. Soon only Mr. Bono and Mr. Croton remained on the landing, peering down at my sister and me huddled in the corner. They seemed angry, but looked so helpless there, with their red faces and clenched fists, that I began to laugh.

"For goodness' sake, the girl's nose is bleeding!" Mrs. Thrush came clattering down the stairs and knelt next to me with a handkerchief. Cleo blindly pushed Mrs. Thrush's hand away.

"Cleo!" I captured my sister's hand.

Mrs. Thrush wiped the blood from my face. "Rebecca," said Mrs. Thrush, "I think you should bring your sister down to the principal's office."

At the top of the stairs, Ben Near stood, watching. He held my books.

SIX

IT WAS PAST NOON by the time Mother, Cleo, and I returned to the store from high school.

"Mortified! That's what I was, mortified!" exclaimed my mother. "First she almost burns down the boatyard—"

"They said it wasn't her fault," said my father, kissing me and putting out his arms to Cleo who moved away from him to stand looking out the window. He followed her. "Cleo, Mr. Weyrich said you saved the boatyard by your quick thinking. He wants you to come back." My father reached her side, paused, and then backed away as if he were afraid to provoke her.

Cleo stood rigidly, with her arms folded and her face expressionless. My dark sister, I thought. She resembled the beautiful, black clouds over the town, dense with hidden power, about to erupt.

"It doesn't matter whose fault it was," said Mother, pacing about the store. "Things happen to Cleo. Things happen. She disrupted the whole high school. It was like a riot, Mr. Scott said. A riot! My daughters caused a riot!"

"It wasn't much of a riot, Mother."

"Rebecca," said Father. "Please tell your sister it's all right for her to go back to work."

I sat down in my father's desk chair, my arms folded. "She won't listen to me. She's mad at me."

"Mad at you?"

"Oh come on, Rebecca," said Mother. "Cleo's never mad at you."

"I called her stupid. She's very mad at me."

"You called her stupid?" asked my father incredulously.

"That isn't all our Rebecca did, Henry Bearwald. She practically decapitated Mr. Croton—he claims he has a concussion—and she swore at him and Mr. Bono."

"Rebecca?"

"That's right, Daddy," I said. "I went crazy, out of control."

Mother shook my shoulder. "Don't say such things."

I cried out, recoiling from my mother's violence. My head still ached from Cleo's kick.

Mother released her grip abruptly and then patted my shoulder as if to soothe the pain. "Don't you ever say such things."

Just then the storm broke with a spectacular bolt of forked lightning that pierced the sky over Lake Charlevoix. The interior of the store lit up as if a searchlight had targeted it. The thunder followed almost immediately, a great, rolling roar.

My parents and I joined Cleo at the window. Large balls

of hail clattered down, resounding like pistol shots as the wind whipped it against the window pane.

"We'd better step back away from these windows," said my father.

The family moved toward the rear of the store. A torrent of rain followed the hail, lashing the street and the building. Fascinated, Cleo returned to the window. The electric lights dimmed, brightened, and dimmed again.

I went into a cupboard and began to set out candles in candlesticks around the store. My mother followed me.

"I want you to write those apologies right now, Rebecca, and get them back to Mr. Croton and Mr. Bono today, before the end of school."

"Mother, everyone in town knows that you can't put your hands on Cleo—even the little kids."

"If you don't apologize, young lady, you won't graduate. Mr. Bono is a vindictive man, I can guarantee you that."

"Who cares whether I graduate or not?"

"We care," said my father.

"Daddy," I positioned myself in front of my father's desk, "what if someone were offered a free college education?"

"Not again," said my mother.

I leaned forward, my eyes fixed upon my father's. "Room and board and classes too."

Father, besieged, could not avert his gaze. "That isn't the point, Becky."

"You've always told us that you considered learning the greatest blessing of all."

"True, dear. But your mother and I—." He faltered, aware that the argument was irrelevant. "It's just that we've always hoped that you would marry someone and eventually take over the store."

Mother took up his plea. "You and your husband would do very well here, carrying on after us."

"Everyone in town knows and loves you," muttered my father. He opened a ledger and began to work on accounts.

"What an odd reason for not going to college." I stared at Mother.

She threw her arms in the air. "How can you keep talking about college after what happened today?"

"What difference does today make?" I trembled with the knowledge that we were approaching the true issue. The ugly incident at school made me abandon all restraint. I thrust my face at my mother. "Well? What difference?"

"You know the answer to that."

I stepped around my mother and confronted my father once again. My voice was shrill and unnatural. "Is Cleo why I can't go to college?" As soon as the question was out of my mouth, I regretted it.

My father raised his head slowly and regarded me. In a very low voice he replied, "You're the only person who can control your sister."

The three of us looked at one another, united both in our dread of Cleo's madness and the resentment we shared at its burden. Uneasily, we looked away from one another.

I grasped for some way to retrieve the words that had been spoken. "I'll take Cleo with me."

"Henry, do you hear that? Our daughter plans to take Cleo to Ann Arbor, to the university."

"She can get a job repairing cars or something," I said. "Mechanics make good money."

"That's the end, the final straw. You and your sister can't act properly in this little town where everyone knows you. And you intend to go down to Ann Arbor and set up housekeeping with a poor—" I clapped my hand over Mother's mouth. My mother struck my hand away. "You should seal your own lips, Rebecca."

"I'll take Cleo with me—wherever I go."

"Rubbish!" Mother's voice rose.

My father stepped between us. He placed a soothing hand on each of our arms. "Rebecca, it's not very practical to think of setting up a household in Ann Arbor with Cleo. She knows our town. They know her. She has good work to do here—Mr. Weyrich says she's got the most talented hands he's ever seen. And you would be here to help her—after we're gone."

"Some common sense, at last," said Mother.

"Arabella," said Father, "the girls have gone through a lot today. Why don't the three of you go home and clean up and get some rest. We're not going to have any customers on a day like this."

Mother looked around. "Where is Cleo?"

"She was over there, by the window, a minute ago," said Father.

"She must have slipped out the front door." I ran to the door and stuck my head out, gazing up and down the empty street. "It's all my stupid fault." The wind billowed my skirt, drenching me with rain. Breathless, I closed the door and turned. "Gone."

"She's run away again," said Mother.

"I told you she understands everything," I said.

"I'm not the only one who's been talking about Cleo."

"I'll go look for her." I began to put on my jacket.

"You will do nothing of the kind," said my mother, snatching my jacket away.

"She was very upset," said Father. "She shouldn't be out in this storm."

"The rain has let up a little," I said. I didn't really want to go searching for my sister. I wanted to get into bed and pull the covers over my head.

Father persisted. "I'll get the car and try to find her."

"Not on your life," said Mother. "The doctor in Traverse City told us that Cleo's disappearances are simply a form of blackmail."

"I thought you didn't trust him," said Father. "He doesn't even have a degree in psychology. You said he got his ideas from the *Saturday Evening Post*."

"Well, on other matters, he talks more sense than—"

"But Arabella, the storm—"

"Henry, if we go chasing around town looking for Cleo, everyone will start talking again about locking her up."

My father bowed his head. He remained silent for some time.

Mother put on her coat. "I am going to the bank and Rebecca is going to write her apologies. Sooner or later Cleo will come home—she always does. In the meantime, we'll carry on exactly as we always do."

*

While my father continued putting out the spring merchandise for display, I sat at his desk, composing an apology to Mr. Croton and Mr. Bono. I was furious at myself. I wished I could take back the question that had sent Cleo out into the storm. This spring I was possessed by a disagreeable spirit.

I tried to reconstruct the morning as it might have occurred in the life of the "familiar" Rebecca, the caretaker—the girl I had been until two months ago. At school I would have gone immediately to my sister's rescue, sent Cleo's tormentors on their way with a mild reprimand, calmed Cleo with my gentle touch, dealt with Mr. Croton and Mr. Bono graciously, and returned Cleo to her work before noon. There should have been no confrontation with my parents at the store.

"Good Rebecca," I muttered, flushing as I remembered the conclusion to my essay on the university application form. "Kind Rebecca, thoughtful Rebecca." I attempted to hypnotize myself, imagining what that former Rebecca might write in apology to the teachers she had offended. After all, I told myself, I intended to graduate from high school at least, and I still hoped to convince my parents to let me go to college. I would not give up on that. I had sent in the applications with my father's forged signature. If I were lucky enough to earn a full scholarship, there remained the problem of Cleo.

"Good, kind, and gentle Rebecca," I chanted and then asked my former Self: "What would you do?"

My anger temporarily calmed, I pondered my difficulty. The plan to take Cleo with me to Ann Arbor was far-fetched, I admitted. If there were only some way of keeping the family together while I went to college. I then succumbed to a fantasy as far-fetched as any my mother had ever concocted. My mother wanted my father to expand. Why couldn't they open a branch in Ann Arbor? It wasn't Florida, of course, but it was a prosperous, interesting town, very near Detroit. They could hire someone to manage the Charlevoix store, rent their house, and the whole family could move to Ann Arbor. My mother could become the belle of Ann Arbor. And I could go to college.

By the time I had folded the apologies and put them in separate envelopes, I had embraced the new plan wholeheartedly. At the library, I would write an inquiry to the Ann Arbor Chamber of Commerce about dry goods stores in that city. There was probably even a synagogue in Ann Arbor which my father could attend.

I sucked on the end of my pen and gazed across the store through the rain-lashed window at the lowering sky. My mind raced ahead, carrying me south through the storm away from Charlevoix. My father could discuss the matter of finances with my uncles and cousins in Detroit. They might want to join forces, to form a partnership.

To my amazement, before my eyes, the turbulent black sky folded in two and then in three and, with a resounding crash, appeared to fall in upon our store. Great shards of glass clattered to the floor.

"Daddy!" I screamed.

"Becky!" yelled my father.

Carefully we moved toward the front of the store. Rain poured through a jagged hole in the left window. Wind swept through the store, flailing at the clothing, knocking over counter displays, rattling mirrors and doors. Glass littered the display case, the counters, and the floor.

I ran outside and cranked down the metal security screen, blocking off most of the rain. The sudden shattering of our window seemed like a judgment of my selfishness and stupidity. I should never have forced the family to admit aloud the burden of my sister's illness.

My father dragged a stack of boards out of the storeroom. With my help, he propped the boards against the inside of the broken window, wedging them firmly in place with two-by-fours.

"I was afraid of this," he said. "It's a full gale."

My knees trembled. The vision of the sky folding remained with me, clouding my sight. It wasn't until we began sweeping up the broken glass that I discovered the brick.

"Daddy!" Fastened securely around the brick with string was an envelope with "BEARWALD" printed across it in crude capital letters.

My father opened the envelope and took out a sheet of paper with the following message, printed in the same crude, capital letters: "THIS IS A WARNING. STRANGERS STAY OUT. NO ONE MUSCLES IN ON OUR TERRITORY. THERE WILL BE NO MORE WARNINGS."

My father's face had turned dead white. "Who on earth would do such a thing?" He sounded breathless.

"What does it mean, Daddy?"

"It must be a prank of some sort." He sat down.

"Are you all right, Daddy?" I leaned over him, gazing at his rigid face. A bead of sweat appeared on his brow.

"We mustn't tell anyone about this," he said in a low voice.

I resumed mopping up the water.

"Did you hear me, Rebecca?"

"What, Daddy?"

"Not a word about this brick or the note to anyone, not even your mother. It would worry her sick."

"Shouldn't we tell the police?"

"No, no, it's too embarrassing."

"Embarrassing?"

"We'll blame the storm. That's what we thought at first anyway."

I came back to my father's desk and sat down in a straight chair next to him. "What does 'strangers' mean?"

"Who knows? Just foreign, I guess, different."

"You mean because we're Jews?"

My father winced. "Don't try to be an amateur detective." He spoke softly.

"Why else would they break our window?"

His hand clutched his breast. He gulped for air. "That's always a possibility. But never, never has anyone in this town ever done anything to us because of that. No, no, it must just be a prank. Look at the language: 'muscle in on our territory.' Charlevoix is our territory. We've been here for forty years."

"I think we should tell the police."

"It was a prank and that's all," he replied, harshly. "I don't expect anything more to come of it, so we'd best just repair the damage and keep it all a secret between ourselves." He slumped in his chair, a look of misery on his face. "You're a good girl."

"Momma said—"

"Just be discreet. I'll take care of Momma. I should have sent you out right away. Go see John Clover. He knows more about what's happening in this town than anyone else."

*

John Clover arrived at the park every morning prepared for the weather. To protect himself from the storm today, he had fashioned a lean-to of canvas and tree limbs over the bench. He wore yellow foul-weather gear, a whaler's hat, and high rubber boots. Even though I had become accustomed to his constant presence in the park, I found his appearance there this afternoon unsettling. I stopped on the sidewalk above the park and peered down at him. He raised his hand in greeting. Reluctantly, I approached the bench.

"It's Cleo, isn't it?" he said, making room for me under his shelter.

Instead of questioning him about my sister, I was tempted to ask him what he was doing in the park every day and why he had quit his job.

"The way she lit out of Weyrich's this morning—" He let the sentence die and sat waiting.

I told him what had happened at school and at the store.

"She slid up Antrim like a fox."

"You saw her leave the store?"

John Clover nodded. "You say she was mad at you?"

I hadn't said anything about that, but I was used to John Clover's ability to understand what went on in people's minds. "I called her stupid." I had also called her an idiot.

John Clover stared out into the rain. He said nothing.

"It's been a terrible day."

John Clover nodded.

"The storm broke our front window."

"The storm?"

I hesitated. "Yes, sort of."

"A black Packard come tearing through town. It stopped in the middle of Main Street right in front of your store and then went hell-bent-for-leather across the bridge going north."

"A black Packard?"

"Big shiny new one—with Detroit license plates. Passed the sheriff going close to ninety up at Chilton's Cabins. He went after it. Didn't catch it. Vernon came dragging back soon after. He's probably cursing that Ford of his."

I looked sharply at John. "Are you saying that our broken window had something to do with that black Packard?"

John stared out at the park, the town, and the lake. The rain poured down over his yellow oilskin hat down onto his slicker.

"I've got to find my sister." I made no move to leave.

"I might take a look around myself." John put his hand on my shoulder.

I looked up into his lined face and felt like crying. "Thanks, John." I ran off abruptly.

I left my letters of apology at the school office and set off to search for Cleo. I plodded about in a daze, unaware of the blustery wind and rain buffeting me. I felt like one of those battle-weary soldiers wandering in the midst of chaos whom Tolstoy described in *War and Peace* during the battle between the French and the Russians. None of it made any sense. "Strangers stay out" echoed in my head until the words became senseless sounds.

My father should have been angry. He should have called the police. I had always assumed that my father was proud of being Jewish. And yet today, he had reacted as if the brick had soiled us. When I mentioned the black Packard with Detroit plates, he simply said that John Clover must have been hallucinating.

It was six-thirty before I returned home. Cleo still had not appeared. My mother lashed out furiously at my father for sending me to look for my sister. "When Cleo's tired enough and cold enough and hungry enough, she'll come home and we'll pretend that we hadn't noticed. Do you hear me?"

"I think we ought to call the police, Momma."

"Never!"

"Your mother's right," declared Father. "We'll go look for her in the car."

"Over my dead body, you will," said Mother.

"We'll be discreet. No one's going to see us."

"Momma, she's never been so upset—ever, ever." I stuffed some food into my mouth without taking off my rain slicker.

"Sit down at this table this minute, both of you."

"I'm sorry dear," said my father. "We're not going to leave Cleo outside on a night like this."

"It's emotional blackmail, that's what it is. You heard the psychologist: she's wringing us out for love, squeezing us like a washing machine wringer."

"You're welcome to come with us," said Father.

"Then who will be here when she comes back? She always comes back. Five times already this year. She's just stubborn, an ox, a mule. Won't give us even a little inch. Rules our lives like a despot. And we give her everything without the slightest acknowledgment or gratitude. I tell you Henry, if the police pick her up again—"

My father and I left the house in the middle of Mother's tirade. In the car, we covered the town from North Point to South Point, from the Boyne City Road to the Belvedere. With flashlights we explored every beach and hiding place that Cleo frequented. We even climbed down onto the catwalks beneath both bridges and slipped and slid our way out to the end of the Lake Michigan breakwater, but we found no trace of Cleo.

SEVEN

WHILE MY FATHER AND I looked for Cleo, Mother paced and rocked. In her diary, she kept returning to the hours she waited alone for news of her eldest daughter. These pages of notes convinced me more than anything else to revise my absurd and childish assumption that Mother had cared more for herself and her frustrated yearnings than she did for us. I was also astonished when I learned how deeply she admired the Clovers, whom she always referred to as "the Indians."

As she walked about the house on the evening of Cleo's disappearance, every time she passed the telephone she stopped, tempted to call the police, the coast guard, the hospitals. Once she lifted the receiver, but through the dark, rattling windows she imagined the knowing glances of the ladies in her bridge club. Hastily, she replaced the receiver, frightened by the thought of doctors in their white coats and judges in their black robes ready to consign Cleo to the tortures of an insane asylum.

She had seen Cleo in a straitjacket once. Cleo had been found wandering through a farm miles to the north. She had fought so violently that the police had locked her up and then bound her—"for her own good." Cleo had been only fifteen years old. The memory of her daughter trussed in the cruel jacket, lying on her back on the floor of a cell and staring at the ceiling, tormented Mother. My father had been wise enough to bring me along to calm Cleo. The police allowed me into the cell to remove the jacket. At the hearing, I stood next to Cleo, holding her hand. Our lawyer and the Traverse City doctor convinced the judge to release Cleo to the custody of the family and, eventually, to drop the case. The judge, however, warned my parents that any further incidents would surely end in a different manner: he would call in an expert psychologist or even a psychiatrist, who would probably commit Cleo to an institution. My mother had vowed never to trust officials again.

As she waited for news of her missing daughter, my mother relived Cleo's anguished day. She began at the boatyard, cowered on the landing at the high school, and then stood in the store while her beloved sister said she wanted to abandon her. Mother cringed. Who could blame Cleo for fleeing out into the storm?

The hours passed.

Mother went to the telephone. There were only two people in town she could trust with the information of Cleo's disappearance: John and Ruth Clover. She opened the phone book and was surprised to find a number listed under John's name. She picked up the telephone.

Ruth answered and informed my mother that John too had been searching since afternoon for Cleo.

"It's all my fault, Ruth. My big mouth. I just got fed up, you know what I mean? It was one thing after another, Ruth. Henry and Rebecca think that I'm insensitive about Cleo's feelings, that I underestimate her awareness. But they're wrong."

"Of course, they're wrong. You're her mother."

"It's not just that." She didn't know how to explain her bond with her eldest daughter. When Cleo had entered the world, the umbilical cord had been cut and tied. Cleo the baby had begun her separate life. But when Cleo's peculiar illness made itself evident, the child had reimplanted herself into the mother's body and soul. Now she could hardly tell where she left off and her eldest daughter began. "It's different from just being her mother. She leads such a life of agony and I can't do anything about it—except to make it worse." Mother began to cry. "If anything happens to her—"

Mother's voice died. Ruth waited for so long that Mother was uncertain she was still there. Then the firm voice sounded through the receiver. "Cleo is a survivor."

The words startled Mother. "Do you really think so?" Relief flooded through her body.

"She won't ever hurt herself on purpose."

"I must sound like a madwoman. I'm so sorry for disturbing you."

"She'll come home."

The moment she hung up the receiver, Mother felt she had humbled herself. She never knew how to act with the Clovers. She could hardly believe that American Indians still existed. To her annoyance, she suspected that the townspeople of Charlevoix thought that Indians and Jews somehow belonged in the same category—outsiders with strange beliefs.

Once more Mother began to rock, thinking now about Rebecca's desire to leave home. At eighteen, she too had fled her home. In spite of her poverty, her childhood had been more adventurous than Rebecca's. Her father had collected bottles and junk from the alleys of Detroit, selling his booty back to large dealers and beverage makers. As a small child, she had joined her father on the wagon rides, scrambling through the garbage to find the precious bottles and valuable junk. She still felt the excitement of those voyages out into the world far beyond the confines of her neighborhood. She had been struck with wonder at the houses and buildings of the city which she saw mainly from behind. She marveled that there could be treasures among the objects that other people threw away.

A violent gust of wind distracted my mother from her memories. She got up and peered out of the front window, hoping to see Cleo stride up the sidewalk toward the house. But the street was empty. She sighed and pictured Cleo, battered by the storm, hating her family. Her own limbs ached, her heart pounded, her head throbbed. Once more she collapsed into the rocking chair, reminding herself what Ruth Clover had said: "Cleo is a survivor."

She regretted her unkind thoughts about the Indians. They were good people. Ruth had known how to comfort her; John was out in the storm, looking for her daughter. She thought of Ruth's acceptance of John's eccentric behavior. She pictured the two of them drinking coffee down on the park bench every morning. A good marriage, she thought, a couple who loved one another after so many years.

Her face flushed. She wondered whether she loved her husband. They had met at his uncle's business, Bearwald's Department Store in Detroit, where she had worked, a star sales clerk. He had courted her with ardor. She had admired him, had recognized his kindness and intelligence and his morality, but she had not fallen in love with him. Her resistance had only spurred him on. The energy with which he pursued her had made her feel that, perhaps, she could love him. A man of such devotion could open new frontiers and carry her with him.

The wind blew and my mother writhed about in the rocking chair, disturbed now by the thought of her youngest daughter's unhappiness. No, no, no. She denied the urge to identify with Rebecca. It was bad enough to suffer Cleo's painful life. Now, she asked herself, must she suffer from Rebecca's frustrated passion for college? No. She refused to experience Rebecca's disappointment. Why should Rebecca escape life's demands?

Forty years old, she thought, and what did she have to look forward to in this town of two thousand small souls? She, too, had dreamed in vain. She had come to Charlevoix a stranger and had remained an outsider. Henry, at least, had been born here. That meant something to people. She was an exotic, too volatile. She was always saying a few words too many, dismaying her neighbors with her humor and imagination. Henry prayed and contemplated the sacred books of Judaism, yet he was hardly Jewish. He was as much a son of Charlevoix as he was of his own parents. But she was Jewish to the core—in speech, gestures, and imagination. A big city girl, born and brought up in a ghetto. Oh she was active in the town, a leading member of the Ladies' Auxiliary to the chamber of commerce, a founding member of the local chapter of the American Red Cross, a school volunteer, a conscientious supporter of the World Awareness Group at the library, a popular member of a sewing group, and a fund-raiser for the League of Nations Famine Relief Society. She played bridge once a week with the wives of the mayor, the banker, and the doctor, and she and her husband exchanged dinners now and then with a number of local families. However, she remained a newcomer, "that Jewish woman from Detroit."

Mother rocked and brooded over her exile. By the time my father and I returned from our fruitless search, she had worked up her anger. She greeted us with the words: "I just called the Indians."

*

By morning, the rain had eased to a fine drizzle. Father, Mother, and I sat at breakfast, arguing.

"We have to notify the police and the coast guard," insisted my father.

"It went below forty last night, Momma. People die from exposure."

"Cleo knows how to take care of herself. She's a regular animal—a survivor."

"I'm going to the police," I said. "It's my fault. I have a right."

"It's God's fault, if you want to know my opinion," declared my mother.

"Arabella!" said my father sternly, but inside he quailed to hear his own condemnation of God spoken aloud.

"An act of God, isn't that what the lawyers say?" Mother challenged him, probing the strength of his piety.

I stood up. "This is ridiculous."

"You'd better not notify anyone, Rebecca!" warned Mother. "They'd just want to send her away. She'll turn up, she always does. The important thing is to remain firm and calm. You can bet your hat, when she sees that we aren't bothered, she won't run off again."

"Momma, I'm going to the police station."

There was a knock at the back door. I ran to open it. John Clover stood on the steps, his yellow slicker dripping.

"I found Cleo."

"Is she—?" For a moment, I was certain that my sister was dead.

"She's fine, but we'll need your car, Hank."

"Of course, let's go."

"We'll all go," said Arabella.

"No," said John. "It's better that just me and Becky go—that's what Cleo wants."

"Come in, John, and have a cup of coffee," said Mother. "You're soaked."

"No thanks," said John, "I'm dry underneath."

"Drive carefully," said my father, handing me the keys to the car.

EIGHT

WE DROVE THE FORD out to the Clover place, rigged a boat hitch onto our back bumper, and attached a heavy, two-wheeled boat trailer. John secured some boards over the bed of the boat trailer. He loaded a heavy coil of rope and a roll of stitched cable into the back seat of the car. He then directed me to drive south through a maze of dirt roads near the lake.

"Where are we going?" I asked. "What's all this about?"

"You'll see. Just keep your eye on the road."

"Why did you quit your job, John?"

John laughed. My face burned with shame. He glanced at me and laughed even harder. When he had recovered his breath, he patted me lightly on the top of my head. "You're the only one who's been honest enough to ask me," he said.

"But why?"

"Maybe I'll tell you, maybe not. For now, it's enough that you asked."

At last we reached a one lane track with grass growing up the middle that followed the Lake Michigan shore. After bumping along for more than five miles, John instructed me to drive out onto the beach itself.

We continued to drive south for more than a mile over the low, wide, hard-packed sand. To the east a slate-gray Lake Michigan moved constantly toward the shore under heavy, low clouds. The water appeared shallow for some distance from the shore. The waves barely broke in long narrow traces of curling foam. Low scrub forests of pine and birch grew along the edge of the beach. Neither house, nor barn, nor even a fence post marked the wilderness through which the Ford moved.

"How did you find her all this way?"

"She found me. Showed up at the house at five-thirty in the morning all excited. Showed me what she wanted and where. My son Jack drove her back out here before he went to work in East Jordan."

Through the wet mist, I made out a boat beached in the shallow water. It lay on its side like a wounded creature. I slowed the car. As we neared the white craft I felt the impulse to turn around and flee. At first sight, I suspected that the ghostly intruder threatened the order of our lives.

"Cleo's there," said John.

We continued on. Ahead, I saw my sister dragging something across the beach, up the sand bank, and into the scrub forest. By the time we reached the boat, Cleo had returned to the beach and was squatting there, waiting for us. I jumped out of the car and embraced my sister, kissing her first on one cheek and then on the other and finally on the mouth.

"I'm sorry, Cleo, I'm really sorry."

Cleo pointed at the boat. The sleek cabin cruiser lay canted to one side in shallow water. The weight of the boat kept it wedged on the bottom so that the waves barely jostled it. There were no numbers on the bow. Something else was wrong about it, something out of place. It was all white, without any distinctive mark or decoration to identify it.

"What's going on, John? Why didn't you call the coast guard?"

"Hell, I just got here myself." He explained that Cleo had appeared at the Clover farm early in the morning. "All she told me was to bring the trailer to Running Shoal."

Cleo tugged on our clothing until we followed her down the beach to a smashed wooden case lying just out of the water. It had contained bottles, several of which remained unbroken. John picked one up.

"It's the real stuff," he said, "*Seagram's V.O.*—the best Canadian whiskey."

"Bootleggers!" I exclaimed. "This has something to do with those bodies they found yesterday off North Point." I stared out at the white boat, imagining the men struggling with one another aboard it, the shots, the bodies.

"Probably," said John.

Cleo pulled us back to the car and kept pointing out to the boat.

"We should go get the police," I said.

Cleo shook her head violently.

"This is none of our business, Cleo."

"Mine," said Cleo, "mine, mine, mine."

John sat down on the running board of the car. He looked at Cleo and then at the boat and finally at the tracks across the sand toward the scrub forest.

Cleo pointed at the forest and at the boat. She nodded at John. "Mine." Then she put out one hand, palm up, and gestured toward it a number of times with the thumb and forefinger of her other hand as if she were counting money. Finally she closed the open hand into a fist and put it into her pocket. Then she stuck a thumb into her armpit.

John thought a while and then said, "Salvage."

"What?"

"She's claiming the boat and the cargo as salvage. She plans to sell the whiskey and pocket the money for herself. I don't know what she's going to do with the boat. Fix it, I guess. I dunno."

"But Cleo, it's not yours." The thought of her taking possession of that doomed craft horrified me. "It belongs to the government! It's contraband. It's against the law."

"Mine, mine, mine, mine!" shouted Cleo, stamping on the shore.

I regarded my sister's red face. With those same words, she had claimed my food, my toys, my books. There had even been times when she had claimed me as her own property, jealously demanding my exclusive affection.

I took in a deep breath and exhaled. "Not yours! Not mine! The government's!" I saluted. "The police!"

Cleo threw herself onto the beach and lay there as if she were dead. I was about to launch myself onto my sister's body and pound her on the back in frustration when I felt John's restraining hand.

"For now, we'd better do what she wants us to."

"But it's against the law."

"I don't know about that. If Cleo salvages the boat, it's hers. With that load, no one else is going to claim it."

"What about the whiskey?"

"Forget about the whiskey. Someone will find it eventually."

"I don't know."

"Listen Rebecca, she's been out in this weather for twenty-four hours and she won't come back with us until she's satisfied. You can deal with the police later if you want to."

*

Once we had convinced Cleo that we would not interfere with her claim on the boat and its cargo, Cleo stood up and took charge of the salvage. First, she pounded the winch on the foredeck until the cabin cruiser's anchor cable was released. The three of us dragged the anchor almost all the way to shore so that the boat could not float free once we unloaded it. Then we unhooked the boat trailer from the Ford and rolled the trailer into the water to the boat's bow. Case by case, we unloaded the boat, piling the whiskey carefully onto the boards over the trailer. When the trailer was loaded, we attached one end of the line to the trailer and the other to the Ford. Slowly, I drove the Ford in toward the scrub forest until the trailer was out of the water on the beach. Then I backed the Ford to the trailer. We attached the trailer directly to the car and hauled the load of whiskey up to the edge of the scrub forest where we unloaded. We hid the whiskey in the forest under a cover of brush and sand.

It took ten trailer trips to empty the cabin cruiser. Free of its load, the boat floated upright in the water, tugging on the anchor chain. I stood up to my knees in water, staring at it. The creature had come alive, promising more brutal murders, drowning, death. Cleo slapped me on the back and pushed me toward the anchor.

Cleo, John, and I carried the anchor back several yards toward the boat until the boat floated in deep enough water to get the trailer positioned under it. Now we ran the cable from the bow of the boat to the Ford. Slowly I put a strain on the cable and pulled the boat forward onto the trailer. John and Cleo stood on either side of the bow, directing the boat. When the boat was firmly lodged on the trailer, we ran the heavy line from the trailer to the Ford so that the car was attached to the boat and trailer by both the cable and the line.

I put the car in gear and let up on the clutch. The rear wheels of the car began to spin. "Stop!" shouted John.

I stopped, hoping that our efforts would fail.

John ran out of the water and stood next to the car. "Straighten your steering wheel," he directed, "and go very, very slowly. The first movement is the most important. Very, very slowly."

This time I let up on the clutch cautiously, feeding the engine more gas only when I felt the first hesitant motion of the car. An inch at a time, we pulled the boat and trailer out of the lake. Finally, we were able to attach the trailer directly to the car and we were ready to head back to town. Only then did I get a chance to examine the wreck. Bullet holes pocked the bulkhead of the cabin. Blood smeared the deck, some of it dried and some still wet. Sickened, I ran down to the water and threw up. Cleo came and dragged me back to the car, where I collapsed, exhausted, onto the running board. Cleo danced about, elated. She pulled me to my feet. She kissed John's cheek and my own and for a moment gazed directly into our eyes. Then she pointed to the boat and to the forest where the whiskey lay hidden and put her finger on each of our lips.

"Mine," she said.

All the way toward town, I kept glancing back to see the white shape hovering above the rear window of the car. It seemed as if we were hauling misfortune back from the waste of scrub, beach, and lake.

*

By the time we had hidden the boat in the barn at the Clover place, it was early evening. To keep Cleo's discovery a secret, John and I devised a story. We would claim that one of the Clover sons had found her marching down the highway past Mancelona; she had fled into an abandoned house and it had taken all this time to convince her to return.

When Cleo and I got home, however, there was no need to make an explanation. "You're late for dinner," said Mother. "Go wash up."

"Don't you think that a hot bath—" my father began.

"Before they go to bed." My mother was determined to make no recognition of Cleo's flight. "Right now it's dinnertime."

No one spoke during dinner. Cleo ate ravenously, using her hands. Mother pretended not to notice. I dozed.

My father could not keep his troubled eyes off Cleo. He linked her disappearance with the brick that had shattered the front window of his store.

The phone rang. My mother got up to answer it in the pantry. It was a collect call from Maureen Lefkowitz.

"Collect?" Mother asked the operator.

"Will you accept the charges?"

"Henry!" Mother stuck her head into the dining room, "Maureen's calling collect!"

"There must be a reason."

"All right, but don't blame me just because Sy's my brother. I warned him not to marry that immigrant."

She accepted the call.

"Are you all right?" Maureen's whisper barely came through the receiver.

"Speak up," said Mother. "Why are we paying for this call?"

"I'm calling from the railroad station."

"Where are you going?"

"Nowhere. Sy thought it best not to call from home. Is Henry all right?"

"We're all fine. A hail storm broke one of the front windows to the store, but we're all in good health."

"When Sy read the newspaper, he sent me out to call. He would have called, but he didn't want to be conspicuous."

"What's in the newspaper?"

"Sy thinks Henry should lay low for a while. Take a trip or something. The whole family."

"Are you crazy?"

"Maybe you don't get a newspaper."

"We get two papers and magazines too, national magazines. What's so bad in the newspaper?"

"Dead bodies in Charlevoix."

"Oh that. Happens all the time. You think we don't have murders up here too, just like Detroit or Chicago?"

"Sy says that maybe Henry's bitten off more than he can chew. The powers-that-be are pretty touchy."

"Henry knows what he's doing. He sticks to business."

"That's exactly what we're talking about—Henry's other business."

"I've got my own troubles, Maureen—"

"He's not exactly cut out for you-know-what. These days, only professionals survive—"

"Henry is a professional. He can take care of himself. He's very well organized. He's getting ready to branch out."

"Oh my God, Bella, at least stick to your own backyard. There are sharks out there."

"Florida, California, the Northwest—we've got the finances and everyone trusts Henry."

"Look, I got to get off the phone. Someone may see me here. You tell your husband that Sy said for him to lay low, take it easy, take a trip. And let me add that I think it's a bad idea to mention Henry's plans to anyone, even to me, especially over the telephone."

To my mother's annoyance, her sister-in-law hung up.

"What nerve!" said Mother, returning to the dining room. "My brother and his wife have gone crazy. They think people are listening in on their telephone."

"Considering some of Sy's clients—"

"Psshhh, nonsense. What if someone hears what she has to say to me—bragging all the time. Now they're terrified that we'll be as successful as they are. They don't think we should open any branches—a lot of nerve. As if they knew anything about the clothing business."

I came out of a doze suddenly. "Daddy!" My voice was bright, a little shrill. "Have you ever thought of opening up a branch in Ann Arbor? The Detroit Bearwalds could go in it with you—partnership."

"Ann Arbor?" asked my father, bewildered.

"No, no," said my mother, "there's snow in Ann Arbor. We've got one winter store already. We need a branch in Florida, in California—resorts, that should be our specialty."

"About Maureen's call—?" began Father.

"Oh they read about those gangsters they found out near North Point. As if they're the only people with gangsters."

"Well, that was nice of them to be concerned."

My mind began to function now. "What about the bodies out at North Point?"

"Bootleggers," said my father. "That's what Sheriff Hayes thinks."

"Was there a boat?" My voice quavered. "Was there a boat?" Across the table, Cleo stopped eating, her eyes fixed on her plate.

"Yes. They found a boat, floating in Little Traverse Bay, full of bullet holes, with three dead bodies and an arsenal of machine guns and pistols."

My father would have ended the conversation, but I persisted in my questions and Cleo stood up, gesturing wildly for him to continue. When he still remained silent, a low growl emitted from somewhere within Cleo.

Daddy put his hands up in surrender and went on. "The sheriff thinks there must have been a gun battle between rival gangs. The Detroit police and the Chicago police are coming up to examine the bodies in the boat and the bodies on the beach. It was clearly a hijacking. There must have been another boat—whether it was the hijacker's boat or the original boat, they don't know. Anyway, the whiskey's gone—either to Chicago or Detroit or sunk maybe, with a dead crew of gangsters and a fortune in booze."

"They're like pirates, these smugglers." Mother's eyes gleamed. "They say that there're so many boats going back and forth across the Detroit River day and night that it looks like a regatta. Great sums of money change hands. Fortunes are being made. Everyone's in the business—the Irish, the Sicilians, even the Jews."

"Jewish smugglers?"

"Your Uncle Sy could—"

"That's enough, Arabella," said Father, firmly. "It's not a subject for the supper table. We're all tired and could use a night's sleep."

"After a bath," said Mother.

*

The next morning I awoke abruptly, my heart clutched with fear. There was something I had to do but for a moment I could not remember what. I lay rigid in my bed, my pulse racing. Cleo was safe, I thought, and I thanked God. Then I remembered the white boat, the bullet holes, and all the dead bodies. I knew what I had to do this morning: go to the police station and explain everything that had happened yesterday. I would ask Sheriff Hayes not to tell my parents. There was no need to go into the matter. No one would hold Cleo responsible. The authorities would take the whiskey and the boat, and that would be the end of it.

There remained only one problem. Cleo. I could not go to the police without telling Cleo first. I had already betrayed my sister once in my desire to escape her and the family.

And Cleo knew my hopes.

Or did she?

I sighed as I forced myself out of bed. I remembered how easily Cleo had forged our father's signature on the college applications. Had Cleo understood what she was doing? Had she realized that those applications might take me away from Charlevoix? The possibility that Cleo had willingly aided me made it unthinkable to betray my sister's secret without warning her. I dressed and ate breakfast with a heavy heart and set off with the family downtown. At the store, we stood before our parents, waiting to be sent on our way.

"Now Cleo," said my father, "Mr. Weyrich is very proud of the way you handled the fire at the boatyard. He thinks you're one of the best craftsmen he has, so there's no need—"

"Daddy," I interrupted, "Cleo knows all that."

"Everything's going to be the same as it was before," said Mother.

Kisses were given and received. This morning my mother did not insist upon a kiss from Cleo. Cleo and I set off for the park. In spite of my assurances to my father, I expected to have a difficult time getting Cleo to go back to work. But Cleo seemed eager to get to the boathouse. She remained with the Clovers in the park only long enough to gobble down her bun and drink her coffee. Then she bounded through the park and waited by the boathouse door.

This was the moment I had chosen to confront my sister. But I did not. Fear and guilt clouded my resolve. That spring I knew that the white boat would bring no good to my family, and yet I convinced myself that the situation would sort itself out: Cleo would forget about the boat hidden in the Clovers' barn and someone would eventually discover the hidden hijacked whiskey.

NINE

THE GREAT MARCH THUNDER and hailstorm proved to be the end of winter in Charlevoix. Fair, windy days followed. Kites sailed through the skies above the ball field and along the beaches. Crocuses and trillium bloomed in the forests under the delicate new branches of birch and oak and elm and ash. Bright needles sprouted upon the pines and then tiny new leaves unfurled at the tips of the hardwood limbs. Farmers set to work plowing and planting the fields, mowing and fertilizing the orchards while their animals browsed in the fresh new grass of the meadows.

Two weeks after Cleo's night on the beach, she arrived at the store late in the afternoon with John Clover. John informed my father that he would like to employ Cleo in the evenings, after work, out at the Clover farm, to repair some farm machinery and to help renovate an old boat.

"I don't know," said Father, taken aback. "Cleo's very tired after a day at Weyrich's."

"Definitely not," said Mother. "Summer's coming on and there'll be a tremendous amount of work at the yard getting the boats ready."

John listened to my parents carefully, studying their faces. Then he looked out the window across the street at Round Lake. He nodded his head. Impatiently, Cleo gestured for him to speak, which he did, very slowly. "Old man Weyrich said it was all right with him as long as Cleo put in her eight hours. She works awful fast, you know."

"I won't have my daughter exploited," my mother responded.

Once again John let the silence expand in the store. He examined the floor in front of him. He spoke deliberately, as if he were thinking out each idea. "I'll pay her half any profit we make when we sell the machinery or the boat. I don't think I could do it without her."

My father glanced at my mother who deferred to him with narrowed eyes. He could tell that she expected him to refuse decisively. It would be easier, he thought, if John weren't an Indian. And then there was the situation concerning John's work for the postal service and his retirement. Such strange behavior made my father feel uncomfortable.

"We'd like to help you out, John," said Father. "And it is very generous of you. But Cleo really doesn't need the money."

Cleo, who had been standing behind John, now edged in front of him and confronted Father and Mother. She looked each of them directly in the eye, commanding their attention. Cleo's large black pupils grew deeper in the gloom of the store. She lowered her gaze slowly to her hands and their eyes followed.

With her right hand she pointed at her left hand; with her left hand she pointed at her right; then she pointed to her chest. "Mine!" she said and stared once more directly into their eyes.

"What on earth is she saying?" asked Mother.

"I don't know," said Father.

Cleo turned to John Clover and repeated the motions with her hands. "Mine!" she repeated.

John nodded toward the Bearwalds, shrugging, as if to say that the matter was beyond his control.

Cleo's face darkened. She stamped upon the floor. She held out her hands. "Mine."

"John," said my father, his voice pleading, "do you know what she means?"

"Why should he know any better than we do?" asked my mother, irritably.

"Because he seems to," said my father. "John?"

"I don't like to interfere any more than I have already," said John.

"John," said Father, afraid they had offended the man, "please tell us what you think she means."

"If you don't want your daughter working out at our place, that's your affair." John looked through the window at Round Lake. "This was sort of her idea, anyway."

"We can't respond if we don't understand."

John sighed. His voice lost its deliberate manner. "Well, the way I figure it, Cleo seems to be saying she thinks her hands belong to her." My father flinched at the implied accusation. John continued, "She feels if she wants to work two jobs, that's her decision. She seems awful anxious, for some reason, to make some money. I can't tell why."

A low sound began deep in Cleo's throat and by the time John had finished, the sound began to issue from her widening mouth.

My parents gazed at one another in alarm and simultaneously burst out, "All right, all right, you can work with John."

After Cleo and John Clover left the store, my parents paced about restlessly, unable to get back to work. Cleo's sudden initiative had unnerved them.

"Oh Henry," said Mother, "what will we do about our daughters?"

Father searched within himself for words that would soothe his wife. He looked around his store, seeking the comfort that the familiar place had always afforded him.

"Henry?"

My father sat down and opened his account book. Mother closed it. When he spoke, he attempted to escape into details. "We could work out a schedule for the girls—Rebecca will have to drive Cleo out to the Clovers every evening, and pick her up before bedtime."

"I don't mean schedules, Henry." My mother's voice rasped. "Something's happening to Cleo and we need Rebecca's cooperation. You have to talk to Rebecca."

"I'll try."

"Trying won't be enough, Henry. She thinks I'm the villain—that I don't understand her love of books. And then there's Cleo, with her hands. She has her own bank account. We put all the money she makes in it."

My father tried to meet his wife's gaze. He weighed the complications which God had piled upon his shoulders and turned back to his work.

"Nothing to say, as usual." Mother sank down in a chair next to the desk. "I should ask John Clover what you're thinking."

Father's right eye squinted, his mouth screwed down. The comforting irony with which he kept despair in check had fled.

Mother threw up her hands. "I give up. We'll talk about schedules."

So they discussed Cleo's new arrangement: she would work at both jobs on the weekdays, on Saturdays she would work only at the boatyard, and on Sundays she would work all day out at the Clover's. Rebecca would ferry her back and forth from the Clover farm.

*

Over the years, I have tried to understand my father's silence. From the very beginning of their marriage that was my mother's constant complaint about him: his inability to express his feelings. Of course, there was a perfectly reasonable explanation. Father was the only child of parents who did not speak about personal matters. Although I had only vague recollections of my grandparents who died before I was three, I felt their presence in our lives. My father's stern parents filled the light and shadowy air of the store with their moral, disciplined work. They gave substance to every square foot.

Was this obstinate silence of my father's simply humility, or something deeper: a desire to hide? After all, why did my grandparents decide to settle so far from their families and community? Indeed, I began to think that Cleo's personality was not so much an aberration as we thought. Cleo and my father were very much alike in their unwillingness or inability to speak. She too had been in hiding all her life.

That spring, however, Cleo emerged a bit into the world. The demanding new schedule of work at the boatyard and out at Clovers' farm appeared to suit her. There were moments, of course, when she didn't get her way that she reverted to her old tricks: screaming, smashing herself to the floor, foaming at the mouth. But much less often. As the weeks passed, she did not once wander off from the boatyard. Mr. Weyrich told my father that Cleo had never before been so dependable. By the end of April, he doubled her wages. "I'll tell you, Hank," he said, "she's as good a machinist and carpenter as you'll find north of Detroit."

Out at the Clovers, the repair of the bootlegger's cabin cruiser proceeded quickly. John and his sons helped Cleo rig up a complete shop. They lifted out the engine, removed the propeller, and replaced the shaft that had been damaged. The hull needed major work, but the cabin and most of the fittings were in excellent shape. Every night when I arrived to take Cleo home, she conducted me through the barn, proudly displaying the results of her work. I could barely force myself to look at my sister's secret project. The incongruous presence of that sleek craft in the ramshackle barn reproached me for my cowardice.

As the weeks passed, the image of that large white boat manned by missing corpses haunted my dreams. I had become an accomplice in the creation of an infernal machine. One evening just as I was about to turn in at the Clovers, Cleo seized the steering wheel and directed the car past the farm. When I tried to stop, she pressed her foot on the accelerator, almost sending us into a ditch. By the time I had fought her off and pulled to the side of the road, we were well past the Clovers.

"What on earth are you up to?"

Cleo pointed ahead.

"I've got homework."

Cleo pointed ahead.

"No, no, no, no!" I began to turn the car around. Cleo grabbed the steering wheel. I stopped the car once more. "Do you want to drive? Is that it?"

Cleo nodded her head affirmatively.

Our parents had never taught Cleo how to drive, afraid that she would have one of her fits behind the wheel. When I obtained my driver's license at the age of fourteen, I secretly tried to give her driving lessons. But Cleo had required no lessons. She had learned to drive simply by watching the rest of us. From time to time I took her out in the car and let her take the wheel. She liked country back roads the best.

"You can take a short drive," I said, "but then you have to get back to the Clovers and I have to get home."

Cleo and I changed seats. It was a mild spring evening. The sliver of a moon rose in the eastern sky. A faint western breeze blew in from the lake. I cranked down my window, lay my head on the back of the seat, and let the wind wash over me. Cleo drove fast and well, much faster than I ever drove. I enjoyed the speed. I closed my eyes and began to imagine what life at college would be like—the books I would read, the professors who would lecture, the many new and interesting friends I would make, friends who shared my belief in the possibility of a just society.

Every afternoon on the way from school to the library, I stopped by the post office to look into the box I had rented for a reply to my scholarship application. Most of the time, I was relieved to find the box empty. I had no idea what I would do if I were awarded the scholarship. Would I confront my parents and force the issue? Would I simply run away at the end of the summer? For now there was no need to take action or even to make any decisions. I had seduced myself with the fantasy of opening a branch of Bearwalds in Ann Arbor. At night after finishing my homework, I composed letters to my father's uncles and cousins, broaching the idea of a partnership. But I never sent the letters off.

The sound of water came to my ears, waves breaking against the shore. I opened my eyes to see that the car was speeding along the beach. Cleo glanced over at me, opened her mouth, and let loose her happiest wail.

"Stop this car!" I ordered.

Cleo stomped down on the accelerator.

Terrified and angry, I did not know what to do.

"Stop!"

Cleo nodded and began to slow down.

"I want you to turn around and get us back to the Clovers!"

Cleo brought the car almost to a halt and swung the wheel. The car headed in toward the scrub forest and then completed its turn. Cleo stopped the car, took the keys out of the ignition, got out, and walked with dignity up the sand bank into the scrub forest. I assumed that she needed to pee.

I moved over to the driver's seat, crossed my arms, and waited. I was not going to let my sister get behind the wheel again. A few minutes later, she reappeared from the forest carrying one of the cases of bootlegger's whiskey that she had hidden after discovering the wreck.

Stunned, I jumped out of the car. I had been so delighted with Cleo's conscientious behavior since her flight from home that I had put the cache of whiskey out of my mind. Before I could stop her, she deposited the case of whiskey in the back seat.

"We are not taking that whiskey anywhere. It's against the law." I reached up to remove the case from the car.

Cleo put her arms around me and lifted me off my feet. She carried me around the car to the driver's door and set me down. She pointed into the car. I slid around her, intending to get the case of whiskey. She captured me again and placed me at the driver's door. Crying in frustration, I got into the Ford and sat behind the wheel. Cleo walked around the car and seated herself in the passenger seat. She handed me the keys and pointed back toward town. With calm determination, she forced me to drive her past the Clovers' farm and turn onto the highway heading south toward Traverse City. Twice I stopped the car. Twice she got out of the car and sat in front of it. Finally I capitulated and followed my sister's directions.

That night we ended our journey at Roadhouse 31, fifteen miles south of Charlevoix. While I waited fearfully behind the wheel, Cleo carried the case of whiskey around to the back of the building. In fifteen minutes she returned with a roll of bills and pointed toward home. Obediently, I started the car and drove down the highway. Before we reached the town limits, she gestured for me to turn. Soon we arrived at the Clovers' farm. John and Ruth sat at the kitchen table, drinking tea. Cleo sat down and placed the bills in front of Ruth.

I sat down with relief. "John, Ruth, she's been selling the whiskey from the boat. That money is illegal. Please tell her that she can't do this."

The Clovers looked at one another and then turned toward me. Ruth spoke. "I'm afraid it's up to her, Becky."

"Why is it up to her?"

"The boat's hers," said John, "the whiskey's hers."

"John, don't you remember, at the beginning you said the whiskey—she doesn't understand that it's against the law."

John looked at Cleo, who smiled.

"Cleo!"

Cleo turned toward me, her smile slowly disappearing.

"She understands," said John.

"And what are you going to do with the money?" I asked Ruth.

"Put it in her account."

"But this makes us all accomplices," I said. I stared at Ruth and then at John. They returned my gaze without flinching, their dark faces somber.

"These days," Ruth said, "everyone in the country is a criminal of one sort or another."

I became aware of Cleo's eyes moving from face to face, watching, waiting. What does she comprehend? I asked myself. How did she communicate her plan to the Clovers? How much of the plan originated with them? Was it possible that all spring my sister, with the Clovers' help, had been bending me to her will? Struck by the absurdity of such a thought, I wanted to laugh.

"Just look at Roadhouse 31 or at that fancy Beechams in town," said Ruth. "Our mayor, our sheriff, our fire chief all know what goes on in those places—"

"Hell, they go there themselves." John snorted.

"My father doesn't. He says—"

"Most people in town don't share your father's views." Ruth reached across the table and patted my hand.

I sat very still. I looked around the Clovers' large, comfortable farmhouse kitchen with its wood stove and the pump over the kitchen sink. Since we were little girls, Cleo and I had eaten many meals here with the Clovers and their children. I loved the Clovers and trusted them. I could not understand why they were helping Cleo in her illegal activities. I stared down at the table, afraid that my expression might reveal disappointment in my friends.

"Listen, Rebecca," said John finally, "your sister wants to be independent."

"Independent?" The idea angered me. I turned to my sister, but Cleo's face remained expressionless. Then I was embarrassed. Why should I feel betrayed by the idea of Cleo living her own life?

John's eyes commanded mine. "You wanted to know why I quit my job, Becky? Why I sit in the park every day?"

I nodded—but now I wasn't sure I wanted to hear him explain.

"Because I am myself and not anyone else. They would have me be something else—something familiar, a thing that fits into their landscape. But that would be a lie."

The image of John sitting at the center of our town rose up before me—on the park bench in his yellow foul-weather gear under a makeshift shelter in the torrential rain. For some reason I thought of Mrs. Thrush and her sister running down South Point Road in the night. "You have no idea who you are," Mrs. Thrush had said.

John and Ruth remained silent while I absorbed his words. I felt Cleo's eyes on me like a great weight. I heard the kitchen clock ticking.

If I were John Clover would I have had the courage to step outside the circle of the town after all those years of acting the exemplary citizen? To say no to everyone and to remain there, every day, saying no?

John was an honest man. Perhaps that was why I loved him.

Ruth laid her hand upon my hands, which were clenched so tight that the knuckles were white. "Cleo's her own person, Becky."

John took up the argument. "It was all her plan from the beginning. The boat's hers; the whiskey's hers; the money's hers." John, Ruth, and Cleo gazed at me. I avoided their eyes.

John was silent for some time, and then continued. "Are we going to help her?"

Caretaking, I thought, what a bedevilment. The more care you give, the more authority you appropriate. And no one admits the anger such relationships generate.

Finally, I conceded to Cleo and the Clovers. And so I, Rebecca Bearwald, who believed in law and social justice, became my sister's confederate in selling hijacked, illegal whiskey to roadhouses within a fifty mile radius of Charlevoix.

TEN

MY LAST SEMESTER AT high school turned out to be a disaster. After a career as one of the top students and everyone's choice as best citizen, I suddenly became the class problem. I scarcely read my homework assignments, turned in papers late, talked during lectures, and fell asleep in class.

While my conduct deteriorated, Cleo's improved. She became almost affectionate to my parents, even a bit playful. She took permanent possession of the key to the boathouse at Weyrich's. Her constant round of work agreed with her. Her eyes glowed and her skin took on a burnished healthy color; she leaped to her tasks with a carefree independence. She became imperious, curiously like my mother, but Cleo wasn't play-acting. She demanded and when the proper response was not forthcoming, she threatened at first and then went into one of her fits. Later I came to understand Cleo's improvement. She now had something of her own to buoy up her injured soul, something substantial, the white boat along with the prospect of independence.

As spring proceeded, this new Cleo took charge of my life. Though I ignored the commands of my parents and teachers, I abandoned my will to hers. Now she dragged me out of bed in the morning and delivered me to school in order to make sure that I got there on time. When school let out, she arrived to escort me to my job at the library and then returned to her own work at Weyrich's. At the end of the day, she walked me home from the library. If Cleo did not appear to pick me up at school or work, I waited listlessly, my mind wandering in misery.

My decline that spring was accelerated by an accident which occurred some time after Cleo and I had begun selling whiskey to the roadhouses around Charlevoix. Betty Jane Kelley, the young divorced mother of the girl who worked at our store, drowned in the channel. She had been babysitting for the pharmacist Jim Morris and his wife while they ate dinner at Roadhouse 31. It was raining very hard. At around ten o'clock at night, Jim offered to drive Betty home. About an hour later, Jim's car skidded through the barrier arm on the south side of the bridge-crossing and fell fifty feet down the embankment into the water. The pharmacist managed to struggle loose, but Betty Jane went down with the car.

As both the Morrises and the Kelleys lived on the north side of the bridge, the sheriff questioned why Jim was on the south side of the bridge. Jim said he had gone back to Roadhouse 31 to retrieve an umbrella. He admitted that he had bought Betty a few drinks while they were there. As soon as I heard the details of the accident, I decided that Cleo and I were responsible.

I felt certain that Jim and Betty Jane had been drinking the whiskey that Cleo and I had sold to the roadhouse.

When Jim's car was hauled out of the channel the next day, Betty Jane's body was not in it. No one knew whether the currents would carry the body to Round Lake or out into Lake Michigan, but everyone said that the body would surface when the wind died at sunrise and sunset. Fishermen posted a lookout on the big lake, while on Round Lake, people went out in small boats to hunt for the body. I insisted that Cleo and I join the search. Every morning and evening we rowed along the shores of Round Lake in one of the Weyrich's skiffs.

On the third day after the accident, Mr. Bono, the assistant principal, called me into his office and informed me that I was in danger of failing two of my four courses, in which case, I would not graduate. Mr. Bono looked pleased. He had never forgiven me my behavior on the day of the big storm when Cleo had come to school to find me.

"Not graduate?" I repeated with surprise.

"That's correct," he said and waited for me to plead my case.

For the first time I realized I had been attempting to provoke such a punishment: I did not deserve a diploma or anything else. To my surprise, I felt relieved at this punishment. All these years I had lived up to everyone's expectations. Now I no longer would be required to try. I stood up and went to the door.

Mr. Bono continued, grudging the words which might offer me hope, "Your study hall counselor, Mrs. Thrush, has defended you, although I fail to see why. She has convinced your teachers to let you write extra papers to make up several of the quizzes you failed."

All day I brooded over my perverse desire to fail. Would I be truly satisfied if I did not graduate? I didn't know. As soon as school ended, I went to the study hall to see Mrs. Thrush. The counselor was correcting papers at her desk. I marched to the desk and stood there, waiting for her judgment. Mrs. Thrush finished the page and looked up.

"I came to thank you for—keeping me in school."

"With your record, no one would seriously consider suspending you."

"I only came to tell you—" I didn't really know why I had come. Perhaps I wanted her to urge me to graduate. "I appreciate your—." I knew that the principal and the school board were reviewing Mrs. Thrush's contract. Rumors about her past continued to circulate. Now, thanks to Jim Morris, the word "lesbian" had been spoken aloud and crept into the discussion. Some of the parents wanted her fired. It was unfair of me to burden her with my personal problems. "I wasn't asking for anything, really." I knew I should leave, but I continued to stand there.

Wearily, Mrs. Thrush placed the fingertips of both her hands upon her forehead. I wanted to sit down and ask the fierce little lady about her life. What had made her into such a prickly, guarded woman? I had seen the woman she lived with—her sister, she said—from a distance, strolling along the deserted road toward South Point. She seemed to wear only clothes from the past, long flowing dresses and great wide hats. She never went down into town. On weekends she went out riding with Mrs. Thrush in their car. On my lips were poised a whole series of questions. Do you have brothers and other sisters? Did your parents want to send you to college? Are you a widow, divorced, abandoned? Whom do you love? How do you love? I asked none of them. Instead, after an awkward silence, I slowly withdrew, my legs leaden, waiting for Mrs. Thrush to call me back. As I closed the door, I saw her still leaning forward, elbows on the desk, her forehead supported by her fingertips.

That night, I dreamed of Betty Jane Kelley creeping along the bottom of the lake, unable to find a way to climb up into the air. Betty Jane wore clothes from the past, like Mrs. Thrush's sister, a great wide hat and a long dress which trailed around her in the water. Every time she reached for the surface, a white boat blocked the way, forcing her back down to the bottom. In the dream, Betty Jane and I were the same person—rotten, stinking, without hope.

On Friday of that week, five days after the accident, just at sunset, Cleo and I returned toward Weyrich's in our skiff after another fruitless search. Cleo rowed. I sat in the stern, staring listlessly at the oars as they dipped into the water, creating small whirlpools behind them, and then rose for another stroke. The drops of water falling from the oars caught the last light of day before shattering onto the lake's surface. As Cleo took her last sweep through the water, I saw a shape swelling up underneath the dock toward which we were gliding. My strangled cry caused Cleo to turn. There, wedged under the Weyrich dock, was Betty Jane, bloated and almost unrecognizable.

"Stop, stop," I whispered, "head toward the harbormaster's." Cleo ignored my plea. She guided our boat to the end of the dock. She made me climb up and hang over the edge while she sat in the boat, prodding at Betty Jane with one of the oars. Slowly the bloated, slimy body edged toward me out from under the boards.

The smell made me choke. I tried to grasp at the coat, but it slipped through my fingers. Finally, I could do no more. I just rolled over on the dock and lay gasping for air. Mr. Weyrich and Richie appeared and took over the task.

I could not forget the sight of the body. My anguish increased when I found a letter at my post office box notifying me that I had been awarded a full scholarship to the University of Michigan. The letter requested that I inform the university of my intentions. Before leaving the post office, I checked the paragraph indicating that I intended to accept the scholarship and posted the document to the university. My criminal career was now complete. I had broken the Eighteenth Amendment of the Constitution, sold stolen goods which had contributed to the death of a good, hardworking woman, committed fraud and forgery, and now intended to evade my responsibilities by running away from home.

*

All through childhood, June was my favorite month, full of excitement and expectation. It was as if the sleeping town with its shuttered hotels and empty stores woke up, determined to transform itself into a rich, strange kingdom capable of satisfying all desires. The new season began with the removal of shutters from the summer houses. I was delighted to see the windows thrown open, bedding aired out, porches repaired, and fresh paint lavishly spread. Then the floors were swept, rugs beaten, furniture scrubbed, and the pantries stocked with canned goods, spices, and all the condiments that would be needed for the summer repasts of families from Cincinnati, St. Louis, Chicago, New Orleans, and even from Detroit.

In the boatyards and boathouses, craftsmen, my sister among them, caulked and painted hulls, sanded and varnished woodwork, replaced and polished fittings, and tuned up engines. One by one, boats slid down ways, were lowered from davits, and backed down boat ramps on trailers until Round Lake was again populated with its handsome fleet of pleasure craft: *The Derring-do*, *The Black Swan*, *The Mar-Jo-Bo-Wink*, *The Savoir Faire*, *The Fairweather*, and so on. Out of the basements of many permanent residents of the town came handsomely lettered signs declaring "Rooms to Let—Day, Week, Month," "Room and Board," "Edgewood Boarding House," "Lakeside Cottage." A host of summer employees arrived to join me and the other local workers to prepare the two hotels and the two private residential associations for the onslaught of pleasure-seekers. In the final week of June, like an industrious army, the children of the town spread through the streets mowing grass, raking up leaves, combing flower beds, planting, trimming, and shaping the gardens and hedges and lawns through which the city visitors would romp, in which they would eat and drink and dance under birches and pines, the sun and stars.

I found June of 1928 to be a month of defeat, miserable guilt, and secrets. Several times I caught sight of Mrs. Thrush gazing at me, a questioning, speculative expression on her face. I admired and feared Mrs. Thrush, but I had no love for her, not even affection. The talk with her, however, after Mr. Bono's threat had convinced me that I had an obligation to graduate. I owed it to her, if not to myself. Reluctantly, I completed my extra essays and passed all of my courses. Then I put on the black robe and mortarboard and marched across the stage to take the diploma. Ben Near was the valedictorian. I had been in the running for that honor until this last semester. As it was, I received no medals or awards.

After the ceremony I was rushing my family off when I found the way blocked by Mrs. Thrush. She introduced herself to my parents and to Cleo. Without pausing for the family to acknowledge her introduction, she continued in an abrupt, clipped tone, "I just wanted you to know that I think Rebecca has the potential to make a significant contribution to society."

She turned now to me, gave my hand a firm shake, and walked briskly off.

ELEVEN

EVER SINCE THE BRICK smashed the front window of my father's store, he had become more and more withdrawn. At first my mother thought he had contracted some sort of illness. She claimed she had never seen him so listless. She served him all sorts of broth, insisted that he eat second and third helpings of red meat and green vegetables, but he barely paid attention. After a while, she became angry. Breakfasts, at which, over the years, she had seemed most content and affectionate, became particularly trying, as if the hours they had spent in bed together had incensed her even more. She nagged at him from the moment he appeared in the kitchen, accusing him of being indifferent to everything—especially to her.

Unable to rouse my father, her attention now turned to me. As summer approached she became obsessed with my marriage. What had begun as a reasonable hope for my future now became a determined plan of action. At first she imagined an alliance with the wealthy German-Jewish families of Cincinnati, St. Louis, or New Orleans. However, she was practical enough to understand that the young men of these families would turn up their noses at life in a small northern town with the responsibility of a disturbed relative. She needed instead a hungry, ambitious young man from that striving crowd out of which her brother and his wife had recently risen. Although she hated to put herself in her sister-in-law's debt, she decided that Maureen offered her the best opportunity for locating the right son-in-law—one who would be glad at the chance to enter a small family business, married to its heir. In spite of all her bragging, Mother consoled herself, Maureen was a good sort of person who would understand the situation immediately. And so she called her sister-in-law in Detroit to discuss my prospects. I know exactly how the conversation went, because Mother reported it to me almost word for word as a sort of bludgeon.

Maureen chortled when she heard Mother's dilemma. Without hesitation, she pledged her support in the project. "Do I love to make matches? Let me tell you, Bella. It's the most wonderful feeling in the world. And I haven't done so bad, even with my own children, who are always the hardest."

"Children? You told me about Seymour and the Weintraub girl, but nothing about Cynthia."

Maureen informed my mother that her daughter had just become engaged to the son of the owner of the biggest laundry supply company in Detroit.

"Congratulations!"

"Let me tell you, there's plenty more where he came from."

"Remember, Maureen, we've got special circumstances."

"You think I don't understand?"

"Henry wants the young man to go into the business."

"Which business?" Maureen's voice faded.

"The clothing business, the store. We're going to expand, you know. Henry has the means."

"It's an excellent opportunity."

"The young man and his family will have to know about Cleo. I'm not trying to hide anything."

"Naturally." My aunt paused for a moment to assess the situation. Then she continued with increasing enthusiasm. "Look, Bella, your Rebecca's an angel. Any young man would be very fortunate—and a thriving small business too. Rebecca's just the right age, too. Not crazy about boys yet and still young enough to take our advice."

"Mind you, Maureen, I'm not talking about an arranged marriage. I want Rebecca to fall in love."

"Let's call it a 'prompted' marriage. It's more American. Our girls are good girls. They really want to please us. Once they see how right it all is, they fall in love. The boys are easier yet. Take my word, you've got a lot to offer. When I get to Charlevoix, we'll make a campaign."

Mother hung up, pleased. She had enlisted a vigorous ally.

Almost immediately, the phone rang. It was Maureen. "I don't want to be critical or anything, but, to tell the truth, Rebecca's wardrobe—well, it could use some improvement."

"You think I'm an idiot? I've spent the winter outfitting my girls for the market. Just wait, we'll knock your eyes out."

Indeed, Mother had spent months measuring us and herself, picking through patterns, studying her fashion magazines, and sewing. Now that she had enlisted Maureen in her crusade, she was ready to launch us. She marched into the living room and announced to the family that she would be finished sewing our summer wardrobes in a week, at which time there would be a formal showing in front of my father. "And you had better show some appreciation and enthusiasm," she warned us, addressing her remark pointedly at Father. "I've made damned good use of that sewing machine and those magazines you gave me and I want some praise, do you hear?" Father sighed, nodded, and shrugged his shoulders. Cleo and I shook our heads up and down. "That's hardly what I had in mind," she said scornfully, turned on her heel and returned to the sewing room.

The final fitting took place a week later. We modeled the outfits for my father who sat in the living room as if he were a client in a smart shop. On his face he wore an odd smirk, by which, I guessed, he meant to express enthusiasm. Mother ignored him.

Cleo, who appeared first in a black-and-white cocktail dress molded to her slim lines, caught the spirit of the occasion, and imitated the poses of fashion models she had seen in movie newsreels. With one hand poised in front of her, wrist cocked, she took half turns about the room, the other hand trailing gracefully. She paused here and there, a toe pointed ahead or behind, cocked her head to the side, and performed a complete turn and a curtsey.

Entranced, Mother, Father, and I gazed at Cleo. For years Cleo had worn only men's work clothes, resisting Mother's attempts to dress her up. Whenever she thought we were observing her, she had deliberately made faces and her gestures turned wooden. Tonight, though, she cooperated enthusiastically. Her enjoyment in the show illuminated her face and animated every gesture.

The style for 1928, which the fashion magazines called the year of "La Garçonne," peculiarly suited her. In the magazines, the short-haired, flat-chested, flat-hipped models wore big belts. Their clothes featured a boyish athletic look that would appeal to the "new woman, an aviatrix, a skier, even a homemaker who demanded freedom of movement." Cleo, with her long, jaunty strides, her boyish slimness, was a perfect "new woman."

We had always thought Cleo could be attractive. We had never before realized the extent of her beauty. This evening we felt as if a stranger had walked into our midst. Indeed, she seemed like a different person: one who would sit down after she had finished showing her clothes off and begin to talk normally about the day's events. No one spoke a word; we wanted only to prolong the illusion.

Finally Cleo stood in front of the mirror, examining her dress with a critical eye. She gestured and turned, gazing over her shoulder at the back of the dress. She bent over and examined the hem and the stitching. Abruptly, she summoned Mother and pointed to several of the seams that appeared badly sewn. Using her hands, she indicated the awkward drape on the left side of the skirt.

Mother turned and announced proudly, "She's like me. She has an instinct for style." For the rest of the fitting session, she consulted Cleo about each costume.

A peculiar exhilaration seized my mother. She allowed herself to believe that Cleo's condition had miraculously begun to improve. For twenty years she had prayed for this possibility without really believing in it. The hope chest had only been one of Mother's extravagant gestures, the product of her ardent imagination. She had never expected Cleo to marry—unless, miraculously, the retarded son of a good Jewish family materialized and asked her hand. Even then, Mother was not certain how she would react. Yet tonight, captivated by Cleo's beauty, my mother found herself desperately believing in her daughter's recovery.

When I marched in to model my new outfits, both Mother and Cleo carped at me, correcting my posture and my bearing.

"A sullen, unresponsive girl can ruin her chances forever," my mother lectured.

I balked, refusing to model any more.

"Rebecca! How on earth do you expect me to finish your clothes for this summer?"

"I don't want any new clothes." I sat down on the floor and crossed my arms.

My parents and Cleo regarded me with astonishment.

"Rebecca," said Mother, "please get up."

"Rebecca?" said Father.

"No!" I declared. An odd glow of satisfaction spread through my chest up to my head.

Cleo leaned over me and tried to raise me by the arms, but I squirmed away, rolling into a fetal position, knees close to my chest.

Mother grasped my arms and tried to get me to stand up. I resisted, clasping my knees rigidly. "We love you very much and we want you to be happy," she said. "But life isn't always just about happiness."

"Oh Momma!" I could not bear this line of argument. I began to feel ridiculous, lying all bunched up on the floor like a naughty child. I wanted to stand up, but I was committed to my position.

"Will you please stand up."

My rigid body relaxed as if I had been bludgeoned into submission. Behind Mother's back Cleo put out her hands as if they held the steering wheel of a car.

"Cleo wants me to take her out for a ride," I said with relief. I sat up.

"I still have to pin your dresses."

"We can finish when we get back."

"All right, but there isn't much time before summer."

"I promise, Momma." I stood.

"And come back with a positive attitude."

"Just remember that I'm not ready to get married."

Mother shrugged, waving my words away. "I think it's wonderful the way you girls have such a good time together."

TWELVE

ONCE WE WERE IN the car, Cleo pointed south. Without need for further directions, I drove out through the back roads and onto the beach. I felt like a dog that has been clubbed and whipped into obedience.

At Running Shoal where the whiskey was hidden, Cleo commanded me to accompany her into the scrub forest. Suspicious, I followed my sister. This was the first time she had asked my help. At the cache she handed me a case and picked up another.

"Two cases?" I asked.

Cleo gestered at all the cases.

"But—" I began to protest. Cleo pushed me ahead of her.

For more than an hour we worked, loading case after case into the Ford until only one was left. As I worked, I became increasingly agitated. In the past we had never peddled so much. I wondered where Cleo would dispose of such a big load.

Who could pay so much money? Tonight, we would surely be caught. For a moment I wished we would be arrested and put in jail. What a relief that would be! And then I remembered the sight of my sister in a straitjacket lying on the floor of the Petoskey jail.

Cleo directed me to the passenger seat of the car, tucked blankets carefully over the load, and took the wheel. We entered Charlevoix along the lake drive and kept to back streets all through town until we got to the bridge over the Lake Michigan Channel. Cleo drove carefully. We crossed the bridge and turned off the highway. We wound our way through the north side of town until we arrived at Beechams, the handsome restaurant, speakeasy, and gambling establishment that had been built on a square block just south of the public golf course. Groves of poplar trees lined the property. The lawn and garden spread out on three sides of the building, with paths and benches for the guests. Here and there unexpected grottoes opened up on ponds and fountains. The place was dark, deserted. It did not open for the summer until the first of July.

"No, Cleo." I was terrified. "Not here. You can't sell it right here in town."

Cleo smiled. Shutting off her lights, she drove the Ford slowly up a side drive to the back of the dark establishment. The formal green and white awnings and the white clapboard of the building shone brilliantly in the moonlight.

"I'm getting out. I'm walking home." I opened my door, but the car kept moving.

My father had spoken often about the disgrace that Beechams brought to the town of Charlevoix. "Openly flouting the law of the land," he said, "with the full knowledge of the mayor and the sheriff—probably the governor too."

I slumped in my seat. My hands were sweating.

Cleo pulled the car up to a small outbuilding behind the establishment. She got out of the car and went to the back door of the main building where she knocked three times in quick succession and then four times slowly. The door opened. In the lighted doorway stood a tall man in a dark, three-piece suit, a broad, colorful tie, and a white fedora trimmed with a black band. I thought he looked like an actor. His face was pale and long. A thin, curled mustache outlined his upper lip.

The man bowed to Cleo, turned, summoned two burly men in work clothes, and followed her to the car. At the well-dressed man's direction, the workmen took two cases from the car and placed them on the ground. One of the workmen jimmied open the cases with a crowbar and removed a bottle from each. The well-dressed man took the bottles back to the lighted doorway and examined them. He opened each bottle and tasted them.

I had never seen anyone taste anything in that manner. First he sniffed the bottle, then he poured a little of the contents into a small glass and held the glass up to the light. Then he smelled the glass and took a sip. He rolled the whiskey around in his mouth for a moment and swallowed. He breathed in deeply. After he had followed this procedure with the second bottle, he returned to the car.

"Excellent. First-rate goods, young lady. You are to be commended."

The workmen proceeded to unload the car and were about to carry the whiskey into the outbuilding when the well-dressed man stopped them. "I hope you don't mind, young lady, but in this business one must be very careful." He directed his workmen to open each case and examine the contents. Only when he was satisfied that all the cases were complete with sealed bottles of Canadian whiskey, did he direct the workmen to carry them inside.

"And now for my part of the bargain." The man drew a large brown envelope from his pocket and handed it to Cleo who nodded and began to turn away. "No, no. You must count it, young lady, exactly as I counted your shipment. In this business, never trust anyone."

Cleo carried the envelope around to the passenger side of the car and handed it to me.

"I don't want anything to do with it," I said, shrinking away.

Cleo opened the door and pulled me from the car. She thrust the envelope into my hand and marched me to the lighted doorway. The well-dressed man followed. "Such beautiful, young smugglers," he said, with a laugh.

I tore open the envelope. I had never seen so much money—brand new green bills—twenty, fifty, hundred dollar bills. I riffled through them. I did not bother to count. I did not know how much Cleo had asked, nor did I care, so long as we disposed of the whiskey. After tonight there would be only one more sale, unless Cleo planned to keep the last case for herself.

I suspected that Cleo had come in contact with the man at Beechams through the Clovers. I did not want to know the details. I stuffed the bills back into the envelope, slapped the envelope on my thigh and, my eyes fixed on the floor, said in short, clipped tones, "All there, every last cent. Thanks."

I strode back to the car and got in. The man shook Cleo's hand. As Cleo walked away, he called out: "Attention! Be careful, young ladies!"

By the time Cleo had slipped into the driver's seat, the man and the workmen had disappeared into the main building, the door shut, and all was dark again. Not a light shone from any of the windows. Beechams appeared totally deserted.

Cleo drove out of the driveway. When I reminded her to turn on her lights, she shook her head. Instead of driving directly back toward our house, she crossed the highway and headed toward the north side of town. She peered into her mirror. I looked back and saw a large black car without lights following us. Cleo stepped down on the accelerator and turned suddenly onto Smith Farm Road. The dust rose behind our car, obscuring the road behind for a moment. It seemed as if we were alone, but then a flash of moonlight reflected from chrome revealed that the black car still followed. I wondered whether this was the same Packard that had raced through Charlevoix on the day of the storm when the brick came crashing through our store window.

Cleo pointed to the envelope of money and then to the floor. I slipped the envelope under the floor covering. Once more Cleo threw her wheel over and the Ford careened onto the private dirt track through Olsen's farm, a short cut which all the kids used to get to North Point. Behind us the big black car followed, now closing the gap rapidly. A loud crack sounded and the back window shattered. Cleo reached over and pushed my head down and began to weave the wheel so that the car moved on and off the track. Another explosion sounded and a hole appeared in the roof of the car, just above the window.

Cleo skidded the car out of the Olsen property onto the dirt road that led from town out past North Point. The car was just behind us.

As we turned I saw another big black car behind the first. I heard two more explosions, but these seemed farther off. The first car swerved from side to side. Cleo jumped up and down in her seat, her happy wail rising and falling. Horrified, I realized that Cleo considered the chase a wonderful game.

Now we reached a place where North Point Road curved sharply right and then left. The moment after Cleo negotiated the second curve, she suddenly skidded the car onto a sandy track that ran along the backside of Mount McSauba, the sand mountain at North Point. The car ground to a halt in the midst of a growth of young birch trees and thick underbrush. As the two big, black cars went careening past us, both still on North Point Road, it became clear that the second car was chasing the first. Explosions and flashes of gunfire erupted from both cars. For some time I could hear the cars speeding through the countryside and then silence fell.

In the moonlight, Cleo and I examined the damage. I could hardly catch my breath.

"What are we going to tell Daddy and Momma?" I asked.

Cleo removed the tire iron from the car and completed the destruction of the back window so that the bullet hole did not show. She then hammered away at the bullet hole in the top until it looked like someone had simply battered the top with a blunt instrument. I winced, knowing how much our father prized his car's mint condition.

By the time she had finished, I had worked out an explanation for our parents. "All right, we'll say we parked out here and took a walk on the beach and that some kids came along and messed up the car."

Cleo nodded solemnly. She pointed to the envelope of money under the floor covering and then to the damage to indicate that she would pay for the repair. We cleaned up the glass in the back seat and searched for any evidence of the attack. We found two spent bullets lying on the back floor. Cleo wanted to keep them, but I insisted upon throwing them away.

We drove home slowly with our lights on. Cleo was subdued. Every few seconds I peered around, afraid that we would be attacked once more. As we proceeded up our block, I saw a commotion in front of our house. The red and yellow lights of the fire engine and of a police car blinked intermittently. The neighbors were out on their lawns. Cleo parked down the street and we approached our house. Father and Mother stood on the porch with the fire chief, Ed Swerdling and Sheriff Vernon Hayes.

Mother greeted us excitedly. "Someone tried to burn down the house! Your father's a hero."

"Nothing of the kind," said my father. He looked very pale.

"He chased them off with a shovel," said Sheriff Hayes, laughing.

"Look, look how they scorched the front porch." My mother took us by the arm and led us down the front steps. She pointed to the corner of the porch where a scorched gasoline can lay on its side. The boards were blackened to three feet off the ground and part of the front hedge was destroyed. "You should have seen them run. Dad put it out with the hose."

"I just don't understand it," said my father. "Why would anyone—?" Sweat lined his brow. He stared around at each face as if he could read an answer there.

Confused and exhausted, I sank down on the front steps.

"It's anti-Semitism, that's what it is," declared my mother.

"Arabella!" said Father.

"I wouldn't rule it out, Hank," said Sheriff Hayes.

"But Vernon, in all the years—" Father's voice trailed off.

Sheriff Hayes shook his head slowly. "There're some ignorant people hereabouts—maybe not in town, but in the county. Or some kids who listen to their parents talking."

"Talking about what?" asked my father angrily.

"No need to get upset at me, Hank." The sheriff patted Henry's shoulder. "It's not my fault that the Jewish people aren't popular in some quarters."

Father sank down onto the porch rail, his face in his hands.

PART TWO

THIRTEEN

EACH YEAR, FROM THE beginning of July to Labor Day, I worked as a waitress. I began my career behind the soda fountain at the sweet store and within a year advanced to the cafe. Then I bussed at the Inn and finally was hired as a waitress at the Belvedere Club. Those who serve others for a living are a different order of creature, even in the eyes of people well-bred enough to treat servants politely. I did not discover my desire for justice and social equality in books. It was confirmed by the lives of my fellow townspeople, who depended for their livelihood upon the whims of the wealthy. In a summer resort the hierarchy of the world stands out in clear relief.

Summer in Charlevoix was not simply one of the four seasons. It was "The Season," an enclosed realm of time and space, suspended from the rest of the year. The summer visitors deliberately chose this period as a rest from their ordinary labor. The permanent residents had a more complex adjustment to make. Our lives depended upon those two unreal months. We earned much of our income from the recreation of our visitors. While they frolicked under the spiky green needles of the pines and fluttering leaves of the birches, we worked.

The first of July marked the beginning of the season. Overnight, the summer visitors made their appearance. They came by automobile, by train, and by boat. Jewish resorters filled the houses, the rooming houses, the hotel, and the inn; Christian resorters preferred the privacy of the resident associations—the Chicago Club and the Belvedere Club. Tennis courts resounded with the twang of balls hitting rackets and the polite cheers and repressed cries of despair among the players; men and women dressed in colorful stripes and checks, wearing brown- and white-cleated shoes, strode boldly up and down the fairways of the golf courses; youths set sail in dinghies, in cat boats, in sloops, ketches, and yawls for Lake Charlevoix and Lake Michigan; their elders motored away in cabin cruisers to fish, to cruise, to carouse on the waves. Crowds sprawled out on the public beaches, while on the private beaches north of the bridge, small, intimate groups sat comfortably on beach chairs, socializing with their neighbors and friends.

On the balmy evenings, long lines formed in front of the movie house; families strolled through the downtown park where shuffleboard players sent disks sliding along waxed surfaces to collide with other disks, producing sharp explosions of sound. Families filled the gift shops, the restaurants, the ice cream parlor and finally straggled back under the leafy foliage and starry skies to their pine- and cedar-scented rooms for sleep to prepare them for another vigorous day of vacation.

During the summer of 1928 I worked dinners at the Belvedere Club from four in the afternoon to ten at night, six days a week. In the mornings and early afternoons, I continued my job at the library. I had little time to anguish over the future. Two months remained before I would have to make a decision about leaving Charlevoix. In the meantime, I would accommodate my family's demands and serve the guests at the club.

One afternoon at the beginning of July, Cleo appeared at the library and marched me down through the park. The docks were already filling with the boats of the summer people. Cleo shook my shoulder to get my attention and pointed to an empty berth about thirty yards from Weyrich's boatyard. "Mine," she said.

"For your boat?" I asked, my voice quavering. From where we stood, I could see the spot where we had found Betty Jane Kelley's body wedged under the Weyrich dock.

Cleo nodded and conducted me to the stone tower in the park that housed the chamber of commerce and the harbormaster. I was not pleased with the prospect of revealing Cleo's handiwork to the world. Her boat had taken on a hellish aura in my imagination. It rose up out of the dreary fog of my thoughts at odd times of the day or at night, piloted by dead men with bullet holes through their foreheads and eyes. I had never before been given to magical beliefs, but by now I associated too many accidents with that white craft. In the harbormaster's office, I filled out the forms for registering the boat and an application for a three month rental of the berth Cleo desired. "It's a wreck that Cleo found and worked on all winter," I muttered, trying to limit the gossip that was certain to circulate in town.

"Well I know Cleo's work," said the harbormaster, a scrawny old sailor with a large Adam's apple that bounced up and down when he talked. "I'll bet it's a fine craft. Don't forget the name."

Actually, Cleo's boat had no name. Instead of a name, Cleo had painted a startling image of forked lightning across the mahogany of the stern. I suspected that the image of lightning referred to the storm during which she had found the boat. I hesitated, trying to think of an appropriate name. Cleo pointed insistently at the blank on the application form. Finally, I filled in the name *White Lightning* and she proudly paid out the full three months berth rental. The harbormaster slid a second form onto the counter. "You folks want to sign up for the Venetian Night contest?" Venetian Night, near the end of July, was the climax of Charlevoix's summer season. For this grand event, the yachting crowd dressed up their boats as elaborate floating sets and vied with one another for honors. The town fathers, my father among them, had invented the contest in order to promote Charlevoix.

"No," I said. I could not imagine joining the rich in their games.

Cleo's elbow jabbed my side. Her forefinger pointed commandingly at the contest form. Dutifully, I filled it out. Cleo paid the fee.

"Hope you win," said the harbormaster as we left.

On the way back to the library, I walked with my head down, my shoulders hunched. I felt powerless, a slave to my sister's whims. At best, I could only muster up a futile gesture of irony by naming Cleo's boat *White Lightning*, a play on words she would never understand. How sad, I thought, how shameful. I could not understand how she had usurped my position of power in the family—or, rather, taken on her true role as older sister. Odd, odd, I moaned to myself. It was no longer a question of being submerged by caretaking. Now I would be drowned in Cleo's emerging achievements and ambitions. If I did not escape this town soon, I would never find out how to live my own life.

The launching of *White Lightning* took place just at dawn the next day. Cleo, John, and I hauled the boat on John's trailer from the Clover farm to Weyrich's boat ramp. Joan Clover and the Clover sons followed in Jack's car. Even in the dim light of the street lamps, the boat gleamed with fresh paint and varnish and burnished brass. I shut my eyes. It seemed as if the craft were flaunting its villainous origins.

A calm enveloped the lake and the town; not a leaf or a bough stirred. A thin mist hovered over the black-mirrored surface of the water which reflected the late stars. As John backed the boat down the ramp, the eastern sky began to brighten. I knelt high up on the bow of the boat, ready to free it from the trailer; Cleo stood at the wheel in the cockpit.

When the boat and trailer canted down the ramp, I had to grab onto the bow cleat to keep from sliding back toward the cockpit. For a moment I saw only the still tops of the trees and the velvety black summer sky to the west, gleaming with bright stars. And then the buoyancy of water floated the stern. I felt the lift of the water travel toward me along the hull until the street lights and buildings of the town, the boatyard, and John Clover's truck became visible. I imagined Betty Jane Kelley crawling along the muddy bottom of the lake, seeking a way to emerge.

Slowly I played out the bow line and the boat floated off the trailer, free of the land, abandoned to the embrace of the watery depths. I stretched out, face down on the deck, possessed by the craft and the lake on which it floated.

Cleo let loose a cry of delight and pressed the starter. With a rumble the powerful engines turned over and then settled into an easy deep bass throb. Hesitantly, Cleo backed the boat away from the ramp and then brought it alongside the dock where John and his family boarded. I coiled the bowline neatly around the cleat and climbed back into the cockpit. Cleo brought the bow around until it was headed east toward Lake Charlevoix. No one spoke. The Clover family stood together, a look of joyful anticipation in their faces they seldom displayed to the world, as if they were about to reclaim the landscape that had been taken from them. Cleo's expression mirrored theirs. Ahead, the rising sun cast its horizontal rays through the Railroad Bridge Channel at an angle, creating a path of brightness across the mist-shrouded water directly to our bow. Cleo pressed slowly forward on the throttles, sending her cabin cruiser on its maiden voyage to meet the sun.

*

The day after *White Lightning*'s launching, Maureen, Sy, their children, and two maids arrived in two sedans crammed with groceries and suitcases. They settled quickly into their rental house on Michigan Avenue and invited us for dinner. "A trial run," explained Maureen, "to see how everything works before our real entertaining begins. Besides, I want to show you how grateful I am for finding us this wonderful house."

As soon as Mother put down the phone, she irritably declared, "We're the guinea pigs."

I yielded to my parents and called in a substitute for my job that night. I knew that the evening was to be a preview of my own launching onto the marriage market. I would have refused to go, but I had no wish to hurt my relatives' feelings. Also, I was curious. I had seen very little of my aunt, uncle, and cousins from Detroit.

As soon as I was dressed for the Lefkowitz dinner, Mother sat me down at her dressing table and prepared to apply my makeup. When I protested, Mother said, "Don't worry, I won't destroy your strong suit."

"And what's that?"

"Good-natured candor." I flinched, even though I knew Mother's words, harmful or soothing, came unbidden from her mouth. She never wounded deliberately.

When she finished, she examined me. "There now, it's perfect, seductive."

"Seductive?" I looked at myself in the mirror and grimaced. "I look odd."

"Of course that face would look odd to a socialist—but to an enterprising young man you will look very fetching—fresh and desirable at the same time, down-to-earth and just a little sophisticated. You're going to be snatched up in a minute."

"Like a fruit or a vegetable."

Mother squeezed my arm. "A luscious tomato."

Cleo appeared, looking like a magazine model. She had applied her own makeup, which she had somehow managed to purchase. "Perfect," my mother murmured, examining her carefully, "you're really good, Cleo." Cleo leaned forward, thrusting her cheek at my mother, who, surprised and pleased at this unusual show of affection, planted a kiss on it, very lightly so as not to spoil the effect. Mother turned to me and said, "If you study your sister, you might learn how to do these things." I'd never seen her so pleased and proud.

We waited for my father on the front porch. Finally, he appeared in a double-breasted navy blue blazer, white duck trousers, and a paisley ascot. Mother had chosen his costume for the occasion. I thought he looked like he had stepped out of the movies—slim, aristocratic, intelligent.

As we set off, Father twisted his mouth to one side and winked at me. "I only hope," he said, "that none of the Rotary or Elks gang sees me in this outfit."

"I hope they see all of us tonight," said Mother. In fact, my father looked so attractive that she felt a desperate pang of desire course through her. She could barely keep herself from falling upon him and shaking him until he explained what was wrong with him. In her diary, Mother underlined this passage and larded it with exclamation marks. Since the arson incident, my father had grown more and more isolated. He slept restlessly and woke at all hours to pace about the house. For the first time since their marriage, his ardor in bed slackened. Mother, who, over the years, had come to depend upon her husband's secret passion and the intimacy of his private touch, felt abandoned. She no longer even bothered to ask him to make love. Each night her anger grew. And in her frustration, her plans for my marriage became more elaborate.

The family strolled across the bridge, up the hill and along Michigan Avenue. Mother's mood improved. She felt rather grand to be marching through the fancy part of town with her daughters—proud that all three of the Bearwald women were dressed in fashionable summer cocktail attire that she herself had sewn.

The house my mother had rented for her brother's family stood near the end of Michigan Avenue on the lake side. It was a broad white clapboard house with a rounded shingle, Dutch-style roof in a grove of old pine trees. Generous columned porches extended all around the first and second floors of the house. Baskets of geraniums hung at intervals between the columns. The opulence of the place delighted Mother; it was a fine setting from which to show off her daughter to the young men of Detroit.

FOURTEEN

THE DINNER WITH MOTHER'S family at the beginning of summer remained particularly vivid in my father's memory. When he visited me in Paris the year after I graduated from college, he talked of it with a candor that shocked me. Perhaps it was Paris, a city he had dreamed of when he was a youth; perhaps he was bent upon passing the burden of truth on to his grown daughter, who had always accused him of condescension; or, more likely, it was because he had drunk most of the bottle of wine we ordered for dinner. Although I had drunk only a glass and a half of the bottle, I went back to my mansard room with my head reeling.

The Lefkowitz family—Sy, Maureen, Seymour, and Cynthia —filed out of the front door and stood on the porch in a row at the top of the stairs to greet us. My parents stiffened and hesitated. My father turned to fasten the gate behind us. He never felt at ease with his wife's family. They look too large, he thought, too clean and well-fed. All wore snug-fitting resort clothes in colors that clashed a little: pinks and aquas, oranges and baby blues, yellow greens and green yellows. It was as if they were crying out, “Look, I’m on vacation.” He was ashamed at how powerfully his own family prejudices worked within him. Recently, he had found himself judging his wife along the same lines. His German-Jewish relatives called everyone who came to America after they did “Eastern European Jews,” by which they really meant “a mass of uncultured, ill-mannered beggars.” His parents had accepted Arabella only because they thought it unlikely that their son could find a proper girl to come live with him in such an isolated place. He was already thirty-two at the time. They were afraid he would remain a bachelor. “At least she’s Jewish,” they had comforted each other, “and healthy enough to have many children.” Now his wife was about to thrust his daughter into a similar marriage of convenience, while he stood by, watching.

Regretting his weakness and his snobbery, he followed his wife and daughters toward the front steps. Arabella, proud and dark and vivid, stood waiting for him. Marriage of convenience? he asked himself. Is that what he thought of his marriage? No, no. He had fallen in love with Arabella, he reassured himself. He had fallen in love with her imagination, her beauty, her vivacious spirit. He was lucky to have captured her. He offered her his arm. They turned to face the Lefkowitzes.

Mother did not trust the smiles with which her brother and his family greeted her. She suspected that the stretched lips, the bared teeth, and crinkled eyes of the Lefkowitz clan projected a certain dull-witted superiority—the wealthy city mice welcoming the poor country mice. She regretted that she had confided her hopes for Rebecca to her sister-in-law. She slowed the family, waiting to be greeted. But the Lefkowitzes remained at the top of the stairs, smiling down upon us. Slowly, we mounted the stairs. I did not notice that Cleo lagged behind. Only when we were a step from the porch did Maureen say, "Welcome, welcome to our summer house—it's just perfect—we can't thank you too much." She leaned over and embraced my parents.

"You did us proud, Sis," said Sy, planting a kiss on Mother's forehead.

"Children!" said Maureen, "Say hello to your aunt and uncle and your cousins. Look at these girls, will you! They're young women." She surveyed us and then my mother. "I've never seen such beautiful clothes and such slim figures."

"We manage," said Mother.

"Henry must have discovered a gold mine," said Maureen. Her voice had an unexpected sarcasm to it. She embraced me and passed me on to Sy.

"Or a new line of goods?" said Sy. I thought he sounded strained, as if something were troubling him.

"Hush!" said Maureen to her husband

Mother moved forcefully up onto the porch so that she was on a level with her brother and his family. She embraced my cousins. Seymour, twenty-four, was six foot one, not quite as tall as his father. He kept his thinning hair cut short and combed with a military precision that did not seem to go with his soft brown eyes, his round face, and amply swelling stomach. Cynthia, twenty, was a large, jolly young woman, with a wide smiling mouth, rosy cheeks, and a full womanly body over trim legs.

Maureen turned toward Cleo who had remained on the porch steps. Cleo stood very still, expecting to be swooped down upon and embraced. Maureen, however, hesitated and spoke cautiously, "Hello, Cleo, I'm your Aunt Maureen, you remember me, don't you?"

Cleo registered her aunt's fear. She reached to take hold of my dress. Only now did she realize that I had moved onto the porch, leaving her alone. She began to tremble. While the Lefkowitz children in solemn succession shook my hand, Sy moved to stand next to his wife, regarding Cleo. "This is your Uncle Sy," said Maureen, pronouncing each syllable with care. The Lefkowitz children joined their parents. "And these are your cousins."

The Lefkowitzes now all stood in a row between Cleo and our family, who stood behind them up on the porch. The Lefkowitzes stared at Cleo. They nodded their heads as if to show their good will. Cleo backed down one step. The Lefkowitzes moved down one step. Cleo retreated a second step, a third, and finally reached the front walk.

From the porch, I recognized my sister's terror. I hadn't seen Cleo so disturbed since the day she discovered *White Lightning*. I started down the steps, surprised at the excitement which gripped me. The prospect of rescuing my sister pleased me. Cleo had already turned away in flight when I broke through the Lefkowitzes and wrapped my arm around my sister's shoulder, detaining her. I looked up at my parents, noting with satisfaction their relief.

"It's all right, Cleo," I crooned into her ear.

I moved Cleo firmly forward. The Lefkowitzes crowded around us in an awkward embrace.

"Well now," said Maureen, "it's time for cocktails on the side porch." As the families walked along the porch, Maureen put her arm through my mother's. "We've got a very attractive product, my dear. Rebecca's a jewel."

I was tempted to vault over the porch rail into the safety of the hedge. Mother could always claim that I was as mad as my sister.

The north porch was furnished in comfortable, white wicker furniture. From a table, Maureen drew a small silver bell which she shook delicately. The Lefkowitzes' two maids appeared. They wore black taffeta uniforms trimmed in white lace. One of the maids was white, the other Negro. Both were middle-aged and appeared to be comfortable with the family, who called them by their first names, Rose and Zorah. They passed silver platters of hors d'oeuvres around, bending to serve each of us. I could not bear to be waited upon like this in a private home. Before they reached me, I got up and moved down the porch, pretending to examine the geraniums. I smiled at the maids as I passed them and murmured, "No thanks."

"Is she on a diet?" asked Aunt Maureen.

"No," said Mother, who knew what troubled me. "She just doesn't want to spoil her appetite."

Whether my mother was sparing me or herself, I was grateful that she hadn't carried on about my principles of social justice. After the maids had departed, I took my seat again.

The two families sat on the white wicker furniture facing one another like strangers. Uncle Sy and Aunt Maureen appeared to be very nervous. They kept glancing at my father as if he held some power over them. I was puzzled. Although I seldom saw them, I'd always thought of the Lefkowitzes as open, warm-hearted and good-natured. Tonight, though, they appeared troubled. I thought of the awkward moment on the steps when my aunt and uncle remarked upon the elegance of our clothes—as if there were something suspicious about our situation in life. Mother had claimed that they were envious, but that seemed very unlike them.

Sy served the cocktails from crystal decanters.

When my father asked for plain seltzer water, Sy protested, "I'm offering you the finest distilled spirits, straight from the source."

"Like coals to Newcastle?" said Maureen, looking sharply at my father.

"Newcastle?" asked Father.

"Say, Henry," said Sy, "in March, when they found those bodies on the beach—I didn't mean to butt in." His tone was hesitant, apologetic. "It just seemed to me that after some things Bella spouted off to Maureen and—other things—that a little trip might be a good idea. You know what I mean?"

Father looked bewildered. He sent a questioning glance toward Mother who regarded her fingernails.

"Sy means that you ought to be more careful, especially now that we're here." Maureen's voice had a pleading note to it.

"Henry," said Sy, taking a deep breath, "I think we ought to talk. Your operations—"

"Look next door," said my Mother interrupting. In the garden next door, a party was starting up—an informal after-boating party. "The Eisenstadts," Mother declared as if she were announcing a possession.

I waited for my uncle to continue his speech to my father, but instead he busied himself renewing the drinks, exchanging furtive looks with his wife. My aunt and uncle were definitely frightened, I thought. But why? We all fell silent, glancing self-consciously over the hedge from our vantage point high on a neighboring porch. The Eisenstadt guests, still in their swimsuits, tennis, and golfing costumes, lounged about casually. Some played badminton, others croquet. Everyone was drinking. A Victrola played sprightly jazz.

"People up here have a lot of fun, don't they?" said Seymour.

"How do you get to know anyone?" asked Cynthia.

"They're our neighbors, dear," said Maureen. "We'll pay them a visit this week."

Mother turned toward Father and lifted her brows and grinned as she imagined the Lefkowitzes in their crisp, ugly resort clothes, marching up the Eisenstadt front walk.

"Anyway," said Seymour, patting his mother's arm comfortingly, "we'll have our own crowd. Natalie and her family are coming up Tuesday."

Cynthia clapped her hands together. "Oh Rebecca, I have ever so many friends who'll be up. Charlevoix is the place to be this summer. We'll introduce you to a lot of boys—Jewish boys. Seymour has this darling friend, Norman—and then there's Sammy's friend, Sidney. Sammy's my beau. He's with his father in laundry supply—they're the biggest in Detroit. Sidney works for Sammy's father and takes courses at night. He dresses very well."

"Dinnertime," announced Maureen, who picked up her little bell and sounded it.

She led the way around the back of the house, stopping for a moment to show off the view of Lake Michigan. Through the pine trees, the sun, a great flattening orange ball, hovered over the lake's horizon.

I lingered for a moment behind the rest, gazing out at the disappearing sun. Cynthia's sprightly talk of Jewish boys had made me dizzy and a little sick to my stomach. Certainly, I had begun to feel peculiar growing up Jewish in the North Woods. But the idea of entering the Lefkowitz world with its Sidneys and Normans and Sammys terrified me. I wouldn't know how to act, what to say. They would all see immediately that I was a freak. Cleo at least had the excuse of being considered unbalanced.

Dinner was a formal affair served on the south side porch where a long table had been laid with linen, china, silver, and glassware. My aunt and uncle kept asking my father if he was comfortable. They had very little else to say. Mother seemed distracted. My aunt filled Father's plate twice, even though he had hardly eaten a bite.

In the silences, once again the neighboring garden, this time on the other side of the house, caught our attention. "The Kuhns!" declared Mother, once more possessive of the town's summer celebrities. "Bankers—relatives of Henry's. Sonny, the wife, was a Bearwald."

"Distant relatives," said my father, waving his hand vaguely in the air to minimize the connection. His wife always made more of the relationship than he deemed proper. In truth, Mrs. Sonny Kuhn, born Cecilia Bearwald, was a cousin. She had been a close friend in his youth, much closer than my mother realized. Since their marriages, though, he had seen little of her. He preferred not to socialize with the resorters. His father had always held that the store would be more respected if the family kept its distance.

The Kuhn garden was decorated with Chinese lanterns. A dance floor had been laid on the grass, surrounded by round tables. A sumptuous buffet and bar took up one whole end of the garden.

"Looks like they're starting the season with a bang," said Sy.

"I only wish we had gotten here sooner," said Maureen. "I'm sure we would have been invited."

"Oh, don't worry, Maureen," said my mother. "The Kuhns entertain all summer long."

"I think all you kids should go to the movies together tomorrow night," suggested Maureen.

"My treat," said Sy, patting his breast pocket.

I explained that I worked nights as a waitress at the Belvedere Club. I emphasized the word waitress.

"The Belvedere Club?" asked Maureen.

"It wasn't my idea," said Mother.

"I thought they didn't allow Jews."

"They make an exception for employees," said my father with a wry grimace.

Sy laughed. "Did you hear that, Maureen—an exception for employees."

"Not a single Jew?" said Maureen with wonder.

"We don't know any gentiles," said Cynthia. "It must be strange to be surrounded by them all year long."

"Well, they all are Americans," said my father, glancing apologetically at me. "Same as us."

"Not exactly, Hank," said Sy. "A little different."

"Not as smart," said Maureen, tapping her forehead.

I waited for my father to protest, but he remained silent. "Well, we don't mind at all," I said airily. "We love our town."

I stifled an impulse to giggle. Everyone treated me as if I knew who I was and how to act. And yet a dozen different tribes claimed my loyalty. To some, I was simply a waitress and a student; to others, a socialist, a German-Jew or a Polish-Jew; to still others, an almost-gentile-small-town girl, a storekeeper's daughter, and finally a caretaker. As kind as our relatives were, they could not understand me or our existence here in the wilds of the north. I cast a glance at my father who hastily looked down into his plate. I was disappointed in him. I had wanted him to reclaim his pride of citizenship in our town.

My father, however, remained lost in his plate. He knew that he should defend his townsmen, but he could not marshal the words.

At the party next door, the guests began to arrive, the band struck up a tune, couples danced, the chiming of glassware and silverware sounded out into the evening, accompanied by lively conversation and laughter. Distracted now, my father looked across the hedge. With regret he recalled the brilliant household of Sonny Kuhn's parents in Detroit where he had lived on two separate occasions: once when he studied for his bar mitzvah and later while he was attending business school. His cousins, prominent in Detroit society, had entertained a sophisticated and lively crowd that had awed him.

He sighed at the memory of his isolated and unhappy youth and then gazed across the table at his two beautiful young daughters, one fair and the other dark. To his dismay, they both seemed to shrink into their chairs, their faces pale, their expressions dull. He could only guess that they were daunted by the energetic self-confidence of his wife's family and the portrait they painted of a Jewish world with Jewish expectations. Watching his daughters' discomfort, he regretted that he had denied his children a Jewish upbringing. In fact, he began to mistrust his own parents. Had it been necessity or choice that had led his father to settle so far from his kind?

As the Kuhns' party became more and more animated, a pall settled over the family dinner on the Lefkowitz porch. When dessert had been finished, Mother announced our departure. She felt that my reintroduction to her family had not been entirely successful—on either side.

Maureen, however, was undaunted. "Rebecca," she declared after kisses had been exchanged on the front steps, "I want you to come back tomorrow afternoon for a swim at our beach. The children will have some of their friends over."

My mother, nodding her head up and down, tried to catch my eye. I glanced at Cleo, who was already clinging to my dress.

"And Cleo too," said Maureen. "The beach is very beautiful over here on the north side of town, Cleo. And private."

Cleo pulled me to the side of the steps and made a swooping and rising motion with her right hand. My mother gripped my father's arm in alarm. She was terrified, I knew, that Cleo would have one of her fits.

Cleo's hand continued on its swooping course. I pretended not to understand her. She gestured with more insistence. I returned reluctantly to confront the Lefkowitzes who were by now all lined up on the porch to wave good-bye. Cleo followed. When I did not speak immediately, she jabbed me in the back. I mumbled. "Cleo suggested that we all go out on our boat tomorrow afternoon."

"Your boat?" said Maureen.

"Our boat?" croaked Mother.

I turned toward my parents. "It's probably not a good idea."

"What are you talking about, Rebecca?" asked my father.

Cleo began to whistle.

"Cleo!" said Mother, hoarsely.

"But we had no idea—" began Sy.

Cleo jabbed me again. "I'm sorry Momma, Daddy," I said. "It's Cleo's surprise. She wants to take everyone out on Lake Charlevoix on our boat. But maybe—"

"Well now, Bella," said Maureen, "you are a sly one."

"I think Henry's the sly one," said Sy. "You son-of-a-gun!"

Father stared helplessly at his brother-in-law, at his wife, and then at his daughters.

"Can we go out on their boat with them, Momma?" asked Cynthia.

"You bet your life we can," said Maureen. "I'll never forgive you, Bella Bearwald, keeping a secret like that."

I waited for my parents to object. Instead, they both glared at me. "One o'clock, then," I said. "At the city docks behind the chamber of commerce, three berths from Weyrich's Boatyard."

FIFTEEN

THE FAMILY HAD BARELY passed the hedge separating the Lefkowitz house from the Kuhns when Mother confronted me.

"What boat?"

"We have no boat!" said Father.

"But we do have a boat."

Cleo whistled again.

"Stop that noise this instant!" said Mother. "We don't have a boat, we never had a boat, and we probably never will have a boat."

Distracted by our argument, we ignored the Kuhns' guests streaming by us toward the party.

"Rebecca, what's gotten into you?" said my father sternly. "I want you to march back there and tell your aunt and uncle the truth."

"Henry, have you taken leave of your senses? If Rebecca ever admitted such a thing—no, no, we'll have to rent a boat from the Weyriches."

"For the whole summer?"

"For five weeks—until my brother and his family leave. But I tell you, Rebecca, you're going to pay every cent of that rental if you have to work until you're an old woman."

Cleo laughed. She laughed so hard that she doubled over. We all stared at her. I wished I had gone to the police as soon as Cleo found the boat. I wanted to disown the boat—and Cleo too. Instead, I found myself attempting to explain.

"Please Momma, Dad, listen to me. Cleo found a wrecked boat on the beach during the storm—remember? The day she ran away? That's what she's been doing all spring out at the Clover's. Fixing the boat. It's her boat, our boat. Cleo's surprise."

"If you think we're taking my brother's family out on some broken-down wreck of a—" began Mother.

A large roadster skidded to a stop beside the curb. A heavy-set, red-faced man in a white suit with an open-necked blue shirt leaped out of the car and landed only a few feet from us. He contemplated our family.

"Well, Goddamn it to hell, if it isn't Henry Bearwald!"

It was Charles Kuhn, younger brother of Felix Kuhn who was giving the party. My father and Charles had gone to summer camp together.

Father introduced his wife and daughters.

"If I had known my brother was going to invite such gorgeous gals, I would have come on over sooner."

"We're not going to the party, Charles," said my father. "We were just passing by."

"The hell you say!" said Charles. "I mean we're relatives of yours—at least Sonny is." Charles took hold of me with one arm and Cleo with the other and swept us through a gap in the hedge into the party. My mother shut her eyes, expecting Cleo's terrified outcry. Instead, she heard Charles announce: "Look everyone! Look what I found on the sidewalk!"

Bewildered, Mother looked at Father. "What on earth—?"

"Charles Kuhn, that damned blowhard!"

"We can't leave them in there alone." My mother was not displeased. "After all, Sonny Kuhn is a relative." She took hold of my father's arm and led him into the glamorous garden.

At the bar, Charles Kuhn insisted that Cleo and I accept drinks. He then asked me to dance, but I refused. He shrugged and wandered toward the dance floor, where he encountered my father and mother, looking for the host or the hostess. Charles Kuhn put his arms out toward Mother.

"Come, we have to dance!"

"I—I really don't—"

"Charles," said my father, "have you seen Felix? I'd like to explain why we're here."

"Old Felix won't be up this summer and maybe never again. He and Sonny have had an amicable parting of the ways—not a separation, mind you, and no divorce. In such matters, Felix is a Puritan—or is it a Catholic? He has opted for 'assisted-living,' as if he hadn't always enjoyed that comfort." Charles laughed heartily at his own wit and dropped to one knee in front of Mother. He grabbed hold of her hand, and begged. "It's the Charleston. They've named the dance after me."

"We're not really—"

Charles leaped up and dragged my mother out onto the

floor. With no alternative, she began to dance. Soon she lost herself in the pleasures of the music.

Father edged his way toward his cousin, the hostess. He was determined to explain his family's intrusion into the party and then leave. Sonny, a slim, tanned, blond woman in her late forties, was dressed in a plain, expensive sheath dress. She wore no makeup or jewelry. She was dancing vigorously with a young man twenty years her junior. Father paused. His heart contracted as he remembered his youthful longing for his cousin. Sonny had been his first close friend. Later he had fallen in love with her.

The music stopped. Sonny pointed to the bar and gave her partner a playful push. The young man dutifully trotted away. My father approached. To his dismay, his cousin appeared to be very drunk.

"Sonny, I wanted to explain—your brother-in-law—"

"Henry Bearwald! What on earth are you doing here?"

"We were walking by and Charles—"

"You have no idea how glad I am to see you, Henry. A ghost from the past." The band struck up a tango. Sonny extended her arms. "Are you going to dance with me, Henry?"

Obediently, my father seized his cousin and began to dance. During the years at business school in Detroit, he had taken lessons. After his marriage to Mother, they had kept up with the latest dances, sending away for sheet music and instruction pamphlets. For the last four years my parents had attended an evening of instruction once a month in Petoskey, twenty miles to the north.

"Why you're a good dancer!" said Sonny as they glided across the floor.

"You were my first dancing teacher."

Sonny looked up at him and smiled. "I remember, country cousin, I remember very well, dear Henry."

On seeing her boyish, impertinent grin, Father found it difficult to breathe. "That was a long time ago."

"You're going to be my partner for the rest of the night."

My father forgot his wife's dissatisfaction, Rebecca's unhappiness, and Cleo's madness. He forgot the mysterious attacks by his hostile neighbors. Sonny's fluid body made his heart ache. Then from the side of his eye, he caught a glimpse of his wife, her eyes closed, her head thrown back, gliding by in the opposite direction in the arms of a tall young man he had never seen before.

*

When I refused Charles Kuhn's invitation to dance, he immediately abandoned me and Cleo. I took Cleo's arm, intending to leave the party, but Cleo balked, her eyes darting about, missing nothing—the colored lights, the music, the laughing faces. At the sight of Charles Kuhn kneeling in front of Mother, Cleo jumped up and down in glee. Embarrassed, I drew her into a dark corner of the garden where we stood arm in arm, watching our parents dance.

We had seen our mother and father dance at home, but never in public and never with other people. All this last winter and spring during my secret battle with them, I had felt part of the family. But now, as Mother and Father glided about the dance floor, clasped in the arms of strangers, I began to experience what it might be like to lead an existence away from them.

I became aware of the warmth of Cleo's flesh and the pressure of the muscles and sinews of Cleo's arm. Was Cleo clasping me? I wondered. Or was I clasping Cleo? As I loosened our grip upon one another, I set myself the task of imagining a life detached from Cleo's.

At this moment, three young men descended upon us. I recognized them all—Dickie Benjamin, Rob Leventhal, Edwin Eisenstadt, sons of wealthy German-Jewish summer families who lived on the north side of town. I had gone to summer day camp with them until we were ten, when the boys had gone off to camps in the East and I began to work, first at the store and then as a waitress. I had seen the young men only occasionally since. Tonight, they didn't recognize me.

Before I could say anything, Rob Leventhal had taken Cleo's hand and led her to the dance floor. Cleo went with him, willingly. As soon as I identified myself, Dickie and Edwin lost interest.

"Who is that girl?" asked Edwin.

"My sister."

"You mean—" began Edwin who stopped in mid-sentence.

"My sister, Cleo," I said in disgust, for I knew that Edwin was about to say, "Silly Cleo."

"Rob's dancing with Cleo?" asked Dickie and he began to giggle.

"Oh, I've got to see this," said Edwin.

"No you don't," I said, stepping in front of them. But they darted around me and ran over to the dance floor. Alarmed, I followed, intent upon rescuing my sister.

"Becky! Becky Bearwald!"

A hand grasped my arm. I turned to see a deeply tanned young man with curly black hair. "Yes?" I said. The young man was not dressed for the party. Everyone else wore jackets and ties. He was in a bathing suit, sneakers, and an unbuttoned white shirt, its sleeves rolled up onto his muscular arms.

The young man's eyes challenged me aggressively. "Don't you recognize me?"

"Not really," I replied in a faltering voice, blushing.

An odd smile revealed perfect white teeth. "It's me, Tony Warburg." There was a magnetism to the smile, but it was not genial. It was shadowed by a slightly bitter cast.

Tony Warburg had been my special friend and protector the first two years I had gone to summer day camp for small children. He was in the oldest group and had adopted me. His family—the Warburgs of Chicago, New Orleans, and Bremen—were the wealthiest and most respected of all the Jewish summer visitors. They owned a large estate on the shores of Lake Charlevoix, with horses, tennis courts, and its own little harbor. I had been invited out to the estate a number of times during those first two years at day camp. The next year, however, and for several years after, the family had spent their summers on the East Coast. By the time the Warburgs had returned to summer in Charlevoix, Tony's friendship with me had been forgotten.

In recent years everyone talked about his drunken, wild adventures which began early in his adolescence. He raced cars and crashed them; he raced boats; he spent his nights at roadhouses with older women; he had been ejected from several boarding schools and several colleges.

I had not spoken with Tony for many years, but I had thought about him now and then—usually with a baffled anger. Although I knew it was foolish of me, I resented that he had forgotten our friendship. Often, the characters of my favorite novels took Tony's shape—Stavrogin in *The Possessed*, Heathcliffe in *Wuthering Heights*, Steerforth in *David Copperfield*—handsome, spoiled men with dark secrets who caused a great deal of destruction around them. They attracted me more than any of the conventionally good heroes. Even at an early age, I was concerned with reform. I did not yet understand this desire for power over the lives of other people.

"Let's dance," he said. Without waiting for a reply, he took my hand and my waist and moved me onto the dance floor.

For a moment, I yielded. Tony held me very close to him. I could smell the fresh odor of his flesh and the whiskey on his breath. And then, over his shoulder, I saw Dickie Benjamin and Edwin Eisenstadt standing next to the dance floor grinning at Rob Leventhal and Cleo as they danced.

"Tony! Will you do me a favor?"

"Anything you want."

"Dance with Cleo, right now. She's over there with Rob Leventhal and I'm afraid the other boys are going to make a scene."

Tony glanced over his shoulder. "That's your sister Cleo?"

"She's still not well, Tony, and—"

"Why she's beautiful!"

"I know she is, but if they—"

In one swirling motion, Tony danced me across the floor until we were between Rob Leventhal and his friends. "Change your partner!" chanted Tony, as if he were calling a square dance, and in a moment had smoothly exchanged places with Rob and danced off with Cleo.

The abruptness of Tony's abandonment left me gasping. For a moment I wished I hadn't suggested the exchange. "If you don't want to dance, Rob—" I began.

"I don't mind at all," said Rob, grasping me.

I buried my head on Rob's shoulder and subtly moved him away from his friends. As we danced around the floor, I felt disoriented and angry. What was my family doing here enjoying the wasteful festivities of these people of wealth? I longed for my waitress' uniform. If I had been wearing an apron, Dickie, Edwin, and Rob would have recognized me immediately.

At the band's next break, my father appeared and suggested that the family leave. I thanked Rob abruptly and excused myself. Father and I managed to round up Mother and Cleo. Luckily, Tony had gone off to get a drink and we were able to move Cleo toward the sidewalk. My mother, tipsy from two drinks, insisted upon stopping to thank the hostess.

"Hell, I should thank *you*, Mrs. Bearwald," said Sonny Kuhn, "for lending me your husband."

"Arabella," prompted Mother.

"That's a peach of name, you got there. Spanish?"

"English."

"Well Arabella, that Henry of ours is a fine dancer."

"It was a wonderful party."

"Damned swell of you to say so. Even the people I invited never remember to thank me. We'll have to get together more often."

By the time we got Mother out on the sidewalk, she was almost weeping with joy. "What a wonderful lady!"

"I wouldn't count on that," said my father, breathing deeply. The encounter with Sonny had shaken him. He was relieved to have escaped.

The family walked in silence down Michigan Avenue toward the bridge. The street lights, nestled in the foliage of the elms that lined the street, cast a soft light on the front lawns and gardens of the handsome houses. As we approached the town, a fresh breeze blew in from the lake, causing the leaves to flutter, breaking the light into gentle patterns.

"Rebecca," said my father, "I'm still a little unclear about this boat of Cleo's. The way you were talking—a cabin, and all that—the Lefkowitzes are going to expect something grand."

"I'm afraid it is grand, Daddy," I said.

We had just crossed to the grassy traffic island that separated Michigan Avenue from the Petoskey highway when a large black car, headlamps off, skidded around the curve and up onto the grass. Cleo hurled her body at our legs, throwing all of us to the ground just out of reach of the car's fender. The car drove on at high speed toward Petoskey.

My father leaped up, waving his fist and shouting after the car. Mother and I clung to Cleo, thanking her for saving our lives.

She lay there for some time, content to remain in our arms. Finally, we managed to get ourselves on our feet. We walked home clumped together, looking around us as if we might be attacked from any direction.

Before I went to bed that night, I drew my father aside. "Daddy, that black car—"

"There's nothing to be afraid of—just some drunken idiots." His voice sounded shaky.

"You should report it to the police. That brick through our window, and the fire at our house, and—and now this. If it's because we're Jewish—"

"Don't carry on about it," he replied, harshly. "There's no connection."

I retreated toward the stairs. I was confused. The brick had come through our store window before Cleo had found the boat with the whiskey. And yet John Clover had said it came from a black Packard with Detroit plates. I wondered whether the brick was a message from gangsters or from anti-Semites? My father did not seem inclined to clarify the question. He followed me, his tone softening. "It's a violent, lawless time. The country will pull through it, dear. We just have to be careful, that's all."

That night I lay in bed, angry at my father. I could not forgive his collapse at the vandalism of his store and home or his timidity about this latest outrage. I wanted him to rise up in wrath and declare his pride in Judaism, in our family, in our town, and in the laws of our country.

SIXTEEN

THE LIQUOR AND THE dancing aroused my mother. In bed she caressed my father. He wanted to reach out and embrace her with fervor as he had over all these years—at least to confess his anxieties to her. Instead, he kept seeing the Lefkowitzes in their summer finery, lined up on their front porch. Arabella was a Lefkowitz. He felt that he had somehow climbed into bed with a stranger. He did his best to counterfeit desire but the encounter did not satisfy either of them. Eventually, my mother fell asleep.

My father lay staring at the intermittent light from the beacon on the bedroom ceiling. A fine sweat emerged upon his forehead as he reviewed the recent attacks upon him and his family. How could anyone in this town hate him so deeply? And his friends—Tom, Dwayne, and the rest—just accepted it. What had Vernon said? It's not his fault that the Jewish people aren't popular. My God, thought my father, the sheriff himself, his close friend since kindergarten. He wondered whether he had realized as a child and youth just how alone he was in Charlevoix. Perhaps that's why he had yearned so passionately for his cousin Sonny's affection—her impertinent grin, her wild, casual joy. He recalled with pain his proposal to Sonny and her dismissal. What would his life have been like, he wondered, if she had accepted?

His feeling for Sonny Kuhn had started during his twelfth year when he had stayed at Sonny's father's house in Detroit to study for his bar mitzvah. Desperately lonely and shy, he had been awed by the luxury of the house and the worldliness of his uncle's family. His cousins, prominent in the Jewish community, were scarcely ever at home except when they entertained. The three sons, all older than he, were kind enough, but paid him little attention. Sonny, nine, a tomboy, took charge of him as if he were her possession. She taught him how he was supposed to act among the sophisticated company that thronged the house. He read her stories and poems. After that year, the two kept up a correspondence. Whenever my father visited Detroit, they renewed their friendship. Later he introduced Sonny to literature and historical works. He took her to the library as if it were a shop, pulling his favorite books from the shelves and leafing through them with her. He taught her the importance of developing her own taste. He sent her books as gifts whenever he could afford it and loaned her his own books.

At the age of eighteen, he once more went to live with his cousins while he studied at the Detroit School of Business. By then Sonny had entered into a wild adolescence. But she retained her strong affection for her cousin from the north. Once more she took charge of him, instructing him on the ways of young women and arranging his social life. As Sonny grew to be a young woman herself, he fell in love with her. Eventually, he proposed and she rejected him.

As my father lay sleepless in bed watching the light of the beacon on the ceiling, the loneliness of his youth and the wound of that rejection returned.

*

Sunday morning, my parents slept late. They awoke irritable and found Cleo and me in the kitchen packing a picnic lunch for the afternoon outing. I served them breakfast and then sent them out of the kitchen while we finished.

I was not at all happy about the excursion. For the first time, *White Lightning* would be exposed to public view. And we, the storekeepers of Charlevoix, would be exposed as aliens to our fellow townspeople. Last night we had dressed up in costumes and accidentally entered the magical realm of the summer visitors. A car had tried to run us down. Today, we would be carrying our elaborate charade even further. This playacting, I felt certain, would end badly.

While they waited for their daughters, my parents lounged on the front porch, eyeing one another.

"I'm nervous," said my mother.

"The boat, you mean?"

"Not just that. Cleo frightens me."

"Too independent?"

"Too happy!" Mother sighed.

Taken aback, my father realized that he too was frightened by his troubled daughter's happiness. "Can that be so bad? All this spring, we've hardly had to take care of her."

Mother took Father's hand. "Do you think Cleo's getting better?"

Resisting the impulse to withdraw his hand, he stared down into his wife's large dark eyes. What would they do, he wondered, if God were at last to answer their most fervent prayer—Cleo's recovery?

Cleo burst through the door, holding the hamper high in both hands. I followed and the family set off for the dock. The Bearwalds together, I thought, just like every morning—except that Cleo could hardly contain her joy. She kept running ahead, turning back, and displaying the basket, a wide smile on her face.

We found the Lefkowitzes pacing up and down the wharf, examining the yachts. They all wore new white sneakers.

"I can't wait," said Maureen. "Which one is it?"

Proudly, Cleo conducted the two families to the *White Lightning*. My parents and the Lefkowitzes stared in amazement at the sleek cabin cruiser.

With grave courtesy, Cleo took Father by the arm and led him out on the dock. She jumped down into the cockpit, placed a handsome mahogany staircase with three rubber-clad steps in position and helped Father descend into the boat. Now I led Mother out and handed her into the boat where Cleo received her. This routine was repeated for each of the guests.

While I fanned the gas fumes out of the bilge and turned the engines over, Cleo proudly conducted a tour of the flying bridge, the cabin parlor and kitchenette, and the forecastle with its four generous berths, head, and shower. At the end of her tour, Cleo brought out two peaked and braided captain's hats which she presented to our parents.

"Captain and First Mate of the *White Lightning*," I announced.

"*White Lightning*?" said Sy. "Do you get it, Maureen, *White Lightning*, as in hooch!" he guffawed.

Maureen sat back in the cushioned stern seat, shaking her head from side to side. "Henry Bearwald, what gall!"

Sy frowned and muttered to his wife, "I'm not sure it's such a good idea that we're out here in plain view."

"Well, we're here now," replied Maureen, "so we might just as well enjoy it."

Father, stunned by the sumptuous craft that his daughters had somehow conjured up, allowed himself to be led by Cleo to the wheel inside the cabin. At Cleo's instruction, he put the boat in reverse. I took a strain on the beam line and then slowly played it out as the boat backed safely into Round Lake without touching its neighboring boat in the slip.

"Underway!" I shouted.

I relieved Father at the wheel, pulling *White Lightning* into a procession of boats leaving Round Lake through the Railroad Bridge Channel. Another similar procession passed on our port side, entering Round Lake. After my father had seated himself in a canvas deck chair, Cleo began the festivities. She handed around empty champagne glasses and removed two bottles of champagne from an ice chest in the corner of the cockpit. Wrapping one with a towel, she removed the wire mesh from the top, and gently twisted the cork. With an explosion that made the guests jump, the cork flew into the air, arcing out of the cockpit and falling into the water. The occupants of a passing sailboat cheered. Cleo poured the foaming liquid into glasses.

The Lefkowitzes grinned guiltily as they received their champagne. They glanced to the right and left at the other boats and the green shore slipping by as if someone was spying on their criminal act. Our parents sat and savored Cleo's assured movements as she balanced the tray of full glasses, serving us all. When Cleo arrived before Father, she hesitated. My father had not touched alcohol since the passage of Prohibition except for sips of ceremonial wine on Jewish holidays. Now he resisted his impulse to refuse. With a flourish, he held out his glass. She poured. "Thank you, Cleo."

Cleo raised her own glass and solemnly went about touching each of the other glasses.

By the time the glasses were empty, we had entered Lake Charlevoix and the procession of boats broke up, proceeding in their separate directions. I headed the boat east, toward Boyne City.

Maureen and Sy could not keep their eyes off my father who sat, his spare body stiffly upright in his deck chair, his legs crossed, the captain's hat cocked slightly over his right eye in the position Cleo had placed it.

The respectful gazes of his in-laws—their astonishment at his supposed good fortune—struck my father like knife thrusts. He was certain that at any moment some authority would repay him for this flagrant disruption of his daily order. Why couldn't his wife's relatives see into his head and his heart? he wondered. Why didn't they understand that he was astonished at this show of wealth and terrified of its consequences? Indeed, the malignant forces of life had already been unleashed upon him. He never thought his family would be attacked by anti-Semites in his own town. Now, what would their enemies say?

Mother, on the other hand, felt as if a fairy godmother had appeared and with one stroke had hatched the fragile fantasies that had been gestating within her imagination for years. She leaned back in the stern seat. The champagne tingled up into her nostrils and her head. She trailed her hand over the gunwale; the spray tingled on her skin. She raised her face to the sun. She felt her soft black hair flying behind her head like the tresses of a water nymph.

Forty years old won't be so bad, she thought, if life has such surprises. The memory of the Kuhn party lingered like a pleasant dream. She had danced the night before in the arms of a number of men. Indeed, her husband had been dancing with the hostess of the party on the same floor. Both of her daughters had danced by under Chinese lanterns, tall pine trees, and the starry sky. How many years had she stood on the shores of life yearning for fulfillment? And today, here she was, Arabella Lefkowitz Bearwald, the wife of a storekeeper, embarking upon that vigorous nautical world of summer enchantment.

We anchored off Evergreen Point where we swam and ate lunch. The champagne, the sun, the food, and the gentle rocking of the boat made us all drowsy. Mother napped. Sy, his nose covered with white paste to keep it from burning, began to snore. Maureen draped a beach towel around her husband's large white body. Cynthia went down into the forecastle and fell asleep on one of the bunks. The water in the bay sheltered by Evergreen Point was flat and clear. The bottom, with its sand and stones and mud, looked as if it were an inch from the surface.

The sun, marching slowly overhead toward the west, had just begun to cast the shadows of the low pine forest across the sand and stones of the beach when a wooden-hulled speedboat appeared from behind Evergreen Point. It headed in a northwest direction. Cleo caught sight of the boat before the roar of its two powerful engines reached us. Its bow jutted high in the air. Two spumes of foam leaped on either side of its stern. Cleo touched my shoulder and pointed. Suddenly the boat changed course in our direction, its starboard gunwale going under water. In a moment it righted itself and proceeded at full speed directly toward us.

Cleo pushed me toward the bow and ran into the cabin. She started the engines and put them in gear, heading the boat toward the anchor. As quickly as I could, I pulled in the anchor cable. Over my right shoulder, I saw the speedboat come bearing down upon us. When *White Lightning* was directly over her anchor, I was able to pull the anchor out of the bottom and up to the boat's bow, securing it.

The roar of the motorboat filled the air, deafening me. Its bow towered high above me. Certain we were about to be rammed, I sprawled, spread-eagled on the deck. At the last possible moment, the motorboat swerved to the port, sending its wake over *White Lightning*, drenching us all. *White Lightning* rocked violently from side to side. The lunch plates and glasses crashed to the deck, awash now with the water from the wake. My father, who had been standing next to the port side, almost fell overboard, saved only by my mother's grasp on his jacket. Uncle Sy pulled Aunt Maureen and Seymour down to the deck and lay over them, sheltering their bodies.

I looked up to see the motorboat's stern receding. Suddenly it slowed. At the wheel, looking back at us, laughing, stood Tony Warburg. He was alone in the boat. He waved.

Cleo swung the bow around and began to follow Tony's boat. I climbed back into the cockpit.

"Who was it?" yelled my uncle. He remained lying over his wife and his son.

"It's just Tony Warburg," I replied, "playing stupid games."

"Oh my God," said my uncle. "What a relief!"

"A relief?" I asked.

"Forget it, forget it," he said as he slowly got up and helped Aunt Maureen and Seymour rise.

"Oh Sy," said Aunt Maureen, "I thought for sure—"

"Don't think so much," said Uncle Sy, laying a finger over her lips.

Aunt Maureen saw me watching them, a puzzled frown on my face. She kissed my brow. "It's nothing, Becky, just fear for our lives. Your friend's a dangerous character."

After I picked up the dishes and glasses and silverware, I pumped the cockpit and bilge of lake water mixed with the remains of lunch. By the time I finished, Cleo had come to within twenty yards of Tony's boat. He put on more throttle, spurting ahead. Cleo followed suit, closing the gap slightly. Now Tony began to make evasive moves, first to starboard, then to port, and back to starboard. Cleo kept *White Lightning* right behind Tony's boat. Tony increased his speed. Cleo increased her speed. Tony made a ninety degree turn to port. Cleo followed. Tony made a ninety degree turn to starboard. Again Cleo followed.

My parents, Sy, and Maureen sat back in the stern seat, holding onto one another and to the sides of the boat. Seymour crawled up to the railing on the forward bulkhead of the cockpit and stood, his legs spread, peering ahead. I secured the deck chairs, the hamper, and the ice chest to cleats.

I could see my parents' mouths open but the sound of the engines drowned out their words. Both pointed urgently to the cabin. I made my way into the cabin and forward next to Cleo. Cleo's gaze was concentrated upon the stern of Tony's boat. I put my hand out toward the throttles. Cleo batted my hand aside. I could see Tony looking back at us. Once more Tony waved and then turned and thrust his throttles full forward. Tony's boat surged ahead.

"Slow down!" I shouted.

Cleo turned and looked directly at me as if annoyed that I dared to tell her what to do.

"Slow down!" I murmured, feeling the strength drain out of me.

Still looking at me, she placed her palm against the chrome throttles and pushed them slowly forward. With dismay, I had the fearful sense that Cleo and the white craft had become a single, implacable force. *White Lightning*, built to outrun the coast guard, responded to Cleo's command. I found myself thrown to the rear of the cabin. Slowly, I inched my way forward. By the time I reached Cleo's side again, we had gained two boat lengths on Tony's boat, then three, four. The waves resounded against the hull of the boat in deep, percussive beats.

Now Cleo thrust her throttles full forward, turning her wheel just slightly to starboard.

White Lightning thrust ahead, crossed Tony's wake, and pulled alongside Tony, a bare boat length off his starboard beam, and then passed him. I could see Tony's face clearly as he looked over at us, an expression of amazement on his face. Cleo raised her left hand slowly and pointed at him as if she were a magician casting a spell. I felt that I had entered a strange land in which Tony too was about to fall under the power of Cleo and the white boat. With a twist of the wheel, she brought *White Lightning* about on a forty degree turn to starboard, heading away from Tony's boat.

Cleo and I looked back in time to see *White Lightning*'s wake hit the hull of Tony's boat. Tony's boat leaped up clear of the water. We gasped. We could see Tony's propeller turning furiously as the hull rotated slowly on its side and then on its back. At the same time, Tony's body arced up in the air above the boat. Then with a crash, the boat fell, capsized, raising an enormous wave of foam in the air.

I turned back toward Cleo, but Cleo had disappeared. *White Lightning* was running out of control. I grabbed the wheel and the throttles, bringing the speed down. I turned back toward Tony's boat. As the roar of the engine moderated, another sound filled the air. It was some time before I realized that the sound was my sister's screaming wail. Looking around, I saw Cleo writhing about in agony on the deck of the cabin.

Seymour was the first to enter the cabin. He stared at Cleo. I called him to my side and told him to keep the bow of the boat aimed toward the hull of Tony's boat which was quite some distance away by now. I turned and threw myself upon Cleo's flailing body.

My parents reached the cabin next. For a moment they stood and stared down at Cleo. "Oh Lord," said Mother, "it's happened."

"Daddy, Momma!" I cried.

Father managed to get hold of Cleo's legs and Mother pinned her arms. I planted myself upon Cleo's chest and slapped her across the face three times.

Cleo's hysteria subsided. She went limp. My parents released their holds.

I glanced up at my parents over Cleo's head. A look passed between us, a look of satisfaction, as if we had been waiting for the inevitable return of Cleo's madness. Now that it had reappeared, we were reassured. The happy, independent Cleo had been an illusion. Here again was our sick, helpless Cleo who needed our constant care. At the same moment, we understood the feeling we shared. With repugnance we looked away from one another.

"We're almost there!" shouted Seymour. "What do I do now?"

I stood and took the wheel. I pulled *White Lightning* alongside the hull of Tony's boat, scanning the water around it. A few yards off the bow, I saw Tony's body lying face down in the water. I cut the engine, ran from the cabin, and dove into the water. With four strong strokes I reached Tony's side. Turning him over, I slung an arm across his body and started to pull him back toward our boat.

"Quite a lifeguard," he yelled, struggling loose. His hand closed upon my head and pushed me under.

I came to the surface, sputtering. "You—you—bastard."

Tony, treading water, laughed. "Just wanted to scare you."

"Well, you did!" Furious, I swam to the boat.

By the time I had reached *White Lightning*, I saw Cleo, still pale from her fit, listlessly secure the ladder over the side. I climbed onto the boat, grabbed a towel, and walked to the stern, drying myself off.

Tony climbed aboard. "Sorry folks," he said, gazing around at the family. "I'm just a damned fool." He reached out and clapped Cleo on the shoulder. "This is some fantastic boat!"

Cleo grinned weakly and handed him a towel.

Cynthia appeared from the forecastle, her eyes wide. "What on earth have you all been doing? First, the boat was pitching back and forth so much that I almost got thrown out of the bunk. I hung on for dear life and didn't come up on deck for fear of being thrown out of the boat. And then there was such a scream."

Maureen hugged her daughter. "It's all right, darling. It's nothing. We were all a bit frightened, but it turned out to be just some kind of a summer joke."

While Maureen comforted her daughter, I gazed angrily out over the stern.

Tony approached me. "I was groggy, Mouse."

I moved away, disturbed. Mouse had been his nickname for me in day camp.

He pursued me. "If you hadn't grabbed hold of me, who knows what would have happened?"

"You were faking."

"I only said that because I felt stupid." He put his hand out. "Friends?"

Grudgingly, I took his hand, but I didn't trust him.

It took several hours for Cleo, Tony, and me to get the capsized speedboat under tow and haul it around Evergreen Point to the dock at Warburg's. With the help of Seymour, we righted the boat, attached it to the davits on the dock, and drained it.

During all this time I brooded over the joyous relief my parents and I felt that our patient had fallen ill once again. Could we be such monsters? I damned Cleo's stupid boat for undermining my family, for destroying our whole way of life. We had spent a stupid, wasteful day pretending to be summer visitors. I reminded myself that my parents kept a store; my sister repaired boats; I waited on table. We did not belong in summer gardens or out upon the blue waters of the lake. Last night at Kuhns' and today at Evergreen Point, my family had been seduced by the summer visitors. To my horror, we had become enmeshed in their trivial pursuits—as if we could discard our ordinary lives. I was particularly disgusted by Tony Warburg's recklessness and my attraction to him.

When we had finished our work, Tony approached me. He wore his enticing, slightly bitter smile. "Mouse, why don't you all come up to the house for drinks." He cocked his head.

I refused to look at Tony or to talk to him. I walked away. He repeated the invitation to my father, who replied, "We've had enough for today, thanks. We'd better head back to port."

I cringed to hear my father say "head back to port," as if he were an "old salt."

"Another time, then," said Tony. "It was stupid of me to swamp your boat."

"And of us," said my father, looking at Cleo, "to capsize yours."

"No, no," said Tony, laughing. "That was justice, right Cleo?" He clasped Cleo lightly around the shoulders and kissed her quickly on the lips.

I was stunned at Tony's easy intimacy with my sister. My heart skipped a beat as if I had been struck. Startled, Cleo brought her fingertips to her lips, touching them. Her eyes followed Tony as he made the rounds of the Lefkowitzes and the Bearwalds, apologizing.

When he got to me, Tony grabbed hold of both my hands. "And for you, a special thanks." He leaned toward me. I turned my head away, refusing to forget that I was one of the servant monsters of this summer world. He took my chin gently between his thumb and forefinger and kissed me on the lips. His lips moved upon mine, coaxing a response. Then he leaped out of the cockpit up onto his dock and cast off our lines, waving goodbye. Both Cleo and I stood gazing at him as our boat drifted away from the dock.

All the way back to Charlevoix my mood dipped and soared. I was seized with rage and a strange excitement which frightened me. I didn't know how I felt toward Tony Warburg or my sister. I was eighteen years old and bewildered.

SEVENTEEN

I WAS NOT AWARE of the next meeting between Cleo and Tony until some time later when I questioned John Clover. He was reluctant to report his outings with Cleo, but he always answered truthfully when asked a question. Evidently, a day after Tony had kissed both Cleo and me good-bye, Cleo awoke before dawn. Stealthily she washed, dressed, and left the house. John Clover was waiting at *White Lightning's* berth. He carried his fishing gear. They greeted each other without words and boarded the boat. It was still dark when they set off—a windless, damp, overcast morning. Once through the channel, Cleo opened up the engines and headed toward Warburg Cove. The water was so calm it looked as if the boat was cutting through black ice. A thick mist enveloped the shore, sending out irregular, invading arms into the lake. John, who knew the best fishing holes, pointed out a spot just before Evergreen Point. By the time Cleo had turned off the engines and allowed the boat to drift, John had broken out the fishing gear and baited both lines. As light appeared in the eastern sky, the outline of the pine forest at Evergreen Point emerged, shrouded in mist and mysterious.

John and Cleo cast. Two barely audible splashes marred the surface of the mirrored water. Two circles of tiny waves expanded, diminishing in size as the periphery moved outward. Just before the waves disappeared, the circles intersected. The surface became still again. Slowly John and Cleo reeled in, pausing occasionally to let the bait fall and then lifting the rod in a graceful arc to provide an alluring motion for the hungry fish. The hooks arrived at the boat almost simultaneously. As the fishermen prepared to cast once more, the surface of the water exploded twenty yards off their stern. John and Cleo grinned at one another. A large fish had just come up for the first snack of the day.

On the third cast, Cleo felt a tentative nibble. She shut her eyes. Her fingers tingled as the urgent, hidden life of the water spoke to her. The fish took a taste, a second taste, and then just as the delicate mouth closed in upon the bait, up went Cleo's arms, setting the hook. The mysterious deep took hold. At this moment all the terrifying chaos that surrounded Cleo's life sorted itself out into a coherent fabric—the depths of the water, the misty pines of the shore, the great stretch of lake, the brightening eastern sky, the white boat, John Clover, and Cleo Bearwald all became one. The fish dove, bending the rod. Cleo played out just enough line to keep it from breaking. Then suddenly the line went slack as the fish reversed its course and broke water in a desperate leap to throw the hook. Cleo reeled in furiously. The fish dove again. Cleo released her line. Three times the fish dove and then began a steady zigzag through the water, struggling against Cleo's inexorable pull. Cleo battled the weakening fish to the side of the boat. John reached down with the net and hauled up a fine small-mouthed bass, not a large fish, but one full of coiled power, twisting furiously to escape the indignity of the hook, the net, and the air. A burst of laughter broke from Cleo and John. Cleo wet her hands over the side and delicately took hold of the wriggling fish just over the gills. With an adept motion, she removed the hook and let the fish slip back into the lake.

As Cleo prepared to bait her hook, John cast. Cleo stood and looked around. The boat had drifted to within a hundred yards of the Warburg dock. A figure appeared out of the forest and strode onto the dock, pausing at the end. A small arm of mist cloaked the figure and the dock, obscuring it. Cleo stared at the figure, casting her will as if it were a fishing line. The figure dove into the water and with long lazy strokes moved out into the lake through the mist toward them. Cleo put her rod down and waited. As the swimmer approached the starboard side of the boat, she put over the ladder. Tony Warburg's glistening wet head and body emerged. To Cleo, the young man looked as beautiful as a fish.

Tony stepped into the boat. She gave him a towel.

"Morning, John." Tony spoke in a hushed voice.

John Clover nodded and kept on fishing.

Tony threw his arm around Cleo who offered her lips to be kissed. He kissed her cheek instead. "How's my reckless speed demon this morning?" He took hold of Cleo's shoulders and held her at arm's length. "What a wondrous sight to wake up to—the calm lake, the rising sun, and a beautiful girl!"

Cleo looked directly into Tony's eyes, her gaze transfixing him. His lighthearted smile faded.

"You don't talk very much, do you?"

Unembarrassed, Cleo shook her head.

"But you understand everything."

She shrugged.

"Probably more than everything." He continued to hold her shoulders and looked shrewdly into her eyes. "I'll bet you see right into people's heads."

She nodded.

"You won't like what you see in mine."

She shook her head slowly from side to side.

He relaxed his grip. "I'm reckless and I'm worthless."

Cleo laughed. She pointed her thumb at herself and cocked her head.

"You too?" Tony scratched Cleo's head, he kneaded her shoulders, and hugged her. "Yesterday I saw just how reckless you could be."

Cleo leaned forward and rubbed up against the young man.

The sound of a fish breaking water and the rapid click of John Clover's reel distracted the two young people.

Cleo handed her rod to Tony and picked up the net, ready to land John's fish.

For more than an hour, the three fished together, silent except for the sound of the bait striking the water, clicking reels, the dripping net, and an occasional exclamation of satisfaction or disappointment. They kept only the largest fish.

At seven fifteen, John looked at his pocket watch and began to stow the gear. Cleo started the engines and brought the boat alongside the Warburg dock.

"Best time I've had since I came up," said Tony, waving at John, who waved back.

Cleo reached into the bucket and pulled out two of the fish, holding them with her forefingers through the gills. Still alive, they twisted violently. She handed them to Tony who placed his forefingers through the gills, replacing hers.

"Thanks, Miss Bearwald."

Cleo, her hands free, took hold of Tony's head, pulled it down, and kissed him on the lips. Tony, helpless, a fish suspended from each hand, remained standing for a moment, gazing down into Cleo's face. He appeared startled by the young woman's ardor. Then he laughed and jumped onto the dock.

"Tomorrow?" he called out.

Cleo nodded and gunned the engines.

*

At quarter to four that afternoon, I walked up Main Street on my way to work at the Belvedere Club. This morning, for the first time in four months, I had awakened free from the weight of furious anxiety. I felt excited, light-hearted, as if I were expecting a pleasant surprise—but I didn't know why.

I turned onto Belvedere Avenue. A car horn honked. I looked up. A convertible roadster moved slowly along the street, following me. Tony Warburg sat at the wheel. A red flush began low on my spine, traveled up my body to my scalp and over my face.

"Come on over, Mouse," he called. The nickname once more recalled our childhood friendship—a vague memory by now. Fighting an impulse to run away, I approached the passenger side of the car.

"Hop in," he said. His voice was curt, matter-of-fact.

"I'm due at work in five minutes." I turned and walked along the street toward the club. He followed in the car, blocking my way with his fender. "Watch out," I called out.

"I'll drive you."

"It's just a few steps."

"Then stand on the running board." He sounded exasperated.

Though his tone annoyed me, I found myself stepping up on the running board.

Tony drove ahead. "Tell me where."

"Here!"

Tony stopped and I jumped down.

"Thanks." I spoke without looking at him and began to walk away.

"Mouse!" I looked at him. "Can I pick you up after work?" He cocked his head and at last his acrid, attractive smile appeared.

I hesitated. Tony Warburg was an aimless young man. I disliked the casual way he assaulted people and then tried to charm them. His life was irrelevant to everything I believed in; yet his charm succeeded—he intrigued me. Fortunately, I had already promised to meet my cousins at a roadside restaurant at the edge of town.

"Tonight I'm busy—" my voice dropped, "—going to the Chow Down with some people."

Tony scowled. Immediately, I wanted to retract my refusal. "Another night, then." He drove off, leaving me in the roadway.

His rudeness confirmed my judgment of him. I entered the kitchen of the Belvedere Club, commending myself on my good sense.

It was a difficult night. The guests kept changing their minds; the cooks misread two orders; my busboy dropped a tray of dishes. After the last customer left, I helped the busboy set up for the next day although it was not part of my job.

Ordinarily it took me only fifteen minutes to walk to the Chow Down on the highway at the edge of town. Tonight I dawdled and gazed at the sky. I wanted to postpone the encounter with my cousins and their friends. I could hardly believe that I was cooperating with this ridiculous attempt to market my charms. After all, I was still intent upon going to college. But I liked my aunt and my cousins, and besides, a soft drink and a hamburger did not constitute a marriage contract. Then there was the chance that my cousins' friends would be interesting. They had grown up in a city where men and women worked in factories building the cars of America—in a city where the battle between the laborers and their bosses was brewing.

I breathed in the soft summer air, sweetened by honeysuckle and given an edge by the poignant smell of tarring on the dirt back streets. I felt a remote twinge of pleasure at the thought that my family was industriously seeking a young man for me even though I knew my parents' motives were not pure. For once the family's attention was focused partly on my welfare and not completely on Cleo's. I fell momentarily into a fantasy that I was the central character of a romance. I imagined myself as the young Princess Kitty Shtcherbatsky in *Anna Karenina*, courted by the dashing Count Vronsky and the sincere and awkward Levin. My distant and ironic father watched sympathetically while my mother pushed me toward disastrous hopes of the more brilliant marriage. The bumbling Ben Near had just performed assiduous athletic feats to impress me at the fashionable skating rink by Moscow's Zoological Gardens while Tony Warburg prepared to sweep me off my feet at one of Moscow's most brilliant balls. I was destined to break Levin's heart. My own heart would be broken by Vronsky, who himself would become enslaved by his passion for the greatest beauty of all of Russia.

Tony Warburg's variable moods had captured more of my emotions than I wished. His mixture of charm, kindness, and irritability produced a strange chemistry within me. I felt bathed in a caustic wash of desire and regret, as if I were missing something essential. I regretted refusing Tony Warburg's invitation.

The sound of my shoes crunching across the gravel parking lot in front of the Chow Down woke me from my reverie. I took a deep breath, squared my shoulders, and reminded myself that this romantic nonsense counted for very little in my life. With a wave of my hand, I banished my mother's fantasies.

The tables of the restaurant were full. People stood at the door, waiting. I edged forward looking for my cousins and saw that the evening would turn out even worse than I had imagined. All the worlds in which I had been granted tenuous citizenship were represented. The owner's wife at the cash register served on the Parks committee with my mother; the waitresses attended high school with me; Ben Near sat at a table with a group of boys on the baseball team. At other tables, I recognized people I served regularly at the Belvedere Club. I spotted my cousins and their friends near a corner next to a table filled with young men and women from the north side of town, including Dickie Benjamin, Rob Leventhal, and Edwin Eisenstadt. Beyond my cousins' table sat two of John Clover's sons with their wives.

"Becky!" Cynthia called out across the room and waved.

Blood rushed to my face. It seemed as if everyone in the room turned their eyes on me. I stood paralyzed by the realization that the whole ridiculous mix of people in our summer resort had jammed together within the walls of this diner to cook, serve, and eat burgers, fries, sodas, and shakes. It was an anarchist's heaven. Why, I wondered, didn't the Chow Down blow up?

"We're over here, Cousin Becky!" Cynthia stood up and signaled me.

Waving and smiling and nodding to the right and to the left, I swiftly made my way to my cousins' table. As I walked I felt myself dividing like those lower creatures under a microscope in biology lab.

Cynthia jumped up and gave me a hug and a kiss. "Sammy, Sidney, Norman—this is our Cousin Becky." I sank down into a chair with the confused impression of a number of young men of various shapes and sizes. "You know Seymour's fiancée, Natalie, don't you?" I waved at Natalie, who smiled. She had a round face and cupid lips painted with lipstick. She wore a light blue fuzzy sweater. Her family owned a summer house on our street. I had always thought her rather dumb and spoiled.

Cynthia's fiancé, Sammy, had been in the midst of a story about cutthroat competition in the laundry business. "It's turned into a war between two trade associations. The other side hired gangsters to do their dirty work."

Sammy's mention of gangsters caught my attention and I asked him for details. While we waited for our order, he continued. "Well, my father's competitors hired these gangsters to attack us. But the gangsters turned against them too, and now they're paying through the nose to keep the goons from blowing up their own plants."

"Sammy likes to exaggerate," said his friend, Sidney. He was a very tall, thin young man, with rimless spectacles—the only man in the place with a tie.

"I suppose Keller's fire was an accident?"

"You mean the gangsters started the fire?" I asked. I remembered the fire on our porch this spring.

"Gangsters start fires in Detroit. That's how they remind people to keep up their payments."

"Do they drive black Packards?" I asked.

"Every gang has a preference," said Sammy. "The Purple Gang—they're Jewish, you know—they drive Packards."

I wanted to ask Sammy more about gangsters and their Packards, but Natalie, who made it clear that she found all this boring, broke in to ask about my work as a waitress at the Belvedere Club. Everyone at the table turned to listen.

"It's work, that's all," I mumbled, feeling that Natalie had intended to put me in my place. Cynthia, with her good heart, added that I worked at the library too. Sammy's friend Sidney found it impressive that I worked at two jobs.

Embarrassed to have become the center of attention, I asked Natalie what she was doing these days. With a little twist of her head, she sent her curls flying this way and that as she informed me that she was in college.

Now I became angry. I felt it unjust that a girl who had no interest in books or ideas should so carelessly enjoy the privilege of college. "Well," I responded, "I'm planning to become a professional waitress—don't need college for that, I guess."

Everyone at the table stared at me. I sank down in my seat, hoping the conversation would proceed on different lines. Instead, Natalie took me literally and began to talk about the plight of labor in our society in a patronizing way. Seymour, embarrassed at his fiancée's insensitivity, hemmed and hawed and came close to apologizing for her. Sidney took my side, arguing that every vocation had its use. I appreciated his kindness. He was formal and looked scholarly, like my father. But he was not nearly as handsome, nor, I decided, as intelligent. Father would have understood my irony.

"Hi folks! Mind if I join you?" I looked up, startled to see Tony Warburg pull a chair up and sit upon it backwards at the corner of the table right next to me. He wore a clean, torn T-shirt and white tennis shorts. "Mousie here and I had a date tonight." He put his arm over my shoulders. I could smell the whiskey on his breath.

This distraction proved even worse for me than the initial conversation. Seymour and Cynthia's friends knew the Warburg name and Natalie claimed that she and Tony had met once. Tony was rude to her, but he did acknowledge having met my cousins. "Tried to drown them just the other day and they saved my life." He clapped Seymour on the back and leaned over and kissed Cynthia's forehead. A broad smile broke over Cynthia's face.

Terrified that Tony would create more of a scene and insult my cousins, I stood up. Tony, who had been leaning on me, fell off his chair. Everyone in the restaurant turned to look.

"Hey, Mouse! That wasn't nice." He stood up and righted his chair.

"I'm sorry, but I have to get home." I bent over Cynthia and gave her a hug. "Thanks a lot." I decided that I really liked her. I patted Seymour's shoulder, hoping he would understand my gesture as an apology, and waved to the rest of the table. "I enjoyed meeting all of you. If you're still around next Sunday, you're all invited out on our boat."

Without waiting for a reply, I fled.

EIGHTEEN

"CAN I COME OUT in your boat too?" asked Tony. He had followed me to the parking lot.

"No, not you, Tony." I kept on walking. "You're drunk and you're rude."

Tony stepped in front of me, his head down, his voice slurred and penitent. "I was just rude to that silly girl who deserved it."

I suspected he was playacting again, but I couldn't be sure. "Oh, what's the use. It's all so stupid, anyway." I pushed by him.

Tony put his arm over my shoulders. "Don't be sad, Mouse. I'm sorry I spoiled your date."

"You didn't spoil anything. It was rotten from the beginning."

"You want to go for a ride?" Now he tried his smile on me, a bright, shining mask.

"You're drunk or pretending or both."

"You drive, then. Please." He took hold of my arm and stopped me. "If you don't, I'll just get into a wreck."

"I don't care. You people with nothing better to do than play games! It makes me sick."

"Please, Mousie." The smile turned rueful. "I'm not in a very good mood."

I didn't want to go home. I knew that when I walked back into the house I would be trapped again. Mother would barrage me with questions and then scold me for spoiling the evening. Well, my parents wanted me to see young men, I thought angrily, and Tony Warburg was a young man—Jewish too, and, best of all, rich. I agreed to drive Tony's convertible.

As soon as I got behind the wheel, Tony leaned over and put his hands over mine. "Here, let me show—"

"I know how to drive." I shouldered him aside.

I started up the car, put it in gear, and pushed down on the gas. The car skidded onto the highway, throwing Tony to the corner of his seat.

"Hey! I'm the one who's drunk."

The warm, sweet wind washed over me. The vibrations of the throbbing engine passed from the steering wheel to my hands and arms. As I drove south away from town and the ugliness of the scene at the Chow Down, I gradually increased speed until my foot was on the floorboard. Tony's roadster was ten, twenty times more powerful than our Ford. I had little control over the fiery machine under me; I had no control over myself or my emotions. Tony pulled himself to a standing position. The wind tore at his curly black hair and at his shirt, billowing it out behind him. His mouth opened in a wide grin, his teeth a brilliant white against the smooth, tanned skin of his face. He looked like a beautiful vision—a knight charging into battle. My spirits rose to a state of dangerous exaltation.

The countryside rushed past. A big truck approached from the opposite direction. Blinded momentarily by its lights, I did not let up on the accelerator. The wind of the passing vehicle swept the roadster to the edge of the road. The two right wheels slipped off the pavement, grinding up gravel. The rear end skidded on and off the pavement and finally settled of its own accord back on the highway. Gradually, I slowed down. I was breathing heavily in joyful terror. Then I caught sight of a familiar side road. With a sudden jerk, I swept the wheel around to the right, skidding onto a dirt road. Tony fell back on the seat, sprawling over me. I thrust him away and continued along the dirt roads until I had reached the beach on the way to Running Shoal where Cleo had found *White Lightning*. I had no idea where I was going or why.

I thought now of those black Packards chasing Cleo and me through the night toward North Point after we had sold the rest of the whiskey to the man at Beechams. Perhaps the fire on our porch and the car that tried to run us over had been retribution for our whiskey sales. Sammy had said that gangsters start fires. But the brick through the front window of my father's store did not fit this theory. That had happened before my sister found *White Lightning* and the whiskey. Could the brick have been just a coincidence? Unrelated? Anti-Semitism, like my father thought? John Clover claimed it had been thrown from a black Packard with Detroit license plates. And my uncle Sy did business with the

Purple Gang—Jews—who preferred black Packards. It all made me dizzy. I wished my sister had never found that cursed boat that had already left three dead bodies on our beautiful shore.

I raced along over the hard sand, my two right wheels in the water, sending spray high in the air behind the car. Tony lunged over and grabbed the wheel, trying to bring it up further on the beach. I struggled to keep that absurd plume of water constant in the moonlight. The car weaved back and forth. I shot an elbow into Tony's ribs. Tony let go of the wheel and the car swerved suddenly to the right, directly into the lake. A wave climbed over the hood and the car died.

"You took us to sea, Captain," sputtered Tony, laughing.

I stared forward through the windshield blurred by water. Slowly the glass cleared and the wide lake appeared on all sides. A half moon sent glimmers of light upon the incoming waves. I, too, began to laugh.

Every time we tried to speak, another wave washed along the length of the car and set us laughing again. We couldn't stop.

"Mousie wrecked my car," Tony sang out.

"Tony is a maniac!" I launched myself across the front seat and began to pummel the young man, tearing his cotton shirt. Wedged against the door, Tony could not defend himself. He reached both arms around me and tried to grab me in a bear hug. My elbow accidentally hit the door handle and we fell out of the car.

We sat side by side in the water, the waves lapping over our knees. I thought of my parents and Cleo waiting at home to hear of my new suitors. All of the dammed up rage of the winter and spring welled up within me. Tony reached out and took my hand. He held it in both of his, tenderly, as if he guessed my thoughts. I leaned my head against his shoulder. He put his arms around me and held me, patting my back and head. He rocked me back and forth. Slowly, an odd realization came to me: that Tony was not simply giving me comfort, he was hanging onto me. I reached around and held him as tightly as I could.

"I'm no good," Tony said. "Worthless, stupid, dumb, miserable, rude—no good."

Stunned, I could think of no reply. Instead, I simply held onto him with all of my strength. He subsided and detached himself from me. He clasped his knees and gazed forward. "Sorry."

I moved over and captured Tony's hand. "Don't be sorry," I said. "We're friends." Tony's remorseful confession had robbed me of my anger. The handsome, nonchalant, insolent Tony Warburg reduced to such weak, suffering need of support? I struggled to absorb this sudden revelation.

We sat in the water. I closed my eyes and held Tony's hand to my face. What now? I asked myself, exhausted. I felt as if my entire past had been erased. Nothing remained—just water and sky and this strange hand. I put my lips to his palm. The breeze shifted to the north. I shivered.

"Hey," said Tony, leaping up. "We're going to catch pneumonia." He pulled me up. "We better push old Marybelle back on dry land before she rusts."

With some effort, we pushed the car back up on the beach. Tony opened up the hood, and with his torn T-shirt dried off the spark plugs and the ignition as well as he could. I pushed the starter. The engine spluttered and died. "It's either still wet or flooded," said Tony. "We'll have to wait."

We got back into the car. Tony wrapped me in a blanket.

"What about you?" I asked.

"Wet and flooded," said Tony, his teeth chattering.

"Let's share it, at least."

"If you don't mind," he replied. "I promise I won't—take advantage."

"How stupid."

We climbed back into the rumble seat and wrapped the blanket around us. We embraced. Slowly, our bodies warmed. I had kissed several boys and had petted with Ben Near at North Point, but I had never lain in such an intimate embrace before. Except for his shorts, Tony's body was bare. The resilience of his flesh against mine excited me. In my confusion over Tony's confession, I concentrated upon simple sensation. I had tasted his palm, now I felt his entire body.

"You know, Mouse," Tony spoke, his mouth close to my ear, "you were really cute at day camp."

"I followed you around like a dog."

"Funny, I really liked that. No one ever admired me the way you did, trusted me."

"You saved my life. All those other kids were so cruel—because we were locals, had a store."

"Bunch of idiots—even at that age."

"Cleo—"

"Kids are damned brutal—just because someone's different."

"It's funny, Tony, but I suppose you were my first real friend."

"We had a lot of fun together. Like tonight. A couple of

hysterical kids. I don't remember much except that you were little and smart. I was such a dumbbell. Still am."

"That's stupid." As the word came out, I realized that I had slapped exactly that word on Cleo just before she kicked me on the day of the storm. In fact, I used the word a great deal. Of course, I didn't think I was stupid. I was smart, superior, intelligent—everyone had always said that about me. And no one, yet, had ever called me arrogant. But maybe, really, I was more stupid than anyone and full of pride, too.

After a long silence, Tony mumbled, "You see, even you think I'm stupid."

"That's not what I meant and you know it." Grateful that the darkness hid my deep blush, I tickled Tony's ribs for lack of a better response.

"Stop fooling around." Tony pinned my hands under his arms. "I'm not kidding." Tony let me go. "What you said about rich people was right."

"I didn't mean—"

"Oh yes you did. Everyone in your family works for a living—and so does everyone else in town. And look at all of us."

"Well," I said, bold suddenly with the instinct of a caretaker, "it doesn't have to be like that. I mean, people can change." Oh God, I thought, now that Cleo has escaped my clutches, I'm going to try to enroll Tony Warburg as a client. But I had settled too firmly in my role. "It's not you," I continued, "it's the system—"

"Oh, I don't want to hear any goddamn thing about the system!" Tony shouted, pulling away from me. I huddled up in the corner of the seat, my cheeks burning as if he had slapped me. He leaned toward me, his face contorted in rage. "It's not the system. It's me. I'm no goddamn good. I've flunked out of every school I've ever been in, I made a mess of the jobs my dad put me in, and I'm just wandering around now like a goddamn bum." He stared down at me. I was certain he was going to hit me. Then he collapsed in the seat, his head back. "No goddamn good."

I sat up carefully, my heart beating rapidly. He remained motionless, his jaw clenched, his eyes staring up at the sky as if he had been shot. He hardly breathed. I got to my knees on the seat and looked down at his stricken face. I bent over him and kissed him on the forehead, eyes, and cheeks.

At first Tony received my kisses like a child accepting comfort. The muscles of his face relaxed. His breathing deepened. Slowly he began to respond, his fingers gently caressing my cheeks and neck, his lips seeking mine. Then, with a muscular twist he lifted me and eased me around across his lap. His tongue came into my mouth. My body shook as the curling, wet, snakelike presence invaded me. The tongue retreated along the length of my own tongue drawing it into his mouth. Now Tony's body and my body moved against one another gently, tenderly, our hands touching each other's skin. One of Tony's hands slid up under my blouse and bra. His other hand moved up under my wet skirt. My legs parted. I wanted him to touch me everywhere. As his fingers slipped under the elastic of my panties, my body began to shudder uncontrollably. I groaned.

Terrified at this unnatural sound, I sat up and pushed Tony's hands away. He didn't struggle.

"What's wrong?" he asked.

"I—I don't know." I couldn't catch my breath.

Tony sat up and leaned over, his elbows on his knees, his head in his hands. He swayed back and forth as if in pain.

"I'm sorry, Tony. I'm such a fool."

"No, no," said Tony, laying his hand gently on my back. "I'm the fool. I promised that I wouldn't do anything, but, of course, you can't trust Tony Warburg."

"But it was me, Tony, not you." I turned and stared at him. In the dim light of the stars and the waning moon, his glistening skin and wet hair made him look frightening and desirable. It was not simply his flesh I craved. I had been lured by his inconstant spirit—his need to be loved, his scornful, lonely fury—and the vague memory of his affectionate kindness from our childhood.

Tony grinned at me and opened his arms. "Come here, you idiot. I promise just to hold you."

I stared at the curling lips, the white teeth. I hesitated and then slipped into his arms. As terrified as I felt, I could not bear to leave the comfort of his flesh. We wrapped the blanket tightly around us and snuggled down together.

"You know, you could go back to school," I said. I caught my breath. The words had come out unbidden. I could not believe that in the midst of my desire I was still intent upon reforming him. My body tensed, prepared for his assault.

His reply was mild. "You don't give up, do you?"

Encouraged, I continued. "I'll bet your folks would send you anywhere you wanted to go."

"You're damned right they would. They hound me day and night. But I don't want to go to school. I'm no good at it."

"I think you could do anything you wanted to do."

"I don't need a guardian angel." His voice was sarcastic, but he stroked my hair as he spoke.

I sighed. "It's really funny. Your folks want to send you to college and you don't want to go. My folks don't want to send me to college, and I want to go more than anything."

Tony listened to my woes patiently. I don't think he really understood what I was saying, but he kept murmuring kind sounds until, exhausted, we fell asleep. Tony woke up first, alarmed that he had kept me out too late. He turned the ignition and the car started up immediately.

NINETEEN

FROM THE END OF the pier, the beacon swept its intermittent light up through the windows and across the ceilings of the Bearwald house. The family anxiously awaited my return. My father sat in his study attempting to read biblical commentary. My mother rocked in the living room, sporadically laboring upon a needlework design of a fresh rosebud with a single drop of dew about to fall from its furled petals. Cleo paced through the rooms, pausing to peer out the windows. From time to time, she ran upstairs to search the bedrooms for me. Then she ran downstairs and out onto the front porch where she stood and listened for my familiar footsteps.

Ten-thirty passed, eleven o'clock, eleven-thirty. The light from the beacon appeared and faded, its departure reminding the family that one of its members was still absent.

My father could not concentrate on his studies. He saw the window of his store crumpling inward, the flames rising from his front porch, the black car hurtling over the curb. He pictured his family dressed in their summer finery, eating dinner with his in-laws on the unfamiliar porch north of the bridge, dancing under the stars in the Kuhns' garden, and drinking champagne in Cleo's cabin cruiser. He had entered a strange nightmare from which he could not awaken. Moment by moment, he waited for the flair of light from the pier below to fill the void that threatened to engulf him. Mechanically he turned the pages of his book, remembering the pleasure of holding his cousin Sonny once again in his arms. Desire for that slim, sardonic creature flickered through his body. For the first time in many years, he mourned for those promises that had seared his youth and then had vanished.

Through the silence of the house he heard Cleo's wandering. Rebecca's inexplicable absence disturbed her. How could the family be sure, he asked himself, that Cleo would accept any suitor for Rebecca's hand—even one who would remain in Charlevoix? "Mine, mine!" he could hear his eldest daughter shriek through the years as she pointed to Rebecca. At eleven o'clock, Arabella's voice came from the other room, urging Cleo to go to sleep. Cleo went upstairs, but soon she came back down and resumed her pacing.

As the hours passed, my mother became more agitated. She rocked back and forth, imagining the romance upon which her youngest daughter had embarked with the young suitors from Detroit. The furled rose at which her hooked needle picked embodied for her all the potential of her daughter's life. Arabella hoped that Rebecca's fiancé would be warm-hearted, talkative and imaginative, an ally in her attempt to bring life to the desolate North Woods. She conjured up her son-in-law's parents, a vigorous couple full of good humor and energy; she imagined his sisters and brothers, each one a happy youth who would laugh and sing and dance at the wedding, and the aunts, uncles, and cousins, respectable professionals and business people who would proudly and generously welcome the Bearwalds into their family.

She decided that the wedding would take place in the summer. She would invite all the Bearwalds from Detroit and, of course, the Samuel Weintraubs, whose daughter would no doubt marry Sy and Maureen's son. She would issue a particular invitation to Sonny Kuhn, Henry's cousin. She would invite Charles Kuhn too, Sonny's brother-in-law, and a number of the other prominent summer visitors from Chicago, Cincinnati, and St. Louis. Into my mother's mind rushed the memory of the soft summer night she had stepped effortlessly into that forbidden world of Michigan Avenue. The way Sonny Kuhn had spoken so warmly to her at her departure, she was certain that she and Henry's cousin would become the best of friends.

"It's after midnight." My father's voice intruded upon her reverie. Mother looked up, startled.

"Rebecca must be having a good time."

"I doubt it."

"Why do you say that?"

"I just don't think that Rebecca will be fascinated by the kind of boys Maureen will dredge up."

Father's remark stung Mother. It dangerously approached her own judgment. "A damn snobbish thing to say."

"I suppose so." My father turned away, embarrassed at the truth in his wife's accusation.

"You should have seen your mouth the other night at their house, all twisted up in judgment. I know what you think of my brother and his family."

My father was about to reply when he saw Cleo, standing by the dining room window, listening intently to them. "To bed, everyone to bed!" He gestured toward the stairs. "Rebecca won't appreciate a welcome from the whole family. And besides, we have to go to work tomorrow morning."

"I want to hear what happened," said my mother.

Father grimaced. "Do you think one of those boys will drop to his knee the first time he lays eyes on our daughter?"

"You won't laugh if she goes off somewhere and leaves us."

"With such a romantic wife, what else can I do. Now upstairs! Both of you." He herded Mother and Cleo up to bed.

My mother lay in bed until she heard my father breathing regularly. Carefully, she rose and stole back down to the living room to wait. Upstairs, she heard Cleo pacing in her room. Finally, the house fell silent. The minutes followed one another at a painfully slow rate. Mother's loneliness grew. She began to feel oppressed, certain now that her daughter was deliberately delaying her return. She sighed. Neither her husband nor her children appreciated her; the townspeople of Charlevoix treated her like an eccentric intruder; the summer people looked down upon her as the wife of a tradesman. She had wasted her life.

Some time after two o'clock, weary of her thoughts, she went back to bed and fell asleep. At three, she woke and crept into the girls' bedroom where she discovered Rebecca and Cleo sleeping soundly. At four-thirty, she heard Cleo leave to go fishing before work. At six, she rose with Henry and discovered Rebecca's wet clothes hanging to dry over the bathtub.

"What on earth could she and her cousins have been doing?"

"Let her sleep," replied my father. "She doesn't have to get to the library until ten."

As soon as Mother entered the store, she called Maureen. "How did it go? What were our kids doing till all hours of the night? I can't wait to hear."

"All hours of the night? My kids were home at eleven."

Mother was taken aback. "Well, I haven't actually talked to Rebecca. She was sleeping when I left home."

"Cynthia said that the boys were really interested—until Becky suddenly went off."

"Went off?"

"That crazy Warburg boy showed up and created a disturbance. Rebecca ran out of the restaurant and he went charging after her. He was drunk."

"Tony Warburg and my Rebecca?" The gables of the Warburg estate rose up in Mother's mind, the circular drive in front of the Big House, the lawns, the gardens, and the tennis court.

"Arabella!" Maureen's voice was sharp. "Stop dreaming!"

"Well," said Mother, "I don't see why—"

"My Seymour's Natalie gave us an earful of Tony Warburg's exploits. He goes out with women twice his age. He'd just ruin your daughter. And besides, he's not exactly what you had in mind."

Mother's mood sank. She couldn't imagine Tony Warburg behind the counter at Bearwalds—or Cleo at the Warburgs' dining table.

"Anyway, we don't know that Rebecca was even with him last night, do we?" Now Arabella remembered her daughter's wet clothes hanging in the bathroom.

"I'd find out if I were you."

"I don't need instructions."

"In any case, Rebecca invited all the kids out on your boat this weekend. Just make sure that she goes through with it. Nothing gets those young men like a boat."

At noon my mother walked over to the library. She discovered me replacing books on the shelves. I threw my arms around her neck and kissed her. "Good morning, Momma."

"How was last night?"

"Oh, I invited Cynthia and Seymour and their friends out on the boat next weekend—if that's all right."

"Of course, it's all right." My innocent tone aroused Mother's suspicions. "Did you like the boys?"

"They seemed nice." I busied myself once more shelving the books. Mother followed me.

"I waited up for you."

"Oh, I'm sorry. I got in late."

"And your wet clothes?"

"I had a little accident. Actually, I fell into Lake Michigan. I was driving—" I hesitated and then continued in a rush, "—Tony Warburg's roadster on the beach down near Running Shoal."

"I thought you were with Seymour and Cynthia."

"It's a long story, Momma. Hilarious. I'll tell you tonight when I get home from work. I promise." I embraced her again and then looked into her eyes. "Look at you, all worried and anxious." I kissed her forehead. "Don't make such faces. You'll get wrinkles."

Pretending alarm, Mother touched her face with her fingertips. "Do I have wrinkles?"

"Not yet, but you will if you worry about me so much."

Reluctantly, Mother left the library. She could not forget the wet clothes hanging in the bathroom. At least, she thought, Rebecca was wearing clothes when she went into the lake. But then what had happened? And why had Rebecca's mood changed so? Why was she so suddenly excited and happy and affectionate?

As she walked slowly back to the store, Mother pondered her younger daughter's future. She put her hand on the doorknob and realized that she envied Rebecca. To drive down a beach in a roadster and fling herself into the water—that would have been life! And here she was, about to be forty.

"Henry," she announced from the door, "we're going to discuss the future." Full of purpose, she marched to my father's desk and sat down facing him. "For five years you've promised to open a branch in Florida. Now's the time."

"What?"

"The economy is strong and we've got the capital—all that gold in the safety-deposit box. We'd hardly need to borrow a dime."

"I don't understand."

"Are you deaf?" Only now did Mother notice that her husband's glasses were lying on the desk and that the desk lamp was off. "What on earth were you doing when I came in?"

"Daydreaming, I guess."

"That's not like you."

My father grimaced and then he laughed. "I used to dream a lot as a young man—before we met."

"You certainly weren't young when we met." Mother peered at her husband. Something about his bearing had changed. In the gloom, the slim, upright, attractive figure without glasses looked almost like a young man.

He leaned forward over the desk and pointed a finger at her. "You're not the only one whose dreams have gone unfulfilled."

She recoiled. "I wasn't talking about dreams."

He sighed wearily and sat back in his chair. "Oh, Arabella, you're a hopeless romantic about business and everything else."

"We're stagnating, Henry—and the rest of the country is growing."

"Your branch in Florida is not the issue. You're simply dissatisfied with me—and you have been for a long time."

Now she entered the fray in earnest. "I married a man who has spent his life hiding his superiority, afraid of any real test of his talent. You're just like one of the farmers around here. Why you're hardly Jewish."

"No one could accuse you of being anything else."

"At last, it comes out. The silent critic has finally chosen to speak out against his vulgar Jewish wife." She sang her words, exhilarated by the argument.

"You're still the woman I married—every bit as exotic," his voice fell to a murmur, and he added, as if in afterthought, "beautiful, and lively." His mouth screwed over to one side in a rueful smile. He placed his glasses carefully on his nose and turned on the desk lamp. "I've never regretted my choice."

"How generous."

"Florida is an illusion created by speculators." He picked

up his pen and opened his ledger. "Besides which, you seem to have forgotten Cleo."

"We've been using Cleo as an excuse for twenty years." As Arabella heard her own words, she winced. What if Cleo really were getting better? How would they manage with only each other to worry about?

She changed the subject. She told my father what she had learned at the library about my adventure with Tony Warburg the night before. Her account distressed my father. They were both glad when a customer entered the store, followed by a flurry of business.

When the store emptied once again, my father returned to his ledgers and my mother stared out the window at the bright day, imagining the streets of Chicago, New York, Paris.

The front door opened, the bell jingled, and in strode Charles Kuhn. He wore a white tennis costume, corded V-neck sweater, flannel trousers, and scuffed, clay-stained tennis shoes. "Arabella, my dear." He stood before Mother, his ruddy face beaming at her. "You must save my life!"

Flustered, Mother straightened. "What?"

"I've startled you, haven't I? Here you were, gazing into the distance, and I bounce in, full of my own problems, to disturb you."

Embarrassed to have been caught out, she put on her haughtiest manner. "Can I help you with something?"

"You can! I need a tennis partner in the worst way. There's a mixed doubles tournament out at the Leventhal court this afternoon and if I don't appear instantly with a belle dame, I will be left out. Be merciful. Say you will come."

My mother examined the imposing, heavyset figure before her, resplendent in his white costume, his skin gleaming with good health, his eyes bright, his manner engaging. She burst out laughing. "Me? A tennis partner? How do you know I play tennis?"

"The way you move. I'm very good about those things."

"Women's bodies, you mean?"

"I've spent my life involved with the damned things. Some women's bodies are suited to certain motions—need I say more?" Turning around, Charles moved toward the back of the store where my father sat at his desk working on accounts. "Henry, old boy, can you spare your wife for a few hours this afternoon? A matter of life and death."

Father looked up. "Oh Charles, it's you. Someone's dying, you say?"

"Not yet, but I will if you don't release your beautiful wife to play doubles with me this afternoon."

"A great tennis tragedy, eh?"

"Yes, Henry, this man wants me to play tennis with him."

"Well, you're quite a good player."

"Ah ha! I knew it," said Charles.

"Do you want to play, dear?"

"I haven't played in years."

"Quickly then!" Charles grabbed her hand and dragged her toward the door. "We'll warm up first at the Eisenstadts' and then we'll sweep them all off the court."

"I have to go home and get dressed."

"I'll drive you. My chariot is right in front."

"Henry? Are you sure it's all right?"

"Fine, dear fine."

My father sounded so hearty that my mother wondered whether he was glad to be rid of her. "You'll be alone in the store."

"Patty Kelley will be in to do inventory at three, anyway."

Mother grabbed her purse and ran out the door.

TWENTY

AFTER MY MOTHER'S HURRIED departure, my father paced restlessly about, unable to concentrate upon his usual tasks. Ordinarily, he enjoyed being in his store alone. Even as a child he had always found refuge and comfort in this grand, high-ceilinged space filled with attractive new goods, displayed in meticulous fashion. He had inherited a love of order from his father, whose methods he had improved upon, using the latest systems he had learned in business college. My father strove for perfect inventory control. His storage shelves and bins and racks were all labeled with headings that reappeared in his ledgers, card files, and file cabinets. He conducted regular surveys of his customers and predicted their needs for each season, basing his orders upon those predictions. There were years when he secretly felt that he possessed the intuition of a magician.

Now the whimsical Charles Kuhn had swept into the store, snatched up Arabella, and departed, leaving everything in disorder.

Father wanted to blame his wife, but he couldn't. When he had courted her, she had expected so much from life. In his desire for the passionate and restless young woman, he had traded upon his grand family name. She had thought Charlevoix would only be the first stage of a journey, not their destination.

He paused to look into a mirror. He found himself pale, slight, ordinary. Perhaps she had been right to accuse him of hiding out in the peace and isolation of Northern Michigan. At the age of eighteen, he too had hoped for a larger life. Once more he recalled his unrequited love for his cousin. No doubt Sonny had understood his cowardice all those years ago. Cowardice? he asked himself. Or had it been respect for his parents? With resentment he thought of that silent, disciplined couple who had stranded him here in this town where his neighbors had been storing up their hatred for years. He had committed only one rebellious act in his life—his marriage. "Exotic," he had called Arabella today and in that word he understood just how much snobbery he still harbored.

The bell on the door rang, ending his introspection. He waited on the customers, a mother and daughter, looking for hair combs and costume jewelry. Alone once more, he paced restlessly around the store. When Patty Kelley called in sick, he felt relieved. He began to worry about his daughters. He blamed himself for Rebecca's angry behavior this spring. What was he to do? More than ever, the family needed Rebecca to control her sister. Without Rebecca the family would be destroyed. But Rebecca was becoming equally undependable—carousing all hours of the night, tumbling into the lake from Tony Warburg's roadster. Another summer visitor, he thought, another intrusion, and danger. He wanted to strike out at Tony Warburg, at Charles Kuhn, but most of all at himself, whom he blamed for everything.

He began to pace once more, imagining his life if God had seen fit to bestow a healthy mind upon Cleo. But, today, my father did not have spirit enough to blame God. No, Henry Bearwald was at fault even for Cleo's madness. Cleo's isolation, her fear of the world, her silence reminded him of himself; he had bestowed those genes upon his suffering daughter.

Feeling abandoned and alone, he went to the storeroom at the back of the store to unpack some new fabrics and clothes for the fall season. He usually saved this work for the evening when the store was locked. The arrival of a shipment of new fabrics and clothes always thrilled him; he particularly enjoyed unpacking them, as if he were discovering hidden treasures. Now, to comfort himself, he took off his jacket and began to cut open the cardboard containers and to store their contents. Everyone in town knew about my father's orderly nature. What they did not know was that he reveled almost as much in the color and feel and style of the clothing he sold. Only his wife understood his sensual nature. Their sex together had always been very good, but it was performed in silence, as if his passion would disappear once it were mentioned. The same was true of his feeling for the silks, the brocades, the woolens, and cottons that he sold. This afternoon he began by unpacking a shipment of special orders. He laid the packets out on the cutting table and opened them. Slowly he caressed the new fabric, breathed in the smell of fresh cloth, and laid the different bolts one on top of the other to appreciate the contrasts. So engrossed did he become that he did not hear the bell.

One particular bolt caught his fancy. He had ordered it for Henrietta Near who wanted to make a suit for her son Ben to wear to college. He and Henrietta had gone through the catalogues and both had decided on this particular tweed, an English suiting of excellent quality. Often materials ordered from catalogues did not live up to his expectation, but this fabric looked even better than he had hoped. Delighted, he shook out the bolt and then wrapped it around himself like a toga. He stepped over to the mirror to see the effect.

"Henry Bearwald!"

Henry turned. In the doorway to the storeroom stood his cousin, Sonny Kuhn. She wore tennis whites and looked damp, as if she had just stepped off the court.

He opened his mouth, but no words emerged. Stunned, he regarded the slim figure of his cousin. With her tanned, moist limbs clothed in white and her damp, sun-bleached hair gleaming in the gloom of the store, she seemed a ghostly spirit risen from his youth.

Slowly she approached him. "Whatever are you doing?"

"Just trying out this suiting." Hurriedly he unwrapped himself. "Can I help you?"

"I need a new swimsuit. My old one is disreputable—tore it to pieces when I took it off this morning."

He threw the cloth up on the cutting table and stepped back into the store. "I didn't hear you come in." He felt dizzy, as if he were suffering an attack of some sort. "Sorry."

"I'm not. You looked magnificent, like a tweedy Roman senator." Sonny, her grin crooked with amusement, stopped and examined him critically. "You know, Henry, you always had great dignity, even when you were a boy."

"Here are the swimsuits." He gestured to a rack.

Sonny went through the stock with a businesslike air and picked out a plain black number. "This will do."

"You can try it on."

"It will fit." Sonny laid a bill on the counter. "Oh by the way, your wife asked me to tell you that she would be home a little late this evening. Charles took her out for a sail after the tournament."

"A sail?" More disorder, he thought.

"They won the tournament, you know. Charles was very excited. He didn't expect to—never has before. Arabella's very good and very competitive."

"She hasn't had much of a chance to play up here. Working all summer and all."

"Why don't you come over to my place for drinks?"

"Can't." The denial spilled out of his mouth like a cry for help. It was quickly followed by excuses. "Cleo will be home for supper. Rebecca works evenings."

"How about inviting me to dinner?"

Dumbfounded, he stalled for time. He made up the bill, gave Sonny her change, and dropped the suit into a bag. He looked wildly around the store, seeking refuge. "I'd like to—invite you," he stuttered, "but I don't know what we're going to eat—Arabella was going to shop on the way home."

"Then you and Cleo come to my place. Our icebox's crammed."

"But—" He could not think of how to halt the disorder.

"Come on Henry, don't be such a prig. I'm at loose ends too. Felix only comes up three times during the summer—he doesn't really like Charlevoix."

Nonplussed, he looked at his watch. It was closing time. "You know about Cleo, don't you?"

"Everybody knows about Cleo, Henry."

He proceeded to lock up the store. Out on the sidewalk, Sonny opened the door of her new touring sedan and slid behind the wheel. "Come on, Henry, I assume you invited me to dinner."

Reluctantly, he stepped in and they pulled away from the curb. The smell of new leather pervaded the car. He breathed in and let his breath out.

"Wonderful, ain't it," said Sonny. "Just feel the dashboard." He reached out and ran his hand over the dashboard. "They only made thirty-four of them. Felix bought it as a surprise. Sometimes he can be very thoughtful."

"Well I hope that Cleo won't be too upset when she sees you."

"Cleo will be fine, Henry. She looked ravishing at my party the other night. Some smart young man's going to gobble that dish up. Just imagine, a wife who doesn't talk!"

Offended, he remained silent.

When they arrived at his house, he insisted that Sonny wait in the car while he went inside to discuss dinner plans with Cleo.

"Fine with me," said Sonny. "In fact, I'll just pop down to the public beach and have a swim in my new suit while you're cleaning up."

Relieved, he entered his house. Cleo had not yet arrived home. He called Weyrich's to see whether she was working late. Richie Weyrich answered and said that Cleo had gone off with Tony Warburg after work.

He put the phone on the hook and stared thoughtfully out of the window. First Rebecca, he thought, and now Cleo—what was the Warburg boy up to? He imagined the young man attempting to seduce his disturbed daughter. What a terrible scene there would be! The afternoon sun hung high in the west over the lake, casting the shadow of the lighthouse back along the high cement pier. "How can a man protect his family?" he asked himself.

In a daze, he went upstairs and washed. He thought of changing into sport clothes, but decided not to bother. He would tell his cousin that he couldn't go out until Cleo returned. He would be rude, if necessary. He had more important problems to solve. Somehow he would have to talk to Rebecca about Tony Warburg and have her talk to Cleo. Why, he sighed, didn't he have sons? As for Charles Kuhn—he had no idea of what he would do about that red-faced fool.

He came downstairs to find Sonny wrapped in a beach towel, standing at the dining room window.

"You have a magnificent view."

"We'll have to make it another night. Cleo hasn't come home yet."

"Do you have any gin?"

"No alcohol, sorry."

"Pure as the driven snow, eh Henry?" Sonny strode into the living room and sat down in the rocking chair. "So we'll wait."

"Why don't you go home—"

Before he could finish, the phone rang. It was Tony Warburg calling to ask permission to take Cleo out for a ride in his boat and a hamburger afterwards. "If that's all right with you, sir. I didn't want the family to worry."

Henry stammered and stuttered. "It's not something that—I'm not at all—she's never done anything like that before. I mean that usually Rebecca—Cleo gets very upset, you know."

"Really, sir, she's very enthusiastic about the plan." Tony laughed. "In fact, it's her idea."

Henry wanted to ask the young man how he knew what Cleo wanted but instead he yielded. "Well, if it's all right with Cleo, then have her back here by ten. And be very careful—if things go wrong, she—" He imagined Cleo writhing about upon the Warburg pier, throwing herself into the lake, hurling dishes and glassware at the customers of the Chow Down, lying on the floor of a police station cell, trussed up in a straitjacket.

"Don't worry, Mr. Bearwald, we get along very well. I promise she won't get upset."

In despair, my father put down the phone.

"You look like someone just died," said Sonny, rising.

"I guess my family has deserted me." The sun had barely moved toward the horizon. The lake stretched out to the west, desolate and empty. He felt that he had failed his wife and daughters. Each of them had rushed off seeking fulfillment—which somehow he had denied them.

Sonny took his arm. "Cousin Sonny hasn't deserted you, Henry. Come along now. What you need is strong drink and rich food."

TWENTY-ONE

LEAVING WORK THAT NIGHT, I walked very slowly up Belvedere Avenue and then down Bridge Street. I hoped and feared that Tony Warburg would appear. Tonight I was prepared to get into his car. I entered the house. No one was home. The car keys lay in their dish. Relieved, I concluded that my parents had walked down to the movie with Cleo. Ever since noon, I had been preparing a story to tell Mother about the night before, but all my inventions sounded false. Now I could pretend to be asleep when my parents came in. By tomorrow I could be vague about the hours I spent with Tony—as if I'd forgotten exactly what had happened.

Happy to be alone in the house, I got ready for bed. I curled up under the covers and opened a book. But I could not concentrate. My body felt strange, as if it were missing something—a limb, two limbs, skin, another body. Over and over again, I called up the precise events of the night before: from the moment Tony and I had fallen into the lake until his fingers had crept between my legs. Feverish, I tried to think about college, about the great ideas I would study, but I had lost the excitement of that adventure. I tried to call up images of women sitting in crowded stuffy rooms at sewing machines and of miners suffocating deep in the earth. Instead, my mind could only grasp at Tony's skin, his wet eyelashes, his shining eyes, his tongue, chest, arms, legs, and fingers. My breath came faster and I began to touch myself gently, pretending that my touch was Tony's.

The sound of an automobile drawing up in front of the house entered my consciousness. Still confused by my intense fantasies, I reached out for the bed lamp, knocking it over. I righted the lamp, turned it off, and went to the window. Down below, at the curb, Tony sat at the wheel of his roadster. Cleo was just climbing out. She stood on the curb and blew a kiss. He returned the kiss and then put the car in gear. Just as the car pulled away, Cleo mounted the running board. Tony braked suddenly, but Cleo held on. She leaned toward Tony who reached up and tousled her hair affectionately. She clasped him around the neck. He kissed her on the lips. I sank to my knees, unable to breathe. Cleo ran laughing up the walk and into the house. Tony drove away.

I got into bed and pulled the sheet up over my head. A wave of revulsion coursed through my body. At first I did not recognize the bitter emotion that seized me. But when Cleo bustled about the room, whistling to herself, I admitted I was furiously jealous—so jealous that I wanted to hurt her. I heard her approach the side of my bed as if hoping I would awake. I lay very still. Finally, she got into her own bed.

A few minutes passed and then a car drove up and skidded to a stop in front of the house. The sound of shouts and laughter broke the night silence of the town. I sat up. Cleo had already gone to the window. I joined her. Down at the curb, my mother struggled to escape the clumsy embraces of Charles Kuhn. She was wearing her tennis dress.

"Can't you take no for an answer, you drunken pirate?" she said, trying to keep her voice low. In the silence of the street we could hear her clearly. She pried her tennis racket against Charles' chest and managed to slip out of the car.

"You've captured my heart and other parts too," said Charles, sprawling along the front seat of the car, grabbing the head of the racket.

"Keep your hands to yourself, you fool!" Mother pulled herself free and ran up the front walk. Charles staggered out of the car, fell on the grass, and then pursued her onto the porch.

I felt sickened. Mother cavorting with Charles Kuhn seemed a vicious parody—no, a stern judgment—of my own encounter with Tony the night before. And where was Father?

I ran downstairs, Cleo just behind me. Mother was trying to open the front door which Cleo had locked, thinking she was the last person home. I turned on the front light and flung open the door. Charles Kuhn had pinned Mother to the screen door.

"Hi there," I said.

Charles drew back.

"Saved by the bell," said my mother. "Thank you very much, Charles." She pronounced each word carefully.

"Thank you, dear lady, for your enchanting company." He bowed and stumbled down the stairs.

"Be careful driving home," she called out.

"An expert in all conditions," said Charles, throwing himself into the driver's seat. He gunned the engine and drove off.

Mother stepped into the house, drooped, and would have fallen if we hadn't supported her. Carefully, we helped her up the stairs to the bedroom.

"No, no," she moaned, "the bathroom."

We got her to the toilet bowl just in time. With a heave, she threw up. After she had finished, she straightened, faced us, and raised one finger before our faces. In a slurred voice, she said, "Do as I say, not do as I do!" She turned back to the toilet and threw up again.

We washed her off and undressed her. Her tennis clothes were wet as if she had been swimming in them. She kept trying to talk, but we hushed her up. Finally, we dressed her in a nightgown, got her into bed, and fed her aspirin with a cup of hot tea. We tucked her in and leaned to kiss her good night.

"What happened to Dad?" I asked.

Looking like a little girl, her face pale without makeup, she smiled weakly up at us, "Remember, alcohol is evil. Do as I say, don't do as I do."

I cringed, ashamed. I turned out the lamp and left the room. Cleo followed me closely, her hand grasping my pajamas. And who's going to comfort me? I thought, reaching for the wall to steady myself. Mother's collapse had left me reeling. I felt even worse about her meek surrender to our care than I did about her foolish antics with the summer visitor. No matter how harshly I judged her romantic nature and her posturing, I had always depended upon her strength of will and practicality.

Unsteadily I proceeded down the hall, Cleo following close behind. The front door opened and closed. Very slowly our father's footsteps ascended the stairs. Finally he appeared, his head down, his hair damp and disheveled as if he had been swimming. He carried his coat slung over his shoulder; his shirt was only partially buttoned. When he caught sight of us waiting in the dim hall, he fumbled with his hair and his shirt. Then he shrugged and put out his hand, palm up, as if asking our forgiveness. He kissed each of us on the forehead. His breath smelled of alcohol.

"Good night, girls," he said and entered the bathroom.

I moved into our bedroom. Cleo followed, still clinging to my pajamas. I sat down on my bed. Cleo sat down next to me and leaned against me. I did not acknowledge her presence.

Cleo picked up my hand and held it to her cheek. The memory of my identical gesture with Tony Warburg's hand the night before filled me with rage. I detached my hand from Cleo's face. I pointed to Cleo's bed. Cleo leaned against me. I sat upright, frozen. Cleo began to move back and forth, still leaning on me. A low moan sounded deep in her throat. My arm rose reluctantly. I gathered Cleo to my bosom and leaned back into the pillows, cradling, rocking, and comforting my sister. I thought of Tony Warburg, his gleaming body, his shining hair, and I hated him. I wished he had drowned in Lake Charlevoix on the afternoon his boat had overturned.

TWENTY-TWO

CONTRARY TO WHAT I believed and to what my father later believed, my mother never had an affair with Charles Kuhn. On that first outing, if Charles' sailboat had not been becalmed, if his outboard motor had worked, or even if someone hadn't removed the paddles from the cockpit, she and Charles would have sailed out onto the lake and back again and she would have been home by six. But Charles had been so overjoyed at their victory in the tennis tournament that he sailed much further out on the lake than he should have. The wind dropped. When Charles tried to start the motor, it only coughed a few times and then died. He searched the boat for the paddles. Instead, he found three bottles of whiskey. Ruefully he explained the situation.

Mother stared at the glassy surface of the water stretching out all around the boat. To the west, she could see the low green shore, the black outline of the railroad bridge and the water tower, the tiny white structures of the railroad station, the Inn, the Belvedere Club, and a few of the houses of the town. She felt as if she had been touched by a magic wand and transported to another planet from which her life appeared small and distant. She laughed.

Grateful, Charles offered her a drink and began to talk. The sun descended, casting a brilliant path across the lake toward them. The western shore turned to a ghostly silhouette. Slowly, as evening drew on, the other shores drifted from green to orange and then to black.

My mother, not much of a drinker, drank too much. The evening was warm. Charles suggested they make love. She told him that it was an absurd idea and began to laugh again. The more she thought of it, the harder she laughed.

"If you won't make love," he declared, standing up, "then I shall take my life." He leaped out of the boat and began to swim around.

Still laughing, Mother jumped out of the boat. The water caressed her body in its cool embrace. She floated on her back and stared up at the emerging stars. This is the way one should live, she thought.

Charles climbed back into the boat and urged her to follow him, but she remained in the water, holding onto a line from the bow. Charles lay on the deck and began to talk to her. Charles talked beautifully. He talked wildly, romantically, comically. Mother found his talk the most beautiful music she had ever heard.

"My dear lady," he called her, "my lovely belle, my belle dame, my beautiful señora, my amazing Amazonian mermaid," and on and on.

Finally, she climbed back into the boat. Once more he urged her to make love and once more she refused. Without pause he went on with his conversation. He gossiped about each woman, each man at the tennis court. He told her intimate details about his marriages and divorces. He discussed restaurants and recipes with her; he described villages in Greece and Portugal and Italy and great passenger ships he had taken back and forth from Europe. In Charles' talk, the joys and pleasures that had only appeared in dim outline in Mother's imagination, became substantial, precise.

A breeze came up and they sailed back to town. She remembered very little about what happened when she got home. The next morning, she rose expecting to be questioned by her husband about her late and drunken arrival. Instead, my father avoided her gaze, as if it were he who had offended her. All morning at the store, she kept waiting to be confronted about her childish behavior, frolicking about the town with that silly Charles. She was prepared to go down upon her knees, vowing never to drink again. But every time she approached her husband, he darted away, finding some pretext to distance himself from her. At noon, the phone rang. She waited for Henry to answer it. Finally, he picked up the phone.

"It's Charles Kuhn," he called out. "He wants you to play tennis at three o'clock."

My mother braced herself on the counter. "What do you think?"

"It's your decision."

"But I'm working, Henry."

"I think you'd better talk to him."

She reluctantly approached the phone. In a low voice, she asked my father, "Should I?"

He handed her the phone and fled to the storeroom.

Charles' laughing voice came echoing through the phone. "Rescue me, belle dame sans merci! Catapult me to joyous heights by your graceful acceptance of my small request."

She accepted. She wanted to hear more of his talk. She wanted to laugh and act foolishly. After tennis that afternoon, she tentatively accepted an invitation to go to a party on the north side of town on Friday night. When she told my father about the party, she expected him to react with anger. My parents did not go out on the Sabbath eve. Mother's challenge failed. Father made no objection to her going alone.

Before she knew it, her week filled up with tennis and boating and picnics on deserted beaches, with lawn parties and dancing parties and cocktail parties. At first my father attended a few evening events with her, but he left early, alone, and soon refused to accompany her. My mother made a point of announcing every plan, every appointment so that her husband had the opportunity to object or to come along. He acknowledged her announcements and went back to his work or his reading. And so Mother continued her adventures, neglecting her family, her household, the store, and all her other duties. To assuage her conscience, she insisted that Father hire Patty Kelley, full-time, for the summer.

My mother hoped for my father to speak up, to protest her absences from work, to forbid her to go out without him. Every morning when she woke, she vowed to stop this pointless gadding about, but the moment Charles Kuhn called or appeared and started talking, her resolve vanished. She accepted his invitations eagerly, like a child who has discovered a delightful game. Charles, an unpredictable stuffed toy, tumbled about her life clumsily, filling her days with nonsensical pleasures.

Two weeks passed before Father made any mention of the change in their lives. At breakfast one morning, he informed her that their household was falling apart. "Cleo has been running around without supervision. She hardly ever eats dinner at home. Rebecca is staying out until all hours—she'd miss work if I didn't call every day to wake her up."

She snapped back. "Well, I'm tired of managing everyone's life. The girls are grown up now, and so are you."

"I've tried to talk to them, but they're preoccupied." He hesitated and then blurted out, "You're as bad as they are. None of you are at home anymore."

"I can't help it if you won't go out at night. You're invited." She stared at her husband, challenging him to lay down the law.

He looked out the window, down at the pier and the lighthouse. He spoke in a low voice. "What's happened to you? I need you down at the store."

"We have summer help. I'm through being a slave."

"You don't even answer phone calls. Here, here's a list." Without looking at her, he handed her a sheet of paper. "People have been calling two and three times. I don't know what to tell them."

"Time," Arabella replied. "There simply aren't enough hours in a day. And so many people to satisfy."

"At least call Maureen," he said. "Your brother and his family have been up here for weeks and you haven't had them over to dinner once."

"We took them out on the boat. Rebecca and Cleo entertained their cousins and their cousins' friends."

My father looked at his watch and stood up from the breakfast table. He waited. It was time to go to the store.

Mother waved her hand in the air. "Go ahead without me. I'll call Maureen—I'll call everyone on the list. I'll spend the morning catching up. This afternoon I'll be swimming at the Eisenstadts."

Father nodded, set his shoulders, and left the house alone. She remained at the table, depressed, her head in her hands. She had hoped he would at last demand that she stop her frivolous pleasures and get back to work. Instead, he had mildly complained about details. How could she respect a man like that? Only his pride kept him from ending her foolishness. Then Mother sighed at her own duplicity. She picked up the phone and called Maureen.

"Who?" said Maureen when she had identified herself.

"Your sister-in-law."

"Oh yes, I vaguely remember."

"I've neglected you and Sy, Maureen, and it's been terrible of me. I can't explain why, either. My life has been turning topsy-turvy. I don't know what to do or where to turn. You just have to forgive me."

"I'm not in the least worried about me, Arabella Bearwald, but you've hurt your brother deeply."

"Come to dinner tomorrow night. I'll make flanken, Sy's favorite dish, just like our mother used to."

"Well . . ."

My mother glanced at her date book and saw that the Leventhals were giving a dinner party tomorrow night. "Not tomorrow, make it Friday night dinner—" Then she saw that Friday night friends of Charles, the Steiners, had invited her to a dinner at Beechams, the gambling club on the north side. "Not Friday, but Thursday night, six-thirty, flanken, with raisin kugel, and strudel for dessert."

"Once you make up your mind about the night, you'll have to ask Sy."

"Come on, Maureen. Sy couldn't care less whether he sees me or not, but he'd walk barefoot to Mecca for flanken and kugel."

"You don't know your brother. His feelings are real hurt. He'll be back from fishing at three. You can call him then."

"Maureen, please don't be so angry with me." It distressed Mother to offend her sister-in-law. "I'd like to see you, Maureen, alone. Let's have lunch today somewhere festive, just the two of us." Perhaps she could unburden herself to her sister-in-law, a fellow romantic. Anyway she was rather proud of her social activities with the North Side swells. "There's a lot on my mind—"

For the first time, Maureen's voice warmed. "You got problems?"

"Do I have problems!"

"Well, I've got big shoulders. But I'm busy today. Sy's clients are in town—he's out fishing on their boat. And I've got the wives coming for lunch. I'm very nervous."

"You want some help with the food?"

"It's not that. They're big mah-jongg players—gamblers. High stakes. I'm terrified that I'll lose my shirt and Sy's shirt too."

Mother, who was a very good mah-jongg player, offered to take Maureen's place in the game. Maureen hesitated.

"I'm not sure it's a good idea. You know who they are?"

"I don't care who they are."

"Well, considering Henry's operations—the brains behind you know what—well, it just makes me nervous, that's all."

"It's my decision, Maureen. I mean, if you want to lose your shirt, that's fine with me."

"Well, if you're sure," said Maureen.

"I'm sure." Mother smiled. The prospect of gambling against the wives of gangsters elated her. "What are you serving?"

"Nothing fancy. A cold broth, a tuna mold, a chocolate pie. It's all made."

"Why don't we play on Cleo's—on our boat. I'll hire Weyrich's son to take us out."

"I don't know. Maybe you shouldn't show off that boat."

"Why shouldn't I show off? Come on Maureen, it'll be an adventure."

"I don't think you know who you're dealing with. You're playing with fire."

"If you won't come on my boat, I won't play. It's fine with me if you want to lose your money."

Reluctantly, Maureen agreed.

When Mother put down the phone, she felt queasy. She recalled the view of Charlevoix from Charles' becalmed boat. Somehow, she had sailed out too far from Henry and the girls.

She felt weightless, prey to the gravity of other planets. Ever since Cleo had found the boat, life had become unmoored.

Cleo? thought my mother. With apprehension, she realized that she hadn't worried about her sick daughter since the beginning of summer. How had Cleo existed? What had Henry said about Cleo this morning? That she didn't eat dinner at home? Where was she eating dinner? And with whom? Panicked, Mother tried to imagine a normal winter's morning: preparing breakfast in the warm kitchen, the sounds of the girls upstairs and Henry in the basement, the family together on the snowy sidewalks of the dark town on the way to the day's work. But that memory was losing substance. If she weren't careful, it soon might begin to resemble one of those fairy tales she told to the children.

Mother dressed thoughtfully for the day's outing. On the way to the boat, she stopped at the bank where she removed one of the leather bags full of gold coins that Henry was hoarding while he waited for the economy to crash. She knew she would need to make a good show this afternoon.

Mother's fear that she had stepped beyond the reasonable boundaries of her life was confirmed when she watched Maureen usher her guests down the concrete steps from Bridge Street. It seemed as if a menagerie of tropical birds were descending upon the docks of Charlevoix. Flaming reds, iridescent blues and greens and purples, burnt yellows and oranges covered their bodies from hair to polished toenails; sequined sweaters and shoes and sunglasses glinted in the sun; gold chains and bracelets and necklaces clanked in a continuous percussion to the rise and fall of screeching laughter. As they approached, Mother admitted that she had been foolish to brush aside Maureen's hesitation about this outing.

PART THREE

TWENTY-THREE

IN PARIS, YEARS LATER, the morning after my father's drunken confession, we met for breakfast in a small café. I pressed him for a more thorough account of his relationship with Mother when they were drifting apart that summer. Although he would have preferred to skip over the details—he remained very embarrassed over his actions—he resigned himself to the punishment of reliving those days. An honest, precise man, he left nothing out.

On the day Mother took the gangsters' women for lunch on Cleo's boat, my father, ignorant of her outing, waited for her to come to the store. In recent weeks she made an appearance once a day, checked the books, discussed business matters with him, and made the bank run. At a quarter to three, he left Patty Kelley in charge and took the day's receipts to the bank. Ruth Clover, who waited on him, mentioned that Arabella had come in earlier to visit the safety-deposit room.

"Safety-deposit?" he asked. "Are you sure?"

"Just took her a minute, whatever it was," said Ruth. "She was in a great hurry."

Disturbed, he returned to the store. He could not imagine what his wife wanted in their safety-deposit box. He sat down at his desk and then let out a long sigh. Jewelry, he thought. She's probably going to one of those North Side parties and wanted one of her valuable pieces. His sigh turned to a groan at the thought of his wife's infidelity. She was clearly having an affair with Charles Kuhn. How could he have let this happen to their marriage? For two weeks she had been begging him to confront her. He had wanted to bring Arabella to her senses, to demand that she cease her foolish rebellion. But he could not reproach her, because on the day Arabella had gone off to play tennis with Charles Kuhn, he too had been unfaithful to their marriage vows.

The memory of that evening with Sonny Kuhn—his adultery—had paralyzed him. He had gone over the details of the adventure many times, unable to understand what had happened. Henry Bearwald had deliberately broken one of the Ten Commandments—more than one, it turned out. Long before he had committed adultery, he had coveted Felix Kuhn's wife—for many years, perhaps. And then there was the long history of his secret denunciations of God's failures—apostasy, if he were truly honest.

He attempted to retrace the steps which led to his downfall. He had hardly thought of his cousin until that night early in the summer when they danced together. In an instant, he realized he still cared for her. Was it "still," he asked himself, or "again"? Perhaps his feeling for Sonny had returned only because of the dislocation of his life this spring—the mysterious crimes against his property, threats to the lives of his family, Arabella's dissatisfaction, Rebecca's rebellion, and the curious improvement in Cleo's behavior. The serene containment of his life had been shattered and he had seized upon that old passion like a shipwrecked sailor might seize upon a piece of floating debris. Embedded in that desire was the pain of Sonny's rejection so long ago.

He had been twenty-two and she had been eighteen. It had taken him weeks to get up his nerve, weeks during which he had memorized and rehearsed the proposal as if it were part of a business school examination. One evening he asked her to drive them out to Belle Isle on the shore of the Detroit River. They had strolled over a stone bridge and suddenly he had turned, grasped her under her arms, and perched her on the railing. There, under a waning moon with the lights of Windsor in the distance, he made his formal declaration. She had been a little startled, tilting her head from side to side as she examined him and contemplated his words and the possibilities they suggested. Then, she had thrown her head back and laughed, saying that they could never be happy together. "I'm too wild and frivolous and superficial for you, and I would suffocate in the North Woods." Then she had jumped down into his arms and kissed him on the cheek. "But thank you, thank you, I'm honored, moved, full of gratitude." She had laughed again and taken his arm, marching him around and around the park, knowing just how deeply her refusal had injured him.

Some thirty years later, at the beginning of summer, when he and his family had been unceremoniously drawn into Sonny's garden party, she had once again thrown herself into his arms. With her slim, elusive body pressed so closely to him and then twirling out at arm's length and back so lightly, the old wound had begun to throb again. Sitting at his desk, he thrashed about, attempting to solve the dilemma of his sin. Two weeks ago Sonny had arrived unbidden at the store, discovered him wearing the fabric of Ben Near's suit like a toga, and spirited him to her house. While they had eaten and drunk and talked about their lives, he had felt as if he were twelve years old again, an only child who had grown up in a silent household. He recognized in Sonny the handsome, energetic nine-year-old who had affectionately ordered him about and the impertinent, adventurous eighteen-year-old who had beckoned and then rejected him. The ardor of his youth returned. Sonny too had become aroused. Hand in hand, he and Sonny had descended to the beach, stripped, swum in the cold lake, and then, after drying one another off with thick, luxurious beach towels, they had made love. Afterwards, they drank a great deal more and Sonny insisted that he read aloud from books of poetry he had given her when they were youngsters. To his surprise, she kept the books on her bedside table.

"But Sonny, why—these books?" he asked.

Sonny had shrugged. "I guess they've been sort of souvenirs—'a road untaken,' someone said. I'm a pretty foolish woman, Henry, but there have been certain memories that I've—treasured."

Then they had made love again.

When Henry left Sonny that night, he hesitated in her doorway. "Sonny," he began, "Sonny, I—" She had touched his lips with her hand. "I know, Henry. We won't do this again. Considering your conscience, it would be very uncomfortable."

Two weeks later, he continued to feel moved by those words. How well she understood him! And yet the memory of that night made him very happy. For an instant, for a few hours, he had fulfilled a yearning, a promise from his youth; he had tasted what might have been. He could hardly believe that she too had carried the memory all this time—that she had continued to read and reread the books he had given her so many years ago. Two weeks later he felt no guilt. This amazed him. He only regretted that he would never embrace his cousin again. His happiness tormented him even more than guilt. It was as if God were intent upon stripping him of his faith. This afternoon he was unable to order his life. He had committed adultery, enjoyed it, and felt no regret. How could he confront his wife with their mutual infidelities?

He sat at his desk until five-thirty. He rose and put on his jacket. He approached the front door, prepared to close up. Just then, Sy Lefkowitz strode in.

"Henry! I have to talk to you."

Sy locked the door, pulled the shade, and drew my father to the back of the store. The two men sat down.

"You're in trouble, Henry, deep trouble."

My father smiled affectionately at his brother-in-law. Sy's sad dark eyes, his thick brows, the heavy folds of his cheeks and jowls inspired confidence. Father felt that God had sent an angel of mercy—Sy Lefkowitz, a good, honest, gentle man. "Well, Sy, I am very troubled." For the first time in his life, my father was tempted to open his heart and confide his troubles.

The full flesh of Sy's face quivered as if the bones beneath had melted. He spoke in a rush, wringing his hands. "Look, it's worth my life to be doing this, but you're my brother-in-law and if you've got any muscle, now's the time to begin using it because all hell is ready to break loose." He was on the verge of tears. "I tried to warn you. I tried."

Bewildered, my father stared at the large, good-natured man crouched on his chair by the desk. "What is it, Sy? What's the matter?"

"I'm an accountant—I handle figures, income tax, estates—nothing criminal, nothing violent. I deal with business, legitimate business. I hear no evil, see no evil, and, above all, I speak no evil. But I got to tell you, brother-in-law, my sister, your wife, has a very big mouth."

The story Sy now told so amazed my father that he could say nothing. He simply sat at his desk, his fingertips joined judiciously. Sy explained that since winter there had been rumors of a new gang of bootleggers operating on the Great Lakes, a mystery gang with a very low profile. There had been incidents and a lot of gossip. Then in March, Sy went on, there had been an attempt to hijack a large shipment of Purple Gang whiskey destined for Al Capone in Chicago. Apparently, a gun battle had ensued, during which it seemed that the crew of both boats had been killed. The bodies on the North Point Beach were connected to the hijacking. The attackers' boat had been found drifting in Little Traverse Bay, empty except for two bodies. But the boat with the Purple Gang's whiskey had disappeared. There had been a big storm on the night of the hijacking and for a while the gang thought their boat and whiskey had been sunk. However, not long after, the hijacked liquor began to appear in roadhouses and speakeasies around Charlevoix. "Do you understand, Henry?"

My father shook his head back and forth. He did not understand.

"Listen to me, Henry. I got a wife and children. You too. I don't want to know what you're up to—but according to Bella, you're up to plenty. Ever since winter she's been bragging about you and your operation over long distance to Maureen—on unguarded phones. And then those trucks at Grayling, the Cheboygan roadhouse and the money you sent me right after it burned to the ground—thousands of dollars for Cleo's annuity—you made up some cock-and-bull story about English woolens." Sy got up and paced in a circle, talking all the while. "Look, I don't know if they suspected you from the beginning, but I was scared. I hired a couple of bums to throw a brick through your window here; then they scorched your house—I told them to be careful not to burn it."

"You broke my window?"

"Yeah, yeah—you wouldn't listen. I didn't mean for the jerks to come so close with the car, they could have run you guys over—but I figured if Carl ever—and now it's happened." Sy slumped down in the chair again. "Today my nutty sister went too far. She stuck it directly to Mimi Greenstein, playing mahjongg, beating the undies off her, and then stuck it to Carl, running circles around his boat. She as much as thumbed her nose at him." Sy pulled a large handkerchief from his pocket and wiped the sweat off his face. "That boat of yours, Henry, ain't an ordinary boat. Carl thinks it's the boat that was carrying his booze down to Capone—the one that got hijacked. The booze you got on it ain't ordinary booze. It's very expensive and hard to get. Any boat that can outrun Carl's *Long John* wasn't built for fishing. Maureen almost wet her pants when Bella dumped those gold coins on the table like she was Croesus' wife, or something."

Gold coins, thought my father. That's what Arabella was up to in the safety-deposit box. His face flushed.

"And then Bella took them all to the cleaners in mah-jongg, like lambs to slaughter. Mimi Greenstein don't take kindly to losing a bundle. And that captain of yours, Richard Weyrich or something like that, from the boatyard. Very high class. All dressed up in a blazer and white trousers. He tried to show up Carl Greenstein's boat."

My father's hands, arms, shoulders, stomach, and legs became rigid. He froze. The idea of Arabella showing off Cleo's boat like that sickened him. How dare she pour out on a gaming table the capital he had laboriously accumulated for his family's security?

"Gold coins, you said? Richard, the captain?" My father could not believe Arabella involved Richie Weyrich in her absurd masquerade.

"That's unimportant. Carl Greenstein's a killer."

"There's been an absurd mistake. In the future, I suggest that you do business with honest men."

"That's a laugh, Henry, coming from you. A real laugh."

"I own a dry goods store. That's what I do for a living. I don't know anything about trucks or roadhouses. Cleo discovered that boat wrecked on a beach south of town. She's a master boatwright. She salvaged it. I believe the laws of salvage state that if there is no claim, whoever salvages a boat can keep it. As for bootleg whiskey, I have no idea what you're talking about. Now, will you please go to your friend and client, Carl Greenstein, and explain all this to him."

"It's too late for that, Henry. Carl's put a contract out on you—I know it."

"A contract?"

"For your death, Henry."

"They make contracts for that sort of thing?"

"I've been warning you for months. I thought he might have been holding off because you're my brother-in-law. Maybe he didn't know at all. But after today he's really mad. Of course, if you want to negotiate with him, to cut him in on your operation—"

"Damn it, Sy. Carl Greenstein isn't interested in dry goods."

"I'm talking about your other operations."

"What you're telling me is a fairy tale."

Sy stood up. "I don't want to talk to you anymore, Henry. You're *mishpocheh*, you're family, and I love you and your girls, but I'm through from now on. I already stuck my neck out plenty by warning you and then coming here. If you and Carl want to duke it out, that's your concern. We're leaving Charlevoix tomorrow morning. I got my kids to think of."

Before my father could stand up, Sy sprinted to the front door, unlocked it, and fled from the store.

Father locked the door again. He paced about the store, muttering to himself. To think that Arabella despised him so much that she had been reduced to bragging about him as a gangster.

He stopped in front of a full-length mirror and looked at himself. Could anyone in the world imagine that this ordinary, mild-looking, fair-haired man with regular features was a gangster? Only his stupid relatives. He grimaced. He stuck his thumbs in his armpits and struck a pose. He waved a fist at himself. What a ridiculous idea!

He turned from the mirror and recommenced his pacing. Astonishing! he thought. The brick through his window this spring, the fire on the front porch, and that black car which had almost run the family over had been the work of his own brother-in-law. He looked through his desk for the note that had been wrapped around the brick. He found it crumpled in the bottom drawer. "THIS IS A WARNING. STRANGERS STAY OUT. NO ONE MUSCLES IN ON OUR TERRITORY. THERE WILL BE NO MORE WARNINGS." How could a man that dumb learn accounting?

He placed the note back in the drawer and sat for some time. Then he began to laugh, a little hysterically. How happy he would be if he could set aside his suspicion that his fellow townsmen, his lifetime friends and neighbors, hated him because he was a Jew. Now he laughed even harder, because the enemy who had been stalking him was Jewish—Sy Lefkowitz—his own brother-in-law. Now, of course, he had a more serious enemy. The head of the Purple Gang. Jewish too. If God were intent upon punishing him, he had chosen a ridiculous device: a discontented wife's bragging, fearful in-laws, a troubled daughter's chance discovery, and an aborted hijacking involving Jewish gangsters. A bitter edge crept into his laughter. How could anyone worship such a devious Master?

On his walk home, my father considered his situation. A gangster's threats were nothing to take lightly. It would no longer be a question of bricks and small fires. Carl Greenstein had crippled his enemies, he had blown up their stores and bars, he had killed dozens of people. Someone had made a terrible mistake about Henry Bearwald's business. What could he do now to protect himself and his family? He couldn't go to Vernon Hayes with such a ridiculous story. It was bad enough that his brother-in-law worked for gangsters. But to admit that Arabella had been pretending that he, Henry Bearwald, was a gangster! What would the sheriff think—and everyone else in town? The Bearwald name would never recover. No one would patronize such a store.

And Cleo's boat? Cleo was so proud of that boat. It was certainly powerful enough to have been a bootlegger's boat—and there was that illegal liquor in the hidden cabinets aboard. My father decided that it must have been a bootlegger's boat. But how could he give the boat up to the police? Cleo would surely break down if she lost her boat.

At home, he found my mother sleeping on their bed. At her side was a large pile of bills: twenties, fifties, and hundreds. The soft skin drawstring bag full of gold coins stood on the dressing table. The gold must be returned to the vault, he thought. He carried the bag to his study and hid it behind some books. Then he drove out to Roadhouse 31, bought a bottle of whiskey and brought it home. In his study, he began to drink.

*

At ten-thirty I came in from work to find Father sitting in the dark, a half-filled bottle in front of him.

"Daddy?" I peered into the study. "What are you doing?"

"Watching the lighthouse," he replied.

The front door slammed and Cleo entered the house. I was too concerned about Father to wonder where she had been. She came to the study door.

"Are you all right, Daddy?" I approached the desk. "Did you have your supper?"

"I drank my supper."

A thump resounded on the ceiling above us and a scream. "Henry! Rebecca!"

"We're downstairs!" I called out.

In a moment, Mother appeared. She turned on the lights and stood staring at the three of us. "How long have you been here?"

"Cleo and I just got in."

Father took a drink from the bottle.

"Henry? How long have you been home?"

"I don't know."

"What's the matter, Momma?"

"I've lost—misplaced something very important. I'm certain I had it when I got home—at least I think I'm certain. Henry, did you come upstairs?"

"I'm not quite sure, dear," my father said drunkenly. He laid his head down on the desk beside the bottle and fell asleep.

Mother looked with disbelief at the bottle. "He's been drinking?"

"I don't think he had any supper."

"Well, let him sleep for a few minutes. I have to make a phone call. Then we'll get him up to bed."

"What did you lose, Momma?"

"I'm sure I'll find it. You girls better get ready for bed."

Cleo went upstairs. I lingered on the stairway to listen to my mother's telephone conversation.

"Hello, Richie? Is that you? . . . . Did you see a small purse when you secured the boat? . . . . I was sure I had it with me when I went home. . . . No, no, I'll go myself."

I heard the back door slam and the car start up.

My mother was so distraught she could hardly drive. She parked at the dock and scrambled onto *White Lightning*. Sobbing, she slipped off the boat-cover and went through the boat from bow to stern. She even lifted the floorboards and scanned the bilges with a flashlight. Breathing heavily, she perched on the gunwale and tried to reconstruct the ending of the afternoon. Could one of the gangsters' wives have slipped her coins into a purse? Mimi Greenstein had been angry enough at her losses and then at the way Richie had shown up the gangster's boat. Arabella pictured the table strewn with mah-jongg tiles, dollar bills of all denominations, and that pile of gold coins. She had been pretty drunk by then, joyous and terrified, busy stuffing all those dollars —20s, 50s, 100s—into her own purse.

It had been a strange, unsettling afternoon—almost like revisiting her past. Once they boarded the boat, she had warmed immediately to her guests. They reminded her of her girlfriends from the old neighborhood. Mimi, the boss's wife and a bully, presided. She had a broad face, broad shoulders, and an ample bottom; her heavy black eyebrows soared and dove, her large mouth writhed around deep, hoarse syllables as she shouted commands at the wives of her husband's henchmen. Adele, the quietest of the lot and a sufferer, seemed acutely uncomfortable—as if an error in her marriage plans had landed her among terrifying companions. She kept adjusting her clothes, giving the impression that she was unused to them. Every time Mimi spoke, she winced. Fern was obviously a second wife, peroxided, young, and so happily self-engrossed that Mimi's ferocity passed by her unnoticed as she glanced appreciatively at her breasts, her legs, her clothing, and her jewelry. Every now and then, she excused herself to go below where Arabella caught sight of her preening before a mirror.

As my mother bet and played with her guests, scenes from her childhood kept flashing through her mind: street upon street around the Eastern Market and the Bishop School—two-family and four-family houses, tiny front lawns, wooden porches and front steps where whole families gathered in the warm summer evenings to watch the children running up and down the street playing games. Still, she felt awkward with these women, as if she had forgotten how to speak their language. Too late, Mother realized she had made a mistake in showing *White Lightning*'s liquor cabinet. Until this moment, it had not occurred to her that the wreck Cleo had found and repaired had anything to do with bootlegging. Almost every boat and every vacation house in Charlevoix had a store of illegal alcohol. She played on, wondering anxiously if Cleo's boat had been the missing boat Sheriff Hayes had speculated about when they found the dead bodies on the beach near North Point. It was one thing to make vague boasts to Maureen about Henry's activities; it was quite another to display what could be construed as evidence to the wives of gangsters. But Mimi's brusque show of authority had challenged her. This was her boat, her town, and she was not going to be bulldozed. She remembered the first day she had arrived at the Bishop School, a fierce five-year-old, ashamed that she was the bottle man's daughter and ready to do battle with anyone who looked cross-eyed at her.

And so she had played for keeps, luring her guests deeper and deeper into the game, and when she had cleaned them out, she urged Richie to run circles around the gangster's big black yacht. Stupid, stupid, she berated herself. Reckless! Crazy! *White Lightning* had slipped alongside that monstrous black boat, so close that she could have stepped aboard. And there, above her, staring down from the flying bridge, was the boss of the Purple Gang. She could not forget the hooded, blazing eyes of Carl Greenstein, a tall, trim muscular man, with a swarthy complexion and black curly hair. He was wearing a bright red shirt and white trousers. His clothes fitted so tightly, they seemed like skin—the skin of a tall, upright snake, ready to strike.

Trembling, trying to remember the moment when her gold coins had disappeared, my mother opened the liquor cabinet, pulled out a bottle, and took a long swallow. She sighed and eased back against the gunwale. Her limbs felt weak. She had put herself in danger; she had put her family in danger. She pounded her forehead with the flat of her hand. She took another swallow, capped the bottle, closed up the cabinet, and replaced the boat-cover.

At home, Cleo and I managed to get Father into bed. Cleo, who had been up since four-thirty in the morning, fell asleep. I remained awake, waiting for Mother. She returned a half hour later, turned on all the lights in the house, and began to search through each room. I came downstairs. "Tell me what to look for," I said, following her.

"A skin bag with drawstrings, very soft skin, some sort of leather. Yellow brown."

We searched the downstairs, the upstairs bathroom and the bedroom where Father slept. He did not wake up.

Finally we returned to the living room. Mother threw herself onto the couch. "Oh Rebecca, I'm such a goddamn fool."

I came up behind her and began to massage her shoulders and then her forehead. "I'm sure it will turn up in the morning."

After a few minutes, Mother calmed down and I reminded her that Friday was my father's birthday.

"This Friday? No, I don't believe it."

"Oh yes. I traded with Estelle so I could help with the celebration."

"But I have a date Friday. I've been invited to Beechams by the Steiners—" Mother hesitated. She got up and paced about the room. "Your father's birthday, you're sure?"

"Of course I am. You'll have to call them up and tell them you made a mistake."

"It's the most important party of the year. They'd never ask me again."

"Momma—"

"He's invited too."

"You know he won't go to Beechams. Besides, Friday night is the Sabbath."

Mother clasped her hands. "I can't help it if that crowd isn't religious."

"But, Friday is his birthday."

"We'll celebrate Monday night—the Belvedere Club is closed Monday night, isn't it?"

"It isn't the same, Momma."

"If we don't mention it, he won't remember that Friday is his birthday."

"Momma—"

My mother raised her hand. "No more, Rebecca. I have to find that bag." She strode from the room and began to search the kitchen.

TWENTY-FOUR

ON THURSDAY MORNING MY father appeared at breakfast, his face very pale, dark rings under his eyes.

My mother peered at him. "You look terrible."

"I feel terrible."

"What happened to you last night?"

"I got drunk."

Mother opened her mouth as if to continue her questioning, but then changed her mind. Instead, she reminded him that she had invited the Lefkowitzes for dinner that night.

"I think you'd better call them. Sy dropped by the store yesterday to say good-bye. They had to go back home early."

"Nonsense. I was with Maureen all afternoon and she didn't say a word about leaving." Mother got up and dialed the Lefkowitz number.

"Maureen? . . . What? . . . But you paid for five weeks . . . What? . . . Oh." Dazed, she put down the phone. "They're leaving, in five minutes—two weeks ahead of time. Maureen sounded—she sounded odd. Like she didn't want to talk to me."

My father stared at his wife. This morning she looked as vulnerable and fragile as he felt. He rose to go to the store. She rose too. On the porch, she took his arm as she had every morning for twenty years. As they marched down the street, he tried to puzzle out the events of the day before, but his head ached too much.

The hours proceeded uneventfully. My mother worked hard, attempting to catch up on all of the details she had been neglecting for weeks. At two-thirty, when it came time to make the bank run, she approached my father's desk.

"Henry," she said, "yesterday I did something very foolish. I took one of the bags of gold coins out of the safety-deposit box and I think I lost it."

"Gold coins?" he asked, dimly remembering something about a bag of gold coins—Sy had told him that Arabella had gambled with gold coins.

"I don't know how I lost it, or where. I used it to gamble with those wives of Sy's clients. I didn't need it, because I won. I won a lot. But then I lost the bag."

"Where did I see—?" He tried to recall what happened the night before when he had returned home.

"So I'm replacing the gold with my winnings. I don't know how much was in the bag, but there's over two thousand dollars here," she held up a roll of bills and placed them on the desk, "and you can buy more gold coins with it—or whatever you want."

He stared at the bills and then remembered coming into

the bedroom where his wife lay on the bed. "I know where it is!" he exclaimed. "I found it on the dresser last night."

"You what?" She sat down.

"I found the coins and hid them in my study."

"That was mean of you, Henry."

"I only hid them to keep them safe."

"You let me think I lost them all this time?"

"Honestly, I forgot all about it until just now."

"I don't believe you."

"I swear to you, Arabella! I wouldn't lie to you." He pushed the bills toward his wife. "You can keep your winnings." He resumed his work.

"Don't you have anything more to say?"

"No."

She leaned toward him over the desk. "But you can't stop talking now."

"What should I say?" He forced the words out. "That I'm angry because you took the family money to gamble with? That I'm pleased that you confessed taking it? That everything turned out all right just because you won a lot of money from some people you hardly know?" As he spoke, he cursed himself for his cowardice and hypocrisy.

"I think that it would help me if I knew that you were angry."

"I'm so angry, Arabella, that I can hardly think. And confused, too. Not just about the money."

"Do you want to talk about it?"

His jaw locked, his throat constricted. He remained silent.

"I would like to work." He bent over his ledgers.

Mother rose and left the store. She did not return that afternoon. When he arrived home, he found that she had cooked up the flanken and kugel and strudel. My father, my mother, and Cleo ate dinner together. My parents did not speak all evening.

On Friday, Mother accompanied Father to work. She left work a half hour early, informing him that she was going to Beechams that night. As she was leaving, she called back, "The Steiners invited you too, Henry—cocktails at their house at five-thirty and a seven o'clock dinner at Beechams."

He did not reply.

He stayed at work late to give his wife time to be out of the house by the time he got there. It was only as he walked home that he remembered that today was his birthday. Hardly able to breathe, he stopped. His wife had forgotten his birthday. He wanted to cry, but he had never cried in his life.

At home he found both his daughters waiting for him.

"Why aren't you at work, Becky?"

"I just thought I'd take a night off and spend it with the family. Friday night."

"Your mother's at a party."

"I know. She told us to eat the leftovers from last night. There's plenty."

"Well, I feel like a drink. We all should have a drink together." I looked at my father, astonished. He patted me on the arm. "It's all right, sweetie. How about it, Cleo?"

Cleo ran to the kitchen to get glasses and ice. Father brought the half-filled bottle from the study.

"Are you sure you want us to drink, Daddy?"

"I'm sure."

When the drinks were made, the three of us stood in the living room and clinked glasses.

"Here's to Daddy," I said.

"As a matter of fact," said my father, "it is a special evening."

"We know. There was a stupid mix-up. Momma planned your party for Monday night because it was my night off."

"That's all right, darling." He hugged us. "You two remembered! That's what counts."

"Momma remembered, she just—" My voice trailed off.

Cleo pulled on my sleeve and pointed upstairs.

"No, Cleo," I admonished. "We'll do all that Monday night."

Unable to contain herself, Cleo broke away and ran upstairs. She returned in a moment carrying two large paper bags.

"Monday night, Cleo," I said. I took hold of the paper bags, intending to return them upstairs. Cleo would not release them. "Momma's not here." I tugged desperately at the presents. "The whole family should be together."

"That's your mother's decision, Rebecca," said my father.

The cold, even sound of his voice took my strength away. I released my grip. "But Momma should be here."

"Cleo's right."

"Wouldn't Monday be better?"

"Tonight is my birthday." He put out his hands. Triumphantly, Cleo handed the gifts to him. He opened them with solemn care. We had given him a desk set, consisting of a blotter trimmed in leather, a letter knife, scissors, and a pen and pencil mounted upon a marble base with a handsome clock set in the middle.

"I've never seen anything so elegant." He kissed us. "It looks very expensive. You two shouldn't have spent so much."

We trooped into the study. He placed the set on his desk. He sat down and tried the pen. He stood up. "We're not going to eat leftovers tonight. We're going out."

"But Daddy, it's Friday night."

"The Lord will forgive me this one time. And if he doesn't, he'll have to punish me." My father never spoke of God lightly. I had my doubts about religion, but my father's beliefs were sacred and I was shocked to hear him invoke God's punishment with such nonchalance. Seeing my anguish, he tried to soothe me. "It's a special occasion for my special daughters." There was something oily and unfamiliar about his voice. "We haven't been out together in ages. Now I want you both to get dressed up in your best clothes. We're going to Beechams."

"I thought that you wouldn't ever go there."

"There's a first time for everything."

"We'll never get in, Daddy, on a Friday night." I felt desperate now, the guardian of my father's righteousness. "Beechams has been booked for the whole summer."

"Don't worry, sweetie, we'll get in. I've never met a headwaiter that refused a large enough tip. Go get dressed. It's my birthday."

I took Cleo upstairs and we put on our summer finery.

My father dressed in his blazer, ascot, and white duck trousers. He tucked in his silk pocket kerchief with great care. Scrutinizing himself carefully in the mirror, he thought that he might just be mistaken for a powerful gangster or perhaps a French count. He had two more drinks while he waited for us. When we were ready, he handed the car keys to Cleo who was pleased that he trusted her to drive. Before he left the house, he went to the study, removed the bag of gold coins from behind the books, and slipped it into his pocket.

*

The foyer of Beechams was jammed with people attempting to get seated at their dining tables before the gala floor show began. The establishment was in no great haste to accommodate the customers, preferring them to drink and gamble while they waited. People wandered in from the gambling rooms, approached the headwaiter's stand, and returned to the gambling rooms. Tonight there appeared to be a good deal of chaos about reservations. The club had overbooked. Several large parties, including the Steiners, had reserved tables for the evening.

My father, a little drunk and in a reckless mood, ushered us through the waiting guests up to the headwaiter's stand. A party of six in summer evening dress crowded around the stand. The men wore bright blue tuxedo jackets with carnations in their lapels, ruffled shirts, diamond studs, and gold cuff links; the women wore evening dresses in chartreuse, carnelian, and aqua, with bouquets of orchids in their hair and an array of gold and precious stones about their necks, wrists, and fingers.

The headwaiter, a very tall, pale man, with hollow cheeks and a thin, curled mustache, lorded over the station with a disdainful air. I recognized him immediately and pulled my father to a stop.

"Let's go somewhere else, Daddy."

"This is the place, Becky."

"Please, Daddy. We'll never get in."

"Nonsense." My father pushed us forward.

The leader of the party surrounding the headwaiter demanded to be seated immediately. The headwaiter listened patiently.

"I understand you perfectly, Mr. Greenstein."

Carl Greenstein, thought my father, Sy Lefkowitz's client, the man who wanted to kill him. Father felt faint. He began to turn, intending to leave, but the other expectant diners hemmed him in. "Becky," he said, "perhaps . . ."

"What, Daddy?" I put out my hand to steady him. "Are you all right?"

"I'm fine." He shook off my hand and squared his shoulders. He examined Greenstein more closely. The gangster's picture in the newspaper had not rendered him vividly enough. He was a swarthy, muscular man with black curly hair. Smooth flesh hooded his eyes and mouth, hiding his expression. My father thought his manner snakelike and offensively cold.

Greenstein's brilliant, narrow, yellow eyes fixed upon the headwaiter. To my father's surprise, he talked very quietly, almost pleading. He sounded as if the headwaiter had hurt his feelings. "Your boss gets first class treatment in my clubs—it's reciprocation."

"I assure you, Mr. Greenstein, you are among our most honored clientele."

"It doesn't look good," said Greenstein, "me standing around like some sort of orphan."

"But, Mr. Greenstein, you arrived without reservations

five minutes ago. It takes time to put out new tables and to set them up."

My father watched the confrontation. He waited for Greenstein to take out a gun and shoot the offending headwaiter. Instead, the gangster hung his head sadly and turned away. One of his companions, a short fat man with long arms, stepped forward, leaned against the stand, and thrust his face up at the headwaiter. "Carl Greenstein don't have to wait one minute anywhere in this lousy state. Just kick some of those hicks out of there. They can wait."

"There's no need to raise your voice." The headwaiter spoke quietly. "Mr. Greenstein's table is being set up at this moment. It will be on the dance floor, in front of everyone else's table." He bent over his stand and issued commands to the hostess at his side. She circulated through the crowd, calling out names. A stream of diners passed by the stand on their way to their tables. Baffled, the short fat man rejoined his party.

The unruffled air of the headwaiter gave my father courage to speak up. "Pardon me, sir, I would like a table for three near the dance floor." He placed several gold coins on the headwaiter's seating chart.

The headwaiter's hand moved swiftly over the gold coins. He looked down at my father, scrutinizing him from head to foot.

"There'll be that much again when we get our table," said my father.

A faint smile came across the headwaiter's face. "My good man, I couldn't promise the Prince of Persia a table tonight."

"My daughters and I would be very, very grateful if you tried."

"Your daughters?" the headwaiter's glance flickered over

Cleo and me. I blushed and turned away. Cleo grinned and stuck out her hand.

The headwaiter stepped toward Cleo, a broad smile of recognition coming over his face. "My young mystery lady!" He leaned over Cleo's hand with a courtly bow. "And her accomplice, too!" He seized my hand and bowed.

My father looked on, bewildered by the headwaiter's gracious greeting.

"Well sir," the headwaiter addressed my father, "what did you say your name was?"

"Bearwald," said my father, dropping his voice. "Henry Bearwald." He coughed and glanced surreptitiously at Carl Greenstein's back.

"A table for Mr. Henry Bearwald and two companions, Rosie," said the headwaiter.

The eyes of the Greenstein party turned upon my father.

"A table for Mr. Bearwald," came the reply and then, further off, "A table for Mr. Bearwald."

Greenstein's short fat companion strode up to the headwaiter, brushing my father aside. He was about to complain again when the headwaiter lolled his head toward the dining room. A hostess appeared and said, "Mr. Greenstein, your table is ready. Just follow me."

One of the ladies in the Greenstein party, a slim, full-bosomed, peroxided blonde in an aqua gown, pushed the short man along behind the others. As she passed, she winked at my father and then followed her party.

The headwaiter apologized to my father for the delay. As he spoke, he slipped the gold coins back into my father's pocket.

TWENTY-FIVE

IN LATER YEARS, MY father referred to the events of that summer as a brief sojourn in a cheap drama. Prohibition, gangsters, and illegal speakeasies might have been ill-conceived, but they existed. In 1928 the Purple Gang appeared in Charlevoix and changed our lives. When I first saw them at Beechams on the night of my father's birthday, they seemed no different from the ordinary summer tourists from Detroit. I didn't know who they were. To me, Carl Greenstein appeared to be an oversensitive father, whom his family tried to protect.

Our table was set up next to theirs on the edge of the dance floor. To fit the table in, the waiters had to move the Greenstein table slightly. "Haven't you people treated us badly enough?" Carl Greenstein complained with an aggrieved air.

"It's all right, Carlie!" Mimi Greenstein patted her husband on the back. "We're quite comfortable."

"They've got no manners here, Boss," said the short fat man.

Four waitresses, carrying table linen, cutlery, plates, and silver for us, followed the two waiters, who positioned our table. Everyone gazed at us as we walked toward the dance floor. The attention daunted my father. He whispered to me, "What's all this about? How do you know the headwaiter?"

"He owns a boat—Cleo worked on it down at Weyrich's. He likes her."

My father frowned. He could imagine the headwaiter might be friendly to Cleo for her work on his boat, but this reception seemed far too elaborate. He shrugged his shoulders and questioned me no further. He spied Mother seated next to Charles Kuhn at the Steiner table. She looked astonished and waved, but Father pretended not to notice her. He tried to whip up his spirits. Arabella, he thought, accused him of cowardice. She had put his life in danger with her romantic fantasies. Well, tonight was his birthday and he refused to hide.

Just as we arrived at the table, a third waiter appeared with a bouquet of roses—all the other tables had single bud vases on them—and two candlesticks. The flowers were arranged and the headwaiter himself lit the candles. Then he seated us with ceremony.

Father recognized many of his fellow diners: the mayor, the sheriff, Weyrich from the boatyard, the pharmacist—all with their families. He wondered what they were saying at their tables about the Jews. On catching his eye, the mayor and the sheriff both smiled broadly. The mayor waved his finger in mock admonition—referring, my father guessed, to my father's opposition to speakeasies in Charlevoix County. Father raised both of his hands as if surrendering. The important families from the north side were represented, as well as the Chicago Club, the Belvedere Club, and Detroit wealth. All in all, he thought, it's an appropriate turnout for my birthday party. He was disappointed not to see Sonny Kuhn anywhere.

The wine steward carried in a standing ice bucket and a bottle of champagne. He showed the bottle to the headwaiter and then to my father. After receiving approval, the wine steward opened the bottle and poured out four glasses. The headwaiter lifted his glass in a silent toast to our table, sipped the champagne, bowed, and left. Immediately, the lights went down and the floor show commenced.

Although no one took our dinner orders, food arrived at the table, course after course, each one with a different wine. Cleo watched the floor show with such avid wonder that she hardly ate. My father wondered at Cleo's shining beauty; he was certain that her condition had improved. With each sip of wine, he murmured a prayer in Hebrew, thanking God for his blessings and then in English, with irony, for his punishments which were certain to follow. Two more commandments broken, he thought: "Thou shalt not take the name of the Lord in vain" and "Remember the Sabbath day and keep it holy." With God and Carl Greenstein after him, he felt peculiarly vulnerable. Nevertheless, he concluded, the greater the danger, the more recklessly he would act. Like King Lear out in the tempest, he thought, here I am in a den of thieves and lawbreakers tempting God's retribution. By now, my father was very drunk.

During the show, I caught sight of Tony Warburg and his parents at a table across the dance floor. When the show ended, the lights came up and the orchestra began to play the latest song, "Am I Blue." My father invited Cleo to dance. As they whirled away, Tony Warburg crossed the floor toward me. I examined the approaching young man. For the last three weeks, he had divided his time between Cleo and me. Unable to control myself, I had allowed him his weakness, answering his call when he beckoned and retreating when he chose Cleo. Apparently, he did not care which sister he courted. He just went about carelessly exercising all sides of his fractured character, determined to prove his worthlessness.

What character? I asked myself as he put out his arms. Obediently, I rose and we began to dance. When the piece was over, my father appeared at our side with Cleo and offered to trade partners. Cleo moved toward Tony, but I would not let go of him.

Father looked at me reproachfully. "Don't you want to dance with me?"

Left with no choice, I gave Tony up to Cleo and moved into my father's arms. The music began and we danced off together. "It's fun, isn't it Dad?" I felt miserable.

"Very festive and a bargain too, for some reason. You wouldn't happen to . . . no, I don't want to know."

We danced a while and then sat down. Cleo and Tony continued dancing. Mother arrived at the table and took Cleo's chair. Her skin was flushed and her eyes glittered.

"I can't believe you're here." She peered at her husband. "You never go out on the Sabbath."

"A man like me makes his own rules."

"What's that supposed to mean?"

"Momma, don't argue here."

Mother turned to me. "It's very embarrassing when I refuse invitations for your father because of his religious beliefs and he turns up anyway."

"It's my birthday and my daughters are treating me to a wonderful night."

"I was planning to celebrate Monday night," declared Mother.

My father grinned wryly and put out his arms. "You're welcome to join us if your party is boring."

Mother cocked her head as if considering the invitation, and then rejected it. "Sounds more like a challenge to me," she said sharply. She glanced over at the Steiner table. "I have to get back, but you and I are going to talk about this, Henry, I warn you." She stood up.

Just as she turned away, the dining room went dark and the orchestra began playing "Happy Birthday." From the kitchen came two waitresses wheeling a birthday cake topped with candles. Everyone sang. The waitresses stopped in front of our table. When the song was over, my father stood, took a deep breath, prayed for his daughters' future, and blew out the candles. Everyone clapped.

One of the waitresses handed him a cake knife and he cut the first piece. Once three pieces had been cut for his table, Father directed the waitresses to serve the Greenstein table and the Steiner table. "And please, I would like to purchase champagne for both tables to go along with the cake." He placed a stack of gold coins on the food cart.

"Henry!" Mother stared at the gold coins. "What on earth?"

"Oh yes, dear." He reached into his pocket and brought out the skin bag of coins. He shook it, jangling the coins. All eyes at the Greenstein table were upon us. Father raised his voice. "I thought I'd take advantage of your good fortune."

"But Henry—"

"It was like a message, a birthday message. Go out and have a good time with the girls, it said, and so that's what I intend to do."

The waitress picked up the gold coins from the tray and handed them back. "I'm sorry Mr. Bearwald, Monsieur Jacques said that we weren't to take your money."

She wheeled the cake to the Greenstein table and began to cut and serve. Carl Greenstein stood up and made a little bow of thanks. My father bowed back, pleased that his gesture had been appreciated. Waiters appeared from the bar with champagne for both the Greenstein and the Steiner tables. Carl Greenstein raised his glass to my father. My father returned the gesture.

Dazed, Mother began to walk away. "See you in the gaming room, dear," Father called out, dropping the gold coins into the skin bag. She nodded and made her way quickly back to the Steiner table. When Father sat down, Tony Warburg joined us. Cleo and I offered Tony birthday cake from our plates. He accepted a forkful from each and then waved us off.

"Would you mind, sir," asked Tony, "if I took your daughters out for a tour of the garden? They say that the fish ponds are spectacular this year."

For a moment, my father did not reply. He was distracted by the tall, slim, young blonde woman at Greenstein's table who had been eyeing him all evening. Now she stood and excused herself from her table. As she brushed past my father's chair, he felt her nails brush across his neck. A cloud of strong perfume accompanied her.

"Mr. Bearwald?" said Tony. "Would you excuse us?"

"Of course." He stood politely as we rose. "After I finish my champagne, I plan to do some serious gambling. Come find me when you're through with your walk."

Tony offered my sister and me an arm each and we walked away.

My father was not displeased to be left alone. His head felt light. His spirits soared. Now that he had broken the Ten Commandments and defied God, he had nothing more to fear. He found himself enjoying the sight of the gangsters at the next table. Carl Greenstein seemed a pleasant enough fellow. It was hard to imagine that he hurt people and that he would be foolish enough to consider Henry Bearwald, haberdasher, merchant, and devout follower of the rites of Judaism, a serious rival. What would Greenstein say, he wondered, if he were to tell him and his gang that Henry Bearwald served a power much greater than theirs?

He shut his eyes and imagined the altar of the synagogue in Detroit where the Holy Ark stood open. The precious scrolls of the Torah, each with its velvet casing and silver medallion, waited there to be picked up by adoring hands and held aloft for all to admire—the Law of the Lord. He and his family would be there in September during the High Holy Days.

He was feeling quite joyous and then he remembered that on that sacred parchment were written the words condemning Henry Bearwald's sacrilege. He asked himself whether he could ever face the Torah again.

When he opened his eyes, he saw the remaining members of the Greenstein party leave their table and walk into the gaming room. The band began to play again and couples filled the dance floor. The blonde from the Greenstein party returned from the ladies' room, brushed by my father's back once more, and stood before her empty table.

"Pardon me," said my father, rising. "Your friends went into the gaming room."

"Oh dear," said the blonde, "and I wanted so much to dance."

"Would you like to take a turn with me?"

"Oh, you're too good a dancer. I saw you with your—your daughters."

"Henry Bearwald." Father put out his hand.

"Fern Plotkin." Fern took his hand, placed it on her waist.

My father stepped onto the floor and they danced off together, their bodies touching from cheek to thigh. They danced until the band took a break. Then my father suggested that they go into the gaming room. They settled at a roulette wheel. He bought two large stacks of chips from the croupier, using his gold coins.

"Tell me the truth, Henry. Who're you connected with?"

"Strictly on my own, Fern."

"Come on, don't kid me. Chicago? Jersey? We know everybody in Detroit."

"My wife wants me to branch out—but I'm just a country boy."

"I'd like to get to know you better, Henry."

"Really?" Drunk as he was, he suspected Fern Plotkin's interest in him was not exactly amiable.

"Do you know the basement lounge of the Charlevoix Beach Hotel?"

"I do."

"Abie goes to bed early, but I'm going to drop in there later, alone. Maybe you could meet me—for a nightcap?"

"Maybe," said my father, staring into the young woman's wide, blue eyes. He wondered whether she had been given orders to lure him to the hotel.

When they had lost their chips, my father bought two more stacks. This time Fern lost, but Father kept winning. Soon he had several piles of chips in front of him.

A large hand came down onto Fern's shoulder. She gave a cry and disappeared. Father turned to see Carl Greenstein's reptilian face next to his. The gangster had taken Fern's chair. "Mrs. Plotkin is married," said Carl Greenstein, an apologetic note in his voice.

"That's OK. So am I." Face to face with the gangster, my father began to shiver. His hands and his feet felt very cold.

"Just who are you, Mr. Bearwald?"

"I run a dry goods store—clothes for the entire family." To mask his nervousness, my father kept gambling. He continued to win.

"My accountant, Sy, your wife's brother, seems to think that you're a reasonable man—a smart businessman, someone who might see the advantages of cooperation, a partnership perhaps."

"In dry goods?" My father was genuinely confused.

"No, wet goods."

"Bathing suits?" My father tried to joke, but his voice faded as Carl Greenstein's gaze bore into him.

"Look Mr. Bearwald, I'm in business, like you. I didn't make this visit to kid around. Maybe you don't understand who you're talking to?"

"I do, Mr. Greenstein, I really do. But you don't know who you're talking to."

"Is that a threat?"

My father laughed weakly and then began to cough. "No, no, no threat. Not in the least. I'm just a small town storekeeper—that's all. You must be smart enough to see that."

"I'm truly sorry that you're such a stubborn man." The gangster stood up. He contemplated my father with a look of sadness and walked out of the gaming room. His party followed him. As Fern Plotkin reached the door, she turned and winked back at him, pointing to her watch.

My father picked up his chips and carried them to the cashier where he cashed them in. He had won five thousand dollars. He felt very tired, defeated. He could not face his daughters or his wife again. He left the club. With detachment, he wondered whether Carl Greenstein's contract would be fulfilled tonight.

TWENTY-SIX

I STROLLED AROUND BEECHAMS leaning on one of Tony Warburg's arms. My mind floated high above the festive crowd—watching, judging, weighing the events of the evening. The illegal club had opened its doors and the people had flocked in, turning their backs upon the clear, freshwater lakes, the green forests, the immaculate beaches, and the productive farms of Northern Michigan. Potted palm trees leaned over passageways, their fronds casting bladed shadows upon tiled floors. Under a kaleidoscope of colored spotlights, rainbow jets of water spewed out of the mouths of alligators and camels. Tropical fish nosed through elaborate grottoes in tanks nestled among live orchid plants. Bedouin tribesmen galloped along muraled walls; harems of scantily clad maidens cavorted around shadowy corners; and overhead, upon the ceilings, long-robed merchants bartered among colorful tents. As the strains of the tango and the slow fox-trot echoed through the building and the gardens, I observed the citizens of Charlevoix absorbed into a corrupt desert oasis.

What was Rebecca Bearwald doing here embraced by the sumptuous setting of an exotic gambling club? I tried to summon up my dreams of stately classroom buildings, formal lecture halls, paneled libraries, and tree-shaded quadrangles, but their images faded—empty mirages dissipating into the cool evening darkness. My family and I had become captives in a mock-North African fantasy-enterprise. Strangely enough, my mother and father and my sister Cleo were acting out their exotic new roles with conviction, as if they had always belonged here.

I was drunk and yet clearheaded about the details of the disintegrating wreck that had been my family. At the long table in the dining room, Arabella Bearwald shone brilliantly, a dark jewel of the Orient, entertaining the languid crowd of North Siders with her needy energy. Over the swelling beat of "One Alone" and "The Desert Song," I could hear her resonant laughter and see her hands sweep through the air as she told one of her involved tales. If she had been wearing a veil under her glowing black eyes, she would have resembled one of those desert temptresses in the movies. At one moment I blamed my mother and at the next pitied her, and then admired her. Did she not deserve these few moments of gorgeous frivolity? And yet, I feared that she had allowed herself to go too far, spending herself on that red-faced idler and fool, Charles Kuhn.

"I'll be in the gaming room, girls." The voice of my father startled me. He passed by, his arm around the blonde woman from the neighboring table, his hand draped over her hip.

"Daddy—" the word died on my lips. How could I judge my parents when I couldn't control my own emotions? At that very moment I wanted both of Tony Warburg's arms for myself and the rest of his body too. But I had only one of Tony's arms; my sister held the other. I was jealous of Cleo, but more than that, I envied the simplicity of her desire, unmixed by judgment or guilt. What Cleo focused upon, she wanted totally and she never wavered. Deep within the blackness of her eyes, a vortex of will formed, her head lowered, and nothing could distract her. In part, her beauty lay in her single-mindedness. "Mine, mine," she said and she prevailed. Such certainty made me doubt my own passion.

I convinced Cleo to join me in the Ladies Room. Leaving her there, I hurried back toward our table, hoping to spend a few moments alone with Tony. As I entered the dining room, a hand touched my arm.

"Will you dance with me, Becky?" I turned and stared up at Ben Near's fresh, glowing face. Over six feet tall, slim, with sandy hair and freckles, Ben Near had regular features with a broad forehead and wide-spaced blue eyes. To my clouded sight, his clean-cut features signaled a happy, productive spirit.

My impulse was to refuse, but as I stood there, Cleo passed me, moving swiftly toward our table. The orchestra started up a new song, "Bill," and the lyrics seemed so appropriate—"He was just plain Bill,/An ordinary guy"—that I clutched at the young man, clutched at his stiff, responsible embrace. At our table, I could see Tony, drinking steadily. Cleo sat very close to him, clinking glasses, and drinking with him.

Her eyes rested upon him, unwavering. She was afraid, I knew, that someone, her own sister, would snatch him up if she looked away.

"Are you going down south for freshman orientation?" Ben Near asked.

"No, I'm not." I had to stifle a wail of despair. Ben's question implied such an uncomplicated life. "I may not go to Ann Arbor this fall."

"What?" Ben faltered in his dancing. "But Becky, you have to come—I'm counting on it."

I flushed, pleased by his reaction. "I may have to postpone it a year—it's all mixed up."

"I really want us to be in Ann Arbor together." Anxiety flooded through me, as if I had misplaced some object. He continued, "Can I take you home tonight?"

I responded in a rush, without thinking. "I'd like that, Ben, but it's my father's birthday, and there's Cleo too, and we promised to give Tony Warburg a ride."

"Oh." Ben relaxed his grip. His entire body drooped with disappointment.

It was only then that I realized how much of an alternative Ben had been offering. And yet I could not respond. At our table, Tony ruffled Cleo's hair and fondled her. His parents had left early. Cleo and I would have to take him home—an embarrassing end to our father's birthday celebration. Even as I thought this, I schemed that I would drop Cleo and Father off before driving Tony to some spot on the beach where we could embrace. Perhaps tonight, at last, we would make love.

The orchestra changed the beat to a fast number. We continued dancing, but neither of us could quite keep up with the music. "We should talk more, Becky," said Ben, trying to capture my attention. He was breathing hard, trying to keep up with the beat.

"Let's just dance." We continued to stumble around the room.

I wanted to punish Tony and Cleo, too. Cleo had no right to flirt with Tony Warburg; she was too troubled. Or was she? When had Cleo ceased to need me? Obviously, I answered myself, Cleo had begun caring for herself when I decided to go to Ann Arbor.

"Becky?" Ben Near looked down at me, unable to understand my distraction. "What are you thinking about?"

"I think I'd better get everyone together and go home." I reached up, seized Ben by the neck, and hugged him. "Thank you, Ben." I ran away. Ben stood alone among the dancing couples, looking after me.

At the table, I thrust myself between Tony and Cleo. "Come on, you two, let's go find Dad and go home."

"We still have half a bottle left," complained Tony as I hauled him to his feet and marched him out of the dining room. Cleo followed.

When I could not find Father in the gambling rooms or the garden, I became alarmed. I sent Tony into the men's room where he remained for some time. Finally, he emerged.

"No Mr. Bearwald there. I looked in every stall."

I was about to return to the dining room, when Mother emerged from the Ladies' Room.

"Momma. Have you seen Daddy?"

Mother paused and thought. "The last I saw your father, he was pawing a blonde at the roulette wheel."

"We're going home. Do you want a ride?"

"Good night, dears." She looked at me, at Cleo, and then at Tony. "Drive carefully." She wandered back into the dining room.

Certain now that my father had left Beechams, I herded Tony and Cleo to the car. Tony crawled into the backseat and fell asleep. Cleo tried to follow him, but I grabbed her and shoved her into the front seat. She handed over the car keys without an argument. Once we were on the street, Cleo slumped down and fell asleep.

I drove as quickly as I dared out to the Warburg estate. I was worried now about my father. I pulled up to the front door of the Big House.

"Wake up, Tony!" I whispered urgently, shaking Tony from his sleep.

"Wha—what?"

"You're home, Tony, please get out of the car, quietly. Cleo's asleep."

Tony reached out and took my face in his hands. "An angel from heaven."

I slapped him. "Get out!" He meekly obeyed. I drove off, the wheels of my car throwing gravel.

At home, I helped the sleepy Cleo out of the car and into the house. After I had put Cleo to bed, I went into my parents' bedroom. Neither of them was home. I lay awake waiting for them. As I stared up at the ceiling of my room, I recalled the winter mornings the family walked down into town—the four of us, huddled together like one creature. How foolish I had been, I thought, to have resented those walks.

TWENTY-SEVEN

THE NEXT MORNING AT seven Mother woke me up. "Where is your father?" she asked.

"Do you mean he hasn't come home yet?"

Mother shook her head. "Where's Cleo?"

"She must have gone fishing."

Mother sat down on the side of my bed. Her skin was pale, her eyes red. She looked exhausted. "He was throwing those gold coins around—in front of everyone. I heard he won at roulette. Thousands."

"But nobody in Charlevoix would—" I remembered the brick through the window and the black sedans. "Oh Momma, we should call the police."

"He would be mortified—I've never seen him like he was last night."

"His birthday."

Mother threw her arms up, on her face a grimace of angry consternation. "His birthday, his birthday, I know, I know."

Together we went downstairs and looked into the study. It was empty. In the kitchen, I put the water on for coffee and sat down at the kitchen table. "Why don't you call the store?" I suggested.

Mother phoned the store. After a number of rings, she put the phone down. "Do you know who those people were at the table next to you last night?" she asked.

"A man named Greenstein. I didn't like any of them."

"He's the boss of a gang in Detroit—the Purple Gang. The men at that table were gangsters. He was dancing and flirting with one of their molls."

Stunned, I imagined my father's body crumpled in a ditch by the side of the road. "Call the police, Momma."

Mother began to dial when the front door opened. I ran into the living room. She followed.

"Good morning, everyone," my father greeted us. He still wore his blazer and white flannel trousers. "It was a beautiful night. I slept on the beach." He held out his arms. Sand from his coat and trousers fell to the floor around him. "Sorry," he said. He looked very happy. "I'll shave and be down in a jiffy. It's almost time for work."

He ran up the stairs, two steps at a time. My mother followed.

My father whistled as he washed, shaved, and dressed. He was, indeed, very happy. During the night, he had deposited all of his problems into God's lap.

After he left Beechams, he had walked to North Point on the road. He climbed down through the woods to the lake. Slowly, he paced along the beach back toward town, pondering his fate. His life was in danger. Absurd as it was, the infamous Purple Gang had decided that Henry Bearwald should be eliminated as a dangerous competitor. Once more he had considered and dismissed the idea of going to the police. Of course, he could close the store and the house, as Sy had suggested, move away and hide somewhere. But how long would he and his family have to hide? Would he have to sell everything and relocate permanently? Could he get enough from the sale to start over again?

He had taken off his shoes and socks, had rolled up his trousers, and had continued on, his feet lapped by the cold waters of Lake Michigan. When he arrived at the beach behind Sonny Kuhn's house, he hesitated. He yearned to climb up to her house, to embrace her, to tell her his love still burned fiercely within him. Instead, he continued on, passing the back of the Charlevoix Beach Hotel where Fern Plotkin had invited him to meet her. Once more he hesitated, imagining the eager embrace of her slim thighs. He sighed and wondered whether her proposal had been genuine or a trap planned by the Purple Gang. He moved on. At the side of the breakwater across the channel from his house he made a burrow of sand, stretched out, and stared up at the stars.

"Blessed art Thou, O Lord our God, King of the Universe—" he prayed, and resigned his fate to the hands of God.

He awoke as the sun rose, stood up, and looked out at the gleaming blue waters of the lake. The lake was clear to the very horizon. The world looked clean and bright and empty in the dawn. God had preserved him for another day. Whatever happened to him, he decided, he had been blessed with a happy life. As far as he was concerned, his life and his death were God's business. In that mood, he returned home to be greeted by his wife and daughter.

While my parents got dressed, I made breakfast.

At the table, no one mentioned the night before. My father continued to be very cheerful, my mother sad and depressed. No one said a word. When our eyes met, we looked away, embarrassed. As soon as we finished eating, I cleared the dishes. "I'll finish up here," I said without looking up from the sink.

My father put his arm around my shoulders and kissed my cheek. "Thanks for the lovely birthday," he said.

My mother hugged me next. "Thanks for making breakfast and cleaning up."

And then my parents were gone. Their diffident embraces had made me restless. My job at the library did not begin until ten. I left the house and began to walk.

*

It was a fresh summer morning. Droplets of dew still dampened the grass and weeds. Traces of morning fog hovered over the fields. A slight breeze from the lake stirred the lush crowns of the trees along the shore. I strolled along toward South Point, my path meandering through pockets of sunlight and shadow under the trees. The barely moving clear blue lake water lapped upon the stones of the rocky beach. I sat for a while on one of the boulders lining the lake drive. And then I realized that I had set out with a destination in mind: Mrs. Thrush's cottage in

Boulder Park. Now that I was no longer a student, perhaps she might feel free to help me.

The low house built of large field stones was set in a birch grove. With its wavy shake roof, leaded windows, and black shutters, it looked to me as if it belonged in a fairy tale. Filled with romantic fervor, I imagined Mrs. Thrush entrenched here with her forbidden love, defying the conventions of the world. Mrs. Thrush had given up everything to live the way she pleased. Her example should give me the courage to find my own way into the world. But today I knew less about myself than I had known on the day she advised me to go to college.

I opened the cast-iron gate and marched hopefully toward the front door. I lifted the iron knocker, cast in the shape of a wild boar's snout, and let it drop twice. The door opened. A willowy woman of about thirty-five, wearing a long silk dressing gown of pale lavender, greeted me. Her soft chestnut hair, gathered loosely behind her small ears, hung down her back to below her slim waist. She looked sickly. Her features were fine and expressive: pale blue eyes set wide over sharp cheekbones, tiny nose, small sensitive mouth, and pointed chin.

"You must be Rebecca Bearwald," she said, smiling wanly. She reached out and took my hand. Her fingers were long and bony; her grasp was gentle, barely a squeeze. "I knew you would come to see us."

In a daze, I looked into the pale blue eyes which appeared to be depthless, like clear shallow lake water. I had seen Mrs. Thrush's friend many times from a distance, but this was the first time I had ever been face to face with her.

I blushed and withdrew my hand. "How—how did you know who I was?"

The woman raised her fingers to her forehead and flicked at it, jauntily. "Please forgive me. I'm always jumping way ahead of myself." Her faint laughter ended with a cough. "I'm Amelia, Jane's sister."

"Her sister?" I examined her closely and began to discern a resemblance to the study hall counselor.

"Why yes, the same parents, you know. Jane has talked a great deal about you. Described you to a 'T.' And here you are."

She stood gazing down at me. She seemed to lose herself in her meditation. I squirmed nervously under her regard.

Once more she flicked her forehead. "Sorry, I get carried away. I'd like to invite you in, but the house is a mess and, well, Jane does not like to have visitors. We're off to Europe tomorrow and I'm supposed to be packing."

We stood there, staring at one another. Could this woman really be Mrs. Thrush's sister, just as Mrs. Thrush claimed? The idea disappointed me. They could be lying, of course.

"We have a hideout in the Dordogne—very near the great caves of ancient man, but you must know all about that."

I nodded even though I'd never heard of the caves near Dordogne. "Well," I said, backing away, "I'm sorry for interrupting. Please tell your—Mrs. Thrush that I came by. Have a good trip."

The woman looked distressed. "She isn't here, you know. I could ask you in, but . . . she might come back at any time. She really likes you, you know. It's just that people are so nosy." She paused and thought, her eyes holding mine. "I am her sister, even though we look like we come from different planets. She received all the good health, and I—I was the unexpected child of our parents' old age. A defective product. Plumbing all wrong, you know. My childhood was full of doctors and nurses instead of nannies. And then our parents up and died, one after the other. Jane, who's quite bossy, appointed herself my guardian and she's been taking care of me ever since. And I say, why not? I have a competent nurse and Jane has a mission. We live a cozy life, comfortable really. And look how everyone suffers trying to be normal—with husbands and children and all that." She stopped and turned a frank, sympathetic, interrogatory gaze upon me. "You're not very talkative."

"I—I don't know what to say." Amelia's peculiar monologue had stunned me. I wanted her to be Mrs. Thrush's lover, the two of them defying the judgment of the world. As I struggled for words, the squat, energetic figure of Mrs. Thrush stalked through the front gate carrying a shopping bag.

"Oh here's Jane!" exclaimed Amelia. "Isn't she wonderful? Like the force of nature. Every step, every gesture full of purpose. Now Rebecca, listen very carefully. Jane will be delighted to see you—very delighted. But she will not show her delight. In fact, she will appear to be very cross—with you, with me, with the cat, with everything. She really wants to help you."

Amelia disappeared back into the house, leaving me to face my study hall counselor. Mrs. Thrush approached me, forced a smile, and then blushed. "I'm sorry, Miss Bearwald. This is a very inconvenient time. You should have called."

"I know. You're going away tomorrow. I'll leave."

"Now, Miss Bearwald, Rebecca, I don't mean to be rude, but we're very much behind in our packing—"

"I'm sorry. I should have called. Have a good trip." I edged past her down the walk.

"Was there something specific that brought you?"

"I just happened to be walking by and—"

"Unfortunately, we're going off by train very early tomorrow morning. Perhaps, in the fall when we return—before you go to college. If you go."

"Yes, I understand." Somehow, I reached the gate. I forced myself to raise my head and face her again. "What you said after graduation—it meant a great deal to me."

"It was the truth, Rebecca." Mrs. Thrush stepped briskly back down the path and put out her hand. I grasped the hand and shook it briefly. "You will make a contribution." I nodded and managed a small strained smile. I withdrew my hand and slipped out the gate. Without turning around again, I marched back up the road.

As I walked along the lake, I recalled Amelia's words, ". . . she's been taking care of me ever since. And I say, why not? I have a competent nurse and Jane has a mission." I was certain now that they were sisters.

TWENTY-EIGHT

THE LIBRARY WAS CLOSED to the public on Saturdays. I worked all day alone, catching up on new orders, binding repairs, and re-shelving. The tedious work suited me. I didn't want to talk to anyone. I could not forget the Thrush sisters trapped in their cottage. By noon, I came to a decision.

I arranged for a replacement that night at the Belvedere Club. At four-thirty I went home, picked up the scholarship papers from their hiding place in my bureau drawer, and walked to the store. My parents were busy with customers until after five. When the last customer left the store, I laid the forms on the counter. "I forged Daddy's name to the application."

My father read through the papers slowly, handing them, sheet by sheet to my mother. My mother read them through, shaking her head back and forth, murmuring. "Forgery, how could you do such a thing?"

"I handled everything through a post-office box. Even Mrs. Thrush at school, my study hall counselor, knew nothing about it."

"Becky! This is a criminal offense," said Mother.

"I've been awarded full tuition and part room and board. I'll work for the rest. They have university jobs."

"But they'll cancel it all when they find out that you forged your father's signature, won't they?"

"They don't have to find out," I declared.

"They won't find out," said my father. "I'm just disappointed at the way you went about it."

"You wouldn't let me apply."

"That doesn't excuse forgery," said my mother.

"Please, Arabella. The signature is no more than a formality."

I paced back and forth in front of them. Father walked around the counter and put his hand on my shoulder. But he said nothing.

"I suppose you'll go to college, then," said Mother.

"You mean you agree?"

"I guess it's up to you, Rebecca." Mother's voice was sharp, bitter. She wiped her cheeks, put away the handkerchief, and began to freshen her makeup in front of one of the store mirrors.

My father went about the store, preparing to lock up for the night. I stood in front of the counter, staring down at my scholarship papers. I felt abandoned. I gathered up the pages and slipped them back into the manila envelope. I approached my mother and tried to keep my voice calm, reasonable. "Momma,

Cleo isn't a cripple. You're not going to have to take care of her for the rest of your life."

"Your sister is not normal, Rebecca."

"She'll find someone."

"I'm not going to let any man touch her."

"You're not going to have much to say in the matter."

"I'm going home." My mother walked toward the door. I followed her.

"Don't be such a hypocrite, Momma."

"Are you coming, Henry?" Mother stepped out of the door.

I followed, indignant that she had robbed me of a proper confrontation.

As my father locked the door, my mother set off up the street alone. Father turned toward me with an apologetic smile. I wanted very much to believe that he would emerge from his hiding place and acknowledge my right to an independent future. I had been waiting for his blessing. And he had seemed to promise it. But today something had changed in his expression. He had stepped further away from me and my life. Over his shoulder I saw him mirrored in the windows of the store: a stooped, thin man in rimless glasses, his suit neat, his cuffs just showing below the sleeves of his jacket. Behind him, the display—a mixed array of clothes for the beach, for the farm, for the water, and for the town—absorbed his figure as if he were another mannequin. He looked neither as tall nor as imposing as he had during the years of my childhood.

We ate dinner late. Mother insisted upon baking a chicken, the first full dinner the family had eaten together in weeks. Her return to domestic virtue simply increased my anger. Cleo sensed the tension at the dinner table and became increasingly upset. She rattled her dishes and shuffled her feet on the floor.

I came around the table and thrust my face before Cleo's. "No you don't! It's my turn tonight! I'm angry, do you hear, I'm angry. If you keep on, I'll fall on the floor and scream." Cleo shuddered and pulled away.

"Stop it, Rebecca!" said Mother. "You're scaring your sister."

"Why shouldn't I? She scares us all the time."

"Rebecca!" said Father.

I returned to my chair. Cleo sat quietly, her eyes on her plate.

As we ate dessert, the front door opened. "Anybody home?" Tony Warburg strode into the dining room, pulled up a chair and sat down. "Looks delicious," he said, gazing down at the fresh fruit cocktail on my plate. He picked up a fork and speared a peach slice, popping it into his mouth.

"Would you care for some?" asked Mother.

"I'll just feed off of Rebecca's plate," he replied, spearing some more fruit.

Cleo shoved her dish across the table in front of Tony.

I stood up and put a hand under Tony's arm. "I want you to take me out for a ride." Tony rose. Cleo got up too. "No, Cleo, you help Momma with the dishes." I guided Tony to the front door. Cleo followed us, her hands out, pleading. In a very low voice, she said, "Mine."

"No, not yours," I said. "Mine." I pushed Tony through the front door and followed. I shut the door in Cleo's face. Through the door, I could hear the moan welling up in Cleo's throat.

Tony hesitated on the top step of the porch. "Don't you think that Cleo—"

"No I don't." I dragged Tony down the steps. From behind the closed door came the sound of Cleo's high-pitched wail. I drowned it out with a shout, "Come on, come on!" I urged Tony to the car.

*

Once Tony and I were in the car, I opened the glove compartment and searched for the flask that was usually there.

"Fresh out, tonight," said Tony. "No money, no booze."

"Doesn't matter. Let's move."

Tony drove off.

"Running Shoal," I commanded.

It was a clear night. By the time we reached the beach south of town, the moon had begun its slow descent. The stars littered the sky. I lifted my face to the sky and closed my eyes, soothed by the wash of the buffeting wind.

When we reached Running Shoal, Tony stopped.

"Do you have a tire iron?" I asked.

"Why?"

"Do you want a drink or don't you?"

"Of course I do."

"Then get the tire iron." Tony rummaged in his car and handed me a tire iron. "Now sit down and wait."

"You're crazy, Mouse, absolutely crazy."

I walked over the dunes into the scrub forest. It took me some time, but finally I found the remaining case of Cleo's whiskey. I pried open the case and removed two bottles with the tire iron. I pounded the top of the case down again and made my way back to the car where Tony waited, sitting on the running board.

"Magic!" I said, holding the two bottles in front of Tony.

"My miracle mouse," said Tony, putting out his hand.

I avoided his grasp and placed the bottles in the sand, just out of his reach. I sat on his lap, wrapping my arms around his neck. I kissed him lightly on the nose, on each cheek, and on the chin. Then slowly and thoroughly I kissed his mouth.

When I had finished, he said, "You sure turned out to be one hell of a kisser."

"You taught me all I know."

"Now, we need some refreshment."

"You're not very romantic."

"You asked for booze in the first place, not me."

"On one condition."

"Anything for a taste of the bottle."

"Two promises."

"They're yours."

"Swear!"

"Cross my heart and hope to die!"

I opened one of the bottles and handed it to him. I watched him drink. After he swallowed, he exhaled sharply. "Damn good stuff, Mouse."

I took the bottle, put it to my mouth, and tipped it. The liquid flowed in over my tongue, biting at the inside of my mouth. The fumes rose through my nostrils, stinging the membranes. I swallowed. A slow burning sensation spread through my chest and stomach.

While Tony gathered wood and made a fire, I scooped out a hollow in the sand and lined it with a car blanket. Soon we were lying in one another's arms next to the fire, watching the long shallow waves break in from the darkness of the lake. As we talked, we drank steadily. After a while, I no longer had to force the liquid down my throat. In the wash of the water the sand and pebbles rubbed against one another with soft slithering sounds. A warm breeze from the southeast rustled the birch leaves and the pine boughs behind us.

"You know, Mouse, I feel bad about leaving Cleo home tonight."

"I'm going to leave her for good, and my folks too, and Charlevoix."

"That sounds pretty final."

"It is." I drank from the bottle and stared into the fire.

"Cleo's not all that crazy, you know, Mouse."

"I don't care what she is anymore."

"You love her, don't you, Mouse?"

"Of course, whatever that means. But she's impossible."

"I can't figure her out, myself."

And who is Rebecca? I thought. Oh, she takes care of Cleo. And when I leave Cleo, who will I be?

Tony spoke again. "She's pretty terrific, you know, in spite of. . . . Exactly what is the matter with her?"

I realized what I had been doing all day: seeking some image of myself in the eyes of Mrs. Thrush and my parents, an outline, at least, of Rebecca Bearwald when she turned her back on Charlevoix.

"Mouse?"

"Oh hell. I don't think anyone knows what's the matter with Cleo. The doctors say she has a developmental disorder—something about living all inside yourself."

Tony nodded his head. He was silent for a minute. "That doesn't sound like her." He took up a handful of sand and let it run through his fingers. "I think she lives everywhere except inside herself. She's like—like the breeze—part of everything."

I was surprised. I hadn't expected such a poetic thought from Tony. In fact, I suspected that he didn't think at all. I studied the dark shore where the foam glowed in small patches as it broke upon the sand and pebbles. I had to admit that he was right. I felt my sister's presence everywhere: in the shifting sand and pebbles, the lapping water, the rustling trees. "She's a mystery and I'm tired of her."

"She knows how I'm feeling better than I do."

"That's no trick. Everything is out there on your face plain to see." I twined myself around him and began kissing his face, his neck, and chest. "If anyone's crazy, it's you." But I felt no excitement. The less I felt, the more vigorously I caressed him.

"Hey, hey, whoa there. This is getting too rough."

"Hold onto your hat, Buster, it's going to get rougher." What a silly thing to say, I thought. Where on earth did "Buster" come from?

"Slow down, Mousie. Let's just lie here together for a while until I catch my breath. I need another drink."

"Promise Number One."

"Ready, set, go."

"Drive me to Ann Arbor in August."

"Hell, that's easy. I'll drive you there and back."

"No, just there. I'm going to school in the fall."

"I thought your folks—?"

"It doesn't matter what they think. I've got a scholarship."

"Just going off like that—it's pretty serious, Mousie."

"If you won't drive me, I'll take a bus."

"I don't break my promises. To tell the truth, I think it's neat you asked me."

"That's why I wanted you along—" I kissed him gently on the mouth, "—because you like to take chances."

"I'm getting a little worried about Promise Number Two."

"Oh, you'll enjoy that more." I began to undress.

"What are you doing?"

"I'm going swimming."

Tony sat up suddenly. "Wait a minute, Mouse." He tried to stop me, but I jumped away from his grasp.

"Come on, Scaredy-Cat!"

"You're pretty drunk and so am I."

In my bra and panties now, I began to dance around him. "Scaredy-Cat, Scaredy-Cat, Scaredy-Cat!"

Tony his shook head solemnly. "I don't know anything about the lake out here—holes, currents, and we're in no state."

I stood across the fire and undid my bra. "Promise Number Two: I want you to make love to me tonight."

"Not on your life!"

"You promised." I removed my bra, slid down my panties, and stepped out of them.

"I don't have—anything to protect you."

"I don't care. You promised."

"Put on your damn clothes and act sensible."

I didn't know what to do. I hadn't expected a refusal. It had taken all my courage and the whiskey to get me this far. Here I was naked for the first time in front of a boy and he wouldn't even look at me. I had intended to throw myself into his arms, but I felt ashamed.

Maybe I had an ugly body. Tony seemed willing enough to embrace me when I was dressed. He had almost made love to me the night we had fallen into the lake. The problem was that I didn't know what men liked about women's bodies.

The whiskey, which until this moment had buoyed me up, now burrowed down through my body, leaving only emptiness. My shoulders sagged. I decided I must look horrible. My breasts were too pointed, too full. My stomach puffed out too much. My legs didn't curve in the right places. I was, indeed, a monster. I turned away from the fire and began to march toward the lake, weeping.

"Hey!" Tony shouted. "Come back here!" He began to run after me.

I ran into the water. I wanted to dive, but the water was too shallow. I waded as fast as I could, seeking the drop-off.

Alarmed, Tony took off his shoes and began stripping to his briefs. Just then he heard the sound of a motor. Up the beach came a car. Tony recognized our Ford sedan. It pulled to a stop next to him. Cleo jumped out.

"Rebecca!" shouted Tony, pointing out at the lake. "She'll drown!"

Cleo drew her dress over her head, threw it on the beach, and plunged into the water. Tony followed.

I reached the drop-off and went under, swallowing water.

I came up spluttering and went down again. I tried to gasp in air, but my mouth and throat were full of water. Drunk, dizzy, and nauseous, I became terrified. I lost track of the shore. I kicked and flapped my arms frantically and kept going under. I lost consciousness.

With her eyes on me in the moonlight, Cleo took a shallow dive and began to swim before the drop-off. She moved swiftly through the water, her head raised. When I went down again, Cleo knew exactly where I had sunk. She dove and caught hold of my hair, pulling me to the surface just as Tony arrived.

The two of them got me to shore quickly and pumped the water out of my lungs. I writhed in their grasp, trying to gulp in the air. Then I vomited. They raised me to my knees and bent me forward. I continued to vomit until I was empty. I retched and retched, but nothing came up. My stomach ached unbearably. After ten minutes of dry heaving, I collapsed in their arms. I was shivering uncontrollably. They carried me to the fire, chafed my body warm, and wrapped me in the blankets. I fell asleep. Now that I was warm and breathing regularly, they relaxed.

They went down to the lake to wash off. Cleo took off her underclothes and moved into the lake. Tony slipped out of his briefs and followed. He caught up to her and took hold of her hand. They fell forward into the water. They embraced, rolling over and over in the water. After washing off, they returned to the fire. I continued to sleep soundly. Tony offered Cleo a bottle. Cleo drank. Tony drank. Naked, they dried off by the fire. Then they moved away beyond the cars.

TWENTY-NINE

VENETIAN NIGHT, THE CLIMACTIC event of the summer in Charlevoix, was approaching. The festival committee had tacked up notices all over town—one in the window of our store. On Monday morning Cleo planted me in front of the announcement and made it clear that she expected us to fulfill our application and compete in the contest for the best float. There was less than a week to prepare.

The task turned out to be a welcome distraction for the family. We labored slowly, tentatively, as if we were invalids on the mend. Neither Cleo nor I saw Tony all week. My father, Cleo, and I decorated the boat in our spare time. During the week, my father prayed to God with renewed vigor. My mother spent her days working at the store and her evenings sewing costumes at home. My declaration at the store on Saturday had left her terrified about the future. When Charles Kuhn called, she refused to see him.

As I worked on Cleo's boat, I wallowed in misery. I had failed to find support from Mrs. Thrush. My parents had turned away from me in disgust. When I had sought to lose myself in the so-called pleasures of the flesh, I had been rejected. I cringed at the memory of myself standing naked and ugly in front of Tony Warburg.

On Saturday evening, my parents went directly from the store to the dock and the family set off in *White Lightning*. The competing boats gathered in Lake Charlevoix off the Railroad Station Beach. I scanned the lake for a glimpse of Tony's boat, but he was nowhere to be seen. While we waited for darkness, the contestants put finishing touches to their decorations.

I had chosen an Egyptian theme for our boat: Antony and Cleopatra floating down the Nile on Cleopatra's barge. It seemed appropriate. A twelve-foot green and gold snake, made from cloth stretched over chicken wire, curled up from the bow, two fangs pointing ahead. A mock sail of dyed purple sheeting stretched from the radio antenna down to the stern of the boat. On the sail, I had painted a snake coiled around a pyramid. In the middle of the pyramid, I had copied the following lines from the Shakespeare play:

The barge she sat in, like a burnish'd throne,
Burn'd on the water. The poop was beaten gold;
Purple the sails, and so perfumed that
The winds were love-sick with them. The oars were silver,
Which to the tune of flutes kept stroke, and made
The water which they beat to follow faster,
As amorous of their strokes.

On the foredeck stood my parents' bedroom chaise longue, draped in gold silk and flanked by two palms borrowed from the headwaiter at Beechams. Mother, in a sequined, close-fitting evening dress and sandals, reclined on the chaise longue. She wore a headband with a scarab brooch in the center of her forehead. Father stood next to her in a short Roman military costume holding a sword from the high school stage department. Dressed as a slave girl, I fanned my mother with a large peacock fan I had borrowed from the mother of one of my girlfriends. Cleo, in a black-and-white striped burnoose, piloted the boat from the flying bridge.

I felt a little embarrassed by the roles in which I cast my parents: my father the Roman soldier, my mother the romantic and guileful queen. Father had not wanted to be on the boat at all, but after reading the play at my request, he was so taken with Antony's tragic, noble character that he agreed. My mother did not have to be convinced to dress up as Cleopatra. Cleo had been entranced with the entire project. Her clever hands and my mother's gave our production a professional finish.

At eight o'clock, the starting cannon sounded and the boats began their parade into Round Lake through the Railroad Bridge Channel. Just as it came time for *White Lightning* to turn into line, I caught sight of Tony's boat planing across the water from Evergreen Point to join the end of the parade. I looked up at the flying bridge to see Cleo gazing across the water at Tony's boat. In the glow of the instrument panel, I got only a general impression of my sister. Something gentle, yearning, and joyous in Cleo's posture and expression reminded me of the conclusion to my drunken night at the beach. After Cleo had taken me home in the early dawn and finally tucked me into bed, I had begun to sob. To my amazement, Cleo gathered me up into her arms and rocked me just as I had rocked her so many times in the past. While she comforted me, she gazed out the window with that same gentle, yearning, joyous expression she now directed across the lake at Tony Warburg's approaching boat.

"Cleo! The parade is beginning." Cleo turned back to the wheel and brought *White Lightning* into line.

Following one another by five boat lengths, the contestants made a slow clockwise circuit of Round Lake. Searchlights from the reviewing stand at the park illuminated each boat as it passed. Sirens sounded and the crowd on the lawns applauded. After two circuits, the boats gathered in the small bays on the north and south sides of Round Lake and waited while the judges collated the results.

The harbormaster, in his old diesel clunker, came chugging around to announce the winners through a megaphone.

"Cleo Bearwald's *White Lightning* out of Charlevoix, First Place. Ron Fairleigh's *Laisser-Aller* out of Boca Raton, Second Place. Jack Jones' *Barbary Pirate* out of Port Huron, Third Place." I climbed up to the flying bridge and hugged Cleo. Joyfully, we danced around in circles. "Will the winners please parade in order past the reviewing stand!"

I returned to the foredeck and Cleo put the boat in gear. Once more we passed the reviewing stand. This time the crowd shouted and clapped. As we proceeded into the darkness again, it took a moment to adjust our eyes. The second and third place boats were applauded.

The fireworks began with an explosion of sound and light. An instant later, *White Lightning* reverberated with a massive blow. I slid across the deck. In the cloudburst illumination of the fireworks, I glimpsed the chaise longue fly over the side into the lake. My parents had disappeared. By chance, my leg got tangled with the lifeline stanchion. Clasping a cleat, I managed to stay aboard.

"Momma, Daddy!" I called out. There was no answer.

Bruised, I struggled to my feet. In the flickering brightness of the fireworks, I saw the towering black bow of a much larger boat burrowed into *White Lightning*'s port beam. The larger boat backed free of *White Lightning*, which listed suddenly toward its damaged side. Up on the flying bridge, Cleo turned on the port searchlight and swept the bow and then the water. At first I could see nothing. Then I caught sight of my parents in the lake, struggling toward shore. My mother's costume had entangled her arms and legs. My father attempted to free her. Amidst the boom of the fireworks, I thought I heard the sound of rapid explosions like gunfire.

I was about to dive in to help them when a motor boat with Tony Warburg at the wheel slid under our bow. Tony leaned over the side to help my parents. Cleo kept the searchlight on the rescue operation. It was impossible to hear anything over the roar of the fireworks. For a moment Cleo's searchlight darted up, sweeping over the length of a black yacht. Then, with a brilliant glare, the searchlight went out.

In a daze, I climbed to the flying bridge where I found Cleo lying unconscious amidst the wreckage of the searchlight.

Another violent shock sent me sprawling over her body. Overhead, the sky lit up with showers of red, green, and white sparklers. I pulled myself up to see the towering black bow pull clear of our port side. This time *White Lightning* listed even more.

Afraid that we would capsize before I could get Cleo clear of the boat, I took the wheel. To my amazement, the engines were still idling. I put the engines in gear. They sputtered, almost stalled, but then the propellers took hold and we began to move through the water. Flames burst out of the after well. I headed directly at the Belvedere shore. The boat ran onto the beach with a sliding crunch. I turned off the engines and dragged Cleo down from the flying bridge. I lay Cleo out on the deck, grasped her wrists and then lowered her body over the port side into the shallow water. I let her drop and jumped after her. As the flames climbed higher and higher, consuming the cockpit, cabin, and bridge of *White Lightning*, I dragged Cleo across the beach. I just managed to get her to the shelter of a grassy knoll when the boat exploded.

THIRTY

EARLY IN THE MORNING a week and a half after the destruction of *White Lightning*, Mother and I set off in Tony's convertible roadster. For the first time since the attack, we were without police protection. Our greatest concern was to get away unrecognized. At Mother's insistence, we wore large hats, sunglasses, and long flowing scarves to disguise ourselves. We kept the top up. In the half-light of dawn, with the mist lying still over the fields, we sped down the empty road, glancing apprehensively behind us every few miles.

We had never taken a long automobile ride without my father and Cleo. They were the ones who took care of mechanical matters. Today the car seemed made up of an infinite number of unreliable parts—fans and fan belts, pistons, cylinders, spark plugs, carburetor, tires—all ready to fly apart and spatter the highway with gasoline, water, and oil. We feared that the car would break down in the middle of the countryside, leaving us stranded, vulnerable to the pursuing gangsters.

Mother guarded the Dixie Oil Company's road map, pointing the way at each junction. "US-31 to Eastport," she chanted, "M-88 to Mancelona. If you ask me, it's a wild goose chase." Her voice was sharp, full of reproach. "US-31 to Kalkaska, M-76 to Grayling. A waste of time and money."

I was furious at her for refusing to take any responsibility for the attack. Until my aunt appeared in the waiting room of the hospital to reveal Mother's role in the affair, I had blamed only myself for the violence against our family. I had thought that if I had forced Cleo to return the boat and the whiskey, my family would have remained safe and whole.

*

A day after the attack, my aunt had arrived at the hospital at two o'clock in the morning. I lay curled up on a bench of the waiting room, dozing. My father and Cleo were still in critical condition. Aunt Maureen woke me. In her black suit and black hat, her mournful face hidden by a black veil, she looked like she had come for a funeral. For a moment I thought my father and Cleo had died while I was asleep.

My aunt blurted out that Carl Greenstein and the Purple Gang had been responsible for the attack. She urged us to go away and hide as soon as my father and Cleo could be moved. She claimed that even the police couldn't be trusted. "We warned your folks that this would happen. I warned your mother last December to keep her big mouth shut."

"Mother? What does she have to do with it?"

"Bella's always been a big braggart, but now she's really done it—telling secrets about your father out loud on the telephone over and over again and then in the boat in front of Carl Greenstein's own wife."

"What secrets?"

"Hijacking, bootlegging, that's what. Look, I don't know what your father's up to and I don't want to know."

"Let me explain. Cleo and I—"

"I already heard too much. And your family is not the only one in trouble. They've had poor Sy on the grill for two weeks—they're threatening me and Seymour and Cynthia too. They got no conscience, those people. I told Sy not to get mixed up with them. But he kept saying that he only dealt with legal businesses—that he didn't have to know where the money came from as long as the businesses were legal. But I said—"

"Auntie, Auntie, please. Daddy is not a hijacker. He's not a bootlegger. He's not a gangster."

"Well your mother said that he was all three. And worse, an omnipotent Greek—"

"A what?"

"Omnipotent. I looked it up in the dictionary—'all powerful' is what it said—like he thought he was the big boss. And not only that, she claimed that he was about to expand his territory. We don't know for sure whether anyone overheard her on the telephone, but Sy tried to warn your father. It cost him plenty. And there she was, throwing gold coins all over the table, winning thousands of dollars from gangsters' wives, and bragging that your father was a bigger gangster than Carlie."

"Mother said that?"

"Listen to me, Becky, Carlie Greenstein is no angel. He's killed a lot of men, dearie, and he'll kill anyone who gets in his way—that includes Henry Bearwald."

I held my head with both of my hands. "It's a crazy story."

Maureen stood up. "This is the message. You tell your father to close up shop for good. Or none of us will survive." She seized me and pulled me up into a convulsive embrace. Through the rough mesh of her veil I felt tears streaming down her cheek. "Seymour's waiting down in the car. We have to drive back in a few minutes."

"You just got here."

"And then hide, all of you, somewhere out of the state. I love you all. I don't know why such things happen. Money's not worth such shame and disgrace." She ran out of the waiting room and down the hallway.

*

Two weeks later in Tony's car on the way to Detroit, I repeated over and over to myself: the Purple Gang wants to murder Henry Bearwald. The words sounded ridiculous—even after all the attacks, Aunt Maureen's visit, and the police chief's warning.

The car performed smoothly past Mancelona and then past Kalkaska. With each mile, Mother's spirits rose. "Don't be so gloomy," she said. "It's a long trip."

"You're not angry that I'm making you come down to confess your lies?"

"It's hard to stay mad on such a beautiful day. Let's put the top down."

"But they might spot us."

"Nonsense. We might as well have fun before we get there."

For a moment I marveled at my mother's ability to live for the moment. And then I shuddered at the memory of how close my father and Cleo had come to death. "Fun? How can you think of fun?" I drove on.

"Come on, Becky," she pleaded.

"No, no, no!" I sped up.

"Damn it, Becky, stop acting like an old maid, which is just what you'll turn out to be if you keep pretending you're your father."

An old maid, I thought, and remembered standing naked in front of Tony at Running Shoal. I slowed the car, but kept driving. My mother's remarks nagged at me. An old maid. Maybe I didn't know how to have a good time; maybe that was why I spent so much of my time trying to impress everyone. Angry now, I pulled over to the side of the road, skidded to a stop, and, without a word to Mother, folded back the top.

"Thatta girl!" said Mother, annoying me even more.

Soon we were cruising along in the open car, the wind billowing through our clothes and hair. It occurred to me that I had never before been on a trip alone with my mother. I felt the wind washing through my insides. In a small voice, as if I were a child again, I said, "It is an adventure, isn't it, Momma?"

"Just you and me, honey—on the road!" Mother stretched her hands along the leather seats. "I like your gentleman friend's automobile."

"Luxurious and powerful," I replied.

"Let's see how fast it can go."

I felt foolish, but I entered into her game. Mother's romantic spirit always had the power to seduce me and buoy me up, for a few moments at least. I slowly depressed the accelerator. The speedometer moved higher and higher. Released from my father's caution, unshackled from Cleo's demands, I shouted out, "Just you and me, Momma. We're free!"

"Free to do as we please."

We sped down the long shadowy aisle of the highway. Forests of tall, straight dark pines alternated with quivering birches. Overhead, white puffy clouds sailed across the deep blue sky. As the road curved to the right and to the left, through the foliage of the forests we glimpsed the shining waters of secluded lakes. Without warning, the countryside opened up, revealing rich farmland stretching off into the distance: black loam of freshly ploughed fields, thick green plants arranged in orderly rows, high corn, low lettuce, tomato trellises festooned with leafy vines. The brilliant sun rose to the east, baking away the mist. And then once again we were racing along between high, shadowy forests. We breathed the fresh air deeply into our lungs.

In Roscommon we stopped for breakfast at a clean, bright cafe with a bouquet of snapdragons on each table in small vases. The coffee was rich and fresh.

"It seems strange to be here without Daddy and Cleo," I said. "You and I have never gone anywhere alone together."

My mother's mood dipped suddenly. She fell silent and then stood abruptly. "If you're still bent on this foolish errand, we'd better get back on the road."

Outside, I put the top up. There was more traffic on the road now. I concentrated on my driving. Mother sank down in the passenger seat, brooding. I regretted mentioning Cleo.

Just past Bay City on US-23, I broke the silence. "You're a good sport for coming."

"I still have no intention of groveling in front of Carl Greenstein."

"You can be as proud as you want, as long as you tell the truth."

"Your aunt is crazy."

"You told Maureen that Daddy is a bootlegger."

"That woman's *meshuggeneh!* I told my brother not to marry her."

"Maureen is a good person, Momma."

"Good is one thing. Crazy is another. She's good and crazy if you ask me."

"And you told Carl Greenstein's wife too."

"I simply said that he was a good businessman and was going to expand our business. The clothing business. That's what I said."

"Did you call Daddy an omnipotent Greek?"

"That's the kind of gibberish Maureen would make up."

"She said you called Daddy something in French."

"Oh that. It was nothing."

"What did you say?"

"I forget—oh yes, *éminence grise*—it's not so terrible. She's so uneducated I even translated it for her: 'a gray eminence,' the brains behind everything."

"I know what it means. Oh Momma, how could you?"

"She brags so much, I just thought I'd shut her up." Mother gazed out the window at the passing landscape. "Rebecca, this is a crazy trip. Let's go back home."

"We've got to explain to that man that you were just bragging, lying."

"If you think that I'm going to apologize to a gangster because my ignorant sister-in-law doesn't understand English or French, you've got another think coming."

"Do you want them to kill Daddy?"

"The police will protect him."

"Don't you realize that all four of us were almost killed?"

"No one in his right mind would think your father was a bootlegger."

"Then we'll clear up the mistake. You're going to tell Carl Greenstein that you just wanted to impress people and I'm going to tell him about Cleo and me."

"My criminal daughters!"

"I'm the criminal. Cleo is—Cleo."

"How could you let your sister sell whiskey?"

"You can't even deny her an extra dessert. And you blame me?"

"They'll never believe us."

"They will. It all fits together. Your bragging, Cleo's finding the boat and the whiskey, us selling the whiskey. We'll show them Cleo's medical files. And we'll offer to pay them back for the whiskey we sold."

My mother did not reply for some time. Finally she said, "I know you think that I don't love your father enough. I would do anything for him—I already have. But to demean myself and our family in front of such people—"

"Oh Momma, why did you make up such lies?"

"I was simply trying to impress upon my sister-in-law that your father is a very talented man. It's not my fault that he hides his abilities under a basket."

"At least he doesn't pretend to be something he's not."

"I wouldn't be too sure about that."

I was taken aback by the bitterness of her tone. In my experience, Father had always acted with propriety except for two nights of drunkenness this summer. On the other hand, I still believed that Mother had been unfaithful to him. I said nothing about Charles Kuhn though, for the sake of our mission's success.

The cities of Michigan now came upon us more quickly: Saginaw, Flint, Pontiac. The hot air blew into the car. Sweat and grime streaked our faces. Our dresses stuck to the damp seats.

"You've always worshipped your father and criticized me. I want you to know that Henry Bearwald's no saint. I know I don't read much and you think I'm vain. But I've worked hard all these years. I've taken care of you."

"Please, Momma."

"I've kept you all entertained too. Do you understand how hard it is to live with a man who doesn't talk?"

"I'm not judging either of you. I just wonder why you felt you had to tell lies about him. Everyone respects him."

"That's not all you've got against me."

I remained silent.

"Is it?"

"I have no right to judge anyone," I mumbled.

We passed through Royal Oak, Pleasant Ridge, and Ferndale. We were approaching the city limits of Detroit when Mother spoke again. "Just remember, your father's no saint."

THIRTY-ONE

WE ARRIVED IN THE outskirts of Detroit in the late afternoon. The sun, masked by the smoke of the city's factories, cast an orange glow over everything—trees, cars, buildings. It seemed as if we had entered an immense, artificially lit theater, in which nothing was real. We drove down Woodward Avenue, the widest street I had ever seen, passing block upon block of houses and storefronts. Lines of cars waited at intersections. Electric streetcars full of people plied up and down the center of the broad roadway.

I was overwhelmed. "It's amazing, Momma! So many people, buildings, houses, and cars! I've never seen a streetcar before outside a book. They move so smoothly, like boats."

"The city's much larger than I remember," said my mother, her voice catching in her throat.

"Where do we turn?"

"I—I'm not sure." She had always thought of herself as a city girl, but this new, vast Detroit terrified her. "We're not even near the downtown yet."

I drove on. Every time I stopped, we were surrounded by other cars. I could almost reach across and touch the people in them. Crowds of people crossed in front of me in both directions.

Mother grasped my arm. "I think, yes, here, here. Get over and turn right at the next corner. The big street—Grand Boulevard."

The moment we turned onto another wide boulevard, two immense new structures towered up before us. The size of the buildings startled me. I almost lost control of the car.

"Stop!" Mother's voice was hoarse and trembling. "All these years," she said bitterly, "your father kept me a captive exile in that backwater village while the world has been rushing forward."

I pulled over to the curb. Across the street, the massive facade of one of the buildings rose fifteen stories high. I read the legend above the door, "The General Motors Building."

"It must be company headquarters," said Mother. "We're still four miles from downtown. I can't believe it."

Crowds streamed out of the doors. "More people than in our whole town," I murmured. The other large building, located on our side of the street, was even taller than the General Motors Building. The spire, bright green with a shining gold cap, reached up into the sky. "It's a castle," I exclaimed. I drove slowly forward and stopped in front. Gold letters carved into marble at the entrance announced, "The Fisher Building."

"The Fisher Brothers," said Mother. "They make the bodies of the General Motors cars."

Through the glass entrance I saw an interior hallway, three or four stories high, as vast as the great European cathedrals I had seen in picture books at the library.

A policeman approached and urged us to move on. I drove west toward 12th Street. "The Jewish shopping district!" exclaimed Mother. And then she added, in a subdued tone, "Well we're here. What do you intend to do?"

"We'll find a cheap rooming house and contact Uncle Sy." I spoke with more assurance than I felt. The city, the color of the sky, the scale of the buildings, and the vast number of people frightened me.

"Those gangsters will be watching your uncle."

"I know." I drove on.

We looked at three rooming houses before we found one clean enough to suit my mother. It was a two-story brick house with bays at the corners of each floor and a wide front screened porch. Mother inspected the room and the bathroom with a businesslike air. She demanded to see the kitchen. She criticized the menus for the meals. The small, energetic lady who owned the house remained unruffled by my mother's behavior.

When we returned to the room my mother demanded fifty cents off the daily tariff. "We'll only be eating two meals a day."

"With an automobile like that," the lady gestured out the window, "you're going to starve yourself?"

"It isn't ours. Fifty cents off."

"It's a nice room, Momma." It was a pleasant, large front room with a bay window overlooking a quiet tree-lined street.

"Oh well," said the landlady, "it's yours for fifty cents off." She slipped out the door.

"It's strange to be back in Detroit," said my mother. She sat down on her bed. She clasped her hands on her lap and stared out the window. "What I hated about my childhood—it wasn't that we were poor, but that my family was so resigned about it. I used to shout and sing and dance, anything to fill those drab rooms. But my family was too tired or distracted to appreciate my show." She forced a smile and continued. "They weren't mean, Rebecca. They simply didn't seem to notice. There wasn't any—any spirit." She sat for some time, thinking over what she had said. Finally, she got to her feet. "Well, let's get settled."

As we unpacked, I pulled out drawers, opened and closed lights, explored the closet, peered out the windows, and then sighed, "It's all so different."

Mother said, "Why Becky! It hadn't occurred to me—you've never been in a rooming house."

I kissed my mother on the cheek. Tonight would be the first time I had ever slept in a room without Cleo. I went back to the window and stared out at the tree-lined street, with its brick houses, cement porches, and scrawny lawns. Then I thought of my father and sister and their ugly wounds. I hadn't meant to enjoy this trip.

After we had unpacked, I went downstairs and looked through the telephone book. There were a number of Greensteins listed, none of them named Carl. I scolded myself for neglecting to get the address or telephone number from my aunt at the hospital.

Because it would be too dangerous now to contact the Lefkowitzes directly, I called Seymour Lefkowitz's girlfriend, Natalie.

"I'm sorry," said Natalie in a distant voice, "Seymour and I aren't seeing one another for a while."

"The engagement is—off?" I was dismayed.

"No. Not exactly. Just postponed. His family is undergoing some sort of—of difficulty and he doesn't want to involve me."

I winced. "Oh my, I'm very sorry."

After a long silence, Natalie asked, "Why did you call me?"

"I wanted to get in touch with Seymour—without calling his house. It's all very embarrassing."

Natalie suggested I telephone the law office where Seymour worked. I thanked her and apologized once more for all the trouble my family was causing. Natalie cut me short and hung up.

I left a message for my cousin at the law office. I waited by the phone. Seymour called back almost immediately. He was not happy to hear who was calling. He responded in a low voice, limiting his responses—as if someone were listening.

"I'm sorry about you and Natalie, Seymour."

"I'm sorry too."

"My mother and I have come down here in order to clear things up."

"That certainly would be a great help."

"Could you have your mother call us here?"

Reluctantly, Seymour agreed. Before he hung up, he asked me not to call Natalie again. "I don't want her mixed up in this."

It was after nine o'clock before Aunt Maureen called from a phone booth, miles away from her house. "I told you to get your family out of Charlevoix."

"We are out of Charlevoix."

"Out of the frying pan and into the fire. I didn't mean for you to come to Detroit."

"No one knows we're here."

My aunt asked about my father and Cleo. She was much relieved to hear they were recovering and safely hidden. "Don't tell me where they are, you hear? I don't want to know anything. Not even where you are."

"My mother and I have to talk to Carl Greenstein—we have to explain everything—it's all so complicated."

"Carl Greenstein? You've got to be kidding. He's a man you don't explain things to. Please go hide with your father and your sister." She could hardly gasp out the words. "And you can't come to us—we're being watched, day and night. We can't help you. We can't help ourselves now."

"Please, Auntie, please. Where does he live? That's all I want to know."

"You couldn't get near his house. Rebecca, please forget it. Carlie is no one to talk to."

"It's our only chance, Auntie."

"He's the one who does the talking."

"Doesn't he have an office or something?"

"An office, ha! He and his mob hang out at a restaurant on 12th Street—The Cream of Michigan, it's called. But it isn't open tomorrow on Shabbos. Just go away somewhere for a while—for a long while."

"It's got to be tomorrow. I can't keep Mama hanging around any longer. She doesn't want to admit . . . oh please help me, Auntie."

"Darling, I want to help you, but this is impossible, impossible. The only place you could find Carl Greenstein tomorrow would be in *schul*—he goes to Beth Abraham. If he isn't there, his wife might be. Your mother knows her."

I thanked my aunt again and again and promised I would not bother her or her family again.

When I told my mother that we would be going to the synagogue to find Carl Greenstein, I expected her to refuse. Instead, Mother went in search of an iron and a board to press our clothes.

"We don't want to look rumpled and dowdy, do we?"

"Well, I didn't think we'd be dressing up."

"Why not? How often does a woman get the chance to stand up to the Purple Gang?"

I remembered my mother's Chanukah gift to my father—tickets to the synagogue and to the Temple for the High Holy Days. Instead, we were going to Beth Abraham to beg for my father's life. All the same, Mother was determined to look her best.

THIRTY-TWO

BEFORE I WENT UP to bed, I called the Warburg estate, collect, person-to-person for Tony Warburg. I identified myself with a false name—the operators in Charlevoix were not very discreet. Tony accepted the charges. Our conversation was brief. We had settled upon a code by which he could communicate my father and Cleo's condition. Tony indicated that both were doing well. Tearfully, I thanked him again for everything he had done.

The doctors said that Father would have bled to death if Tony had not reacted so quickly. My father had been shot three times. Miraculously, the bullets missed his major organs. When the attack occurred, Tony had been approaching *White Lightning* in his speedboat to congratulate us on our victory. Despite the shooting, he had been able to pull my parents from the water. When the gangsters shot my father, they hit Tony's hull just at the water line. Using his shirt and towels, Tony had slowed my father's bleeding while he steered his own slowly sinking boat to Weyrich's boat-ramp. Richie Weyrich had driven him and my parents to the hospital in the Weyrich truck.

When I put down the telephone, I offered another prayer of thanks for Tony's help. Without Tony, I wouldn't have been able to make the trip to Detroit. I felt that the boy who had protected me as a child in day camp had returned to watch over my family. At the hospital, Tony had remained with us through the night and then he had provided a safe hiding place for my father and Cleo while we were gone. At first, though, matters had not gone smoothly between us. On the night of the accident, Tony and I had argued fiercely.

My father and Cleo had shared a room at the hospital under twenty-four hour police watch. Mother and I took turns sitting in the room. It was past midnight. I dozed in the waiting room and then sat up. Through the corridor window, I could see the back of the policeman standing guard.

The knowledge of my responsibility tortured me. The drab waiting room was an appropriate setting, I thought, for such a depraved person. The walls, ceiling, and furniture breathed out a stale smell of cigarettes so strong that I could hardly breathe. Only one of the two dim lamps worked. The torn leather cushions on the sofa had been picked at by generations of nervous relatives and friends until the cushions appeared ready to yield to the coiled springs beneath. The edges of the wooden benches had all been worn round, the varnish darkened by a patina of dirt.

When Tony entered, carrying coffee and donuts, I declared: "It's all my fault. Tomorrow morning I'm going to confess. I sold the gangsters' whiskey."

Tony sat down and drank his coffee before he spoke. "So what's the big deal?"

"But that's why they want to kill Daddy."

"Don't be silly. You found some whiskey and you sold it. Everyone else is making money on whiskey."

"It was all my idea." I had already worked out my confession. "I needed the money for college."

He got up and began to pace back and forth in the waiting room. He stopped in front of me. "Don't lie to me." His voice was harsh, accusing. "The Clovers told me exactly what happened. The whole idea was Cleo's from the beginning to the end."

His vehemence frightened me. "Cleo isn't responsible. She's—she's not responsible. I should have stopped her."

"No one stops Cleo when she wants to do something."

"For God's sake, Tony, Cleo is sick in the head—"

He grabbed my arms with his hands and shook me. "Don't use that language." He sounded like my mother.

"What's wrong with you? Cleo is not normal."

He released me and sat down. He put his hands to his face, rubbing the skin violently. "You just don't understand her."

I turned toward the window and stared out. I could see Little Traverse Bay and the lake beyond in the distance. A quarter moon was setting on the horizon of the lake to the west, casting a path across the water. A dawn breeze ruffled the surface of the great lake.

Tony spoke very slowly. "If you confess, it'll all come out. They'll go after Cleo."

"But she's sick, everyone knows that."

"Maybe she's not so sick."

"Since when are you such an expert on my sister?"

"The Clovers give her a lot more credit than you do. You'd probably get her tossed into an institution where she really will go crazy and you'd go to jail. What good would that do?"

"I deserve to be in jail."

"And does Cleo deserve to be locked up too?"

"That isn't the question."

Tony glared at me. "What a stubborn brat you are!" He leaped up and began to pace back and forth. "You just want to be noble or something."

"That's not fair."

"A heroine."

"I'm not like that," I replied, my voice fading.

"You've got a choice. It's your conscience." He walked from the room.

For the rest of the day I anguished over our argument. Tony's proprietary air toward Cleo upset me. Now I was jealous of both my sister and of Tony: each of them had supplanted me with the other. Grudgingly I admitted to myself that a confession to the authorities could only harm Cleo.

In the end, I said nothing about the whiskey that Cleo and I had sold. When it came time for my father and Cleo to leave the hospital, I told everyone the family was going to California for a vacation so that the invalids could recuperate safely. Mother and I closed up the house and the store. Late one night, with Tony's help, we moved my father and Cleo to the gardener's cottage on the Warburg estate. The police, relieved to have the family off their hands, convinced the doctors to agree to the plan. The next morning, Mother and I had set off for Detroit in Tony's car.

*

After calling Tony at the estate, I went upstairs. I found that Mother had meticulously laid out our clothes for the morning—hats, gloves, smart dresses beautifully ironed, and high heels. She surveyed her preparations with a satisfied smile.

"Just remember, Momma, we're here to tell the truth."

I lay awake that night looking at the shadows upon the ceiling cast by the muted street light in front of the rooming house. I marveled that I had forced my will upon my mother and here we were, three hundred miles from home, in a strange rooming house, on a strange street, in a strange city.

I thought again about my argument with Tony in the hospital. He had accused me of trying to be noble, a heroine. He had been wrong. I inherited Cleo's life without asking for it. By now, though, caretaking had become a habit. If, as Tony maintained, Cleo was not as ill as we assumed, then who was I? An idea that had lurked in my mind for months became frighteningly clear. I didn't believe in myself as a separate person. Without my sister to guide, I had no function. As I tried to absorb this knowledge, I began to understand Tony's anger at me. I remembered his figure pacing back and forth across the ugly hospital waiting room, while outside the window of the hospital, the quarter moon cast its path across the ruffled surface of the lake. How passionately he had declared that we didn't understand Cleo! And how proudly, at seven years old, he had protected me; he had become my guardian at camp! Had he been wounded by life and unhappy even then, in need of a weaker creature to validate his life? I had followed after him and worshipped him, just as Cleo had this summer.

I tossed about uncomfortably as I imagined Tony watching over my sister's life. Just before I fell asleep, I recalled the brilliant shock as *White Lightning* exploded into pieces. Behind that conflagration, my childhood faded into dim shadow.

On Saturday morning Mother and I stood together in front of the mirror in the downstairs hall of Sadie Abrams' rooming house. I hardly recognized this person in the mirror dressed like an adult in hat and gloves and a stylish dress. If I had been alone, I would have retreated upstairs and crawled back into bed. But there beside me, my mother primped quite contentedly. When she had finished, she turned and straightened my hat.

I set out beside my mother to walk to the synagogue. The houses, the lawns, gardens, the awning-covered porches, the large apartment buildings stood like stern sentinels on either side of our path. I had entered an entirely different world, a heavier world of brick and cement and pavement, built to last forever. Even the warm damp air was thicker than the air of my countryside. There were handsome trees but no forests, grass but no fields, and no lakes at all. I gasped, unable to catch my breath in the strange atmosphere. The feeling was not entirely unpleasant. As we walked along, the exotic landscape began to appear more attractive. My fear remained, but now it was mixed with anticipation. I had launched us into an adventure of my own making. I was going to put myself in danger in order to repair a wrong.

My rising spirits were shattered when Mother declared, "You might as well know right now, Rebecca, that I have no intention of confessing anything to the mobsters. Or apologizing."

"Why start protesting when we're almost there?"

"I don't want you to have any false hopes of me down on my knees, begging those bums."

"Momma, it's a matter of Daddy's life."

"I simply exaggerated a little. How can I admit to such men that I . . . exaggerated."

"Exaggerated? You lied."

"Well, I fibbed a little, that's no reason to kill a man. You can tell them all you want about you and Cleo, but I'm not going to say a word about myself. It's too demeaning."

"Aunt Maureen and Uncle Sy warned you. You just wouldn't listen. And then the way you carried on this summer—" I stopped, afraid that I had gone too far.

My mother clamped her mouth shut and walked on in silence. As she walked along the boulevard she weighed her sin against her husband's. She knew whose sin was worse. Her thoughts on the subject were noted meticulously in her diary.

My father had confessed his adultery to her one night in the hospital room he shared with Cleo. Mother had been dozing in the chair between Father and Cleo. My father's voice had awakened her. She had tried to get him to sleep but he had insisted upon talking. "You're always saying that I never talk. You have to listen." He had spoken in a rush. "That first time you went to play tennis with Charles Kuhn and didn't come back for dinner—well I made love to Sonny that night. We went swimming down at her beach—and, and it just happened." My mother had stared at my father. The dim night-light had barely illumined his features. She had felt she'd entered a nightmare, but my father had leaned toward her and seized her hand. "Sonny and I were very close when we were young. And, well, it was like unfinished business between us. I lived at her house—on two occasions. I was in love with her back then, I guess. Or thought I was. But, of course, it wouldn't have worked out. I'll explain when I have more strength, but I wanted you to know. It's nothing I would ever do again. Sonny understands that." His voice had faded. He had released her hand and had immediately dropped off to sleep. It was as much as he had ever said at one time since she had known him.

The phrase he had used to describe his adultery, "unfinished business," had stunned my mother more than the unbelievable transgression. It rankled her even now as she walked toward the synagogue. Somehow, such a ridiculous explanation made him seem more guilty—as if he didn't regret what he had done. Since his confession, her rage had come and gone. She could not imagine any more formidable rival than Sonny Kuhn: fair, athletic, Germanic, aristocratic, very rich. Could Henry have been secretly longing for this woman all these years? Had he counterfeited his ardor for her, Arabella, simulated his reticent adoration? His betrayal had been working at her, undermining her feeling for him. To the betrayal, she had begun to add his every fault through the years. Every day, his stature had shrunk a little. And now Rebecca expected her to confess all sorts of things to a crude gangster in order to save Henry's life. She strode on, furiously debating with herself.

I could barely keep up with my mother. I was afraid that we had confused the landlady's directions, but I kept silent, not wanting to provoke further argument. Finally, I spoke up. "Mother, are you sure we're on the right street?"

"Of course I am," she muttered and continued on, pulling away from me. "I was born in this city."

Ahead I saw a building unlike any other we had passed. It rose above the street like a great, beached ark. A bank of wide steps flanked with polished brass rails approached the facade of stone and stained glass windows. A few well-dressed men, women, and children climbed the stairs and entered one of the three pairs of handsomely carved wooden doors, each twenty feet high. I approached the steps and stood on the sidewalk gaping up at the noble edifice. Mother, lost in thought, walked on.

"Mother!" I called out. "We're here."

She stopped and turned. "I told you I knew where I was going." She stared at the building for some time without moving. She drew in a breath and spoke sharply, "Well, we might as well go in." She took hold of my elbow in a firm grasp and propelled me up the steps toward the high doors.

THIRTY-THREE

IN THE FOYER, THE ushers directed us to the balcony. The cantor's voice filled the great hall. A row of green marble-like columns supported the vaulted ceiling. On the carved wooden platform in the front, men in black robes, ornamental black yarmulkes, and white tallises led the prayers. Daylight streamed through the stained glass windows, bathing the hall with mild yellow light. The sparse congregation sat widely spaced on long, curved wooden-benched seats cushioned in green velveteen.

My mother looked around and sat down, shaking her head. "No one worthwhile."

"Why aren't there more people?" I asked.

"Everyone who's anyone is away on summer vacation." She picked out two prayer books and pointed out the proper page in the service. To my surprise, she began to follow along with the prayers.

Although I had grown up hearing my father pray aloud in Hebrew on holidays, the full-voiced song of the cantor thrilled me, as if I had been transported to an exotic eastern land. My mother, murmuring responses, seemed quite at home. The Eternal Lamp burned with a red glow over the ark containing the Torahs. The congregation stood in reverence every time the ark was opened to reveal the scrolls containing the words of the Five Books of Moses. The sight of the Torahs made me think of my father. This was his house of worship. He had his tickets to come here in September carefully propped up on his study desk so that he could see them every day. I realized with annoyance that the synagogue didn't feel like my house of worship at all. I knew that I was Jewish and that was the end of it. My father's piety had always been his alone; I had been left to share only our difference from our neighbors.

Feeling disloyal toward my beloved father, I scanned the audience. "Do you see the Greensteins, Momma?"

"With my eyes? I can hardly see the prayer book."

"How did you know then that there was no one worthwhile?"

Mother continued to pray.

Then I noticed that there were only men on the platform. In fact, there were almost no women on the main floor of the synagogue. "Why are all the women and children up here in the balcony?"

"It's a custom from the past," mother replied absently. "The synagogue is the men's place. The home is ours."

And the law? I asked myself. Is that just for men? When I had come home from grade school with my lessons on the Declaration of Independence, the Constitution, and the Bill of Rights, my father had placed those documents within the tradition our people had begun thousands of years ago. Repeating his words with pride, I had stood in front of my classmates and claimed the importance of Judaism which had given law to the world on those Torah scrolls. And here in the place where the ancient sacred scrolls of the Jews were kept, I had been relegated to the balcony. Weren't those laws mine also? I thought of my father yearning for a son. And what about the officials who allowed Beechams and Roadhouse 31 to thrive? And even the gangsters who flourished and destroyed at will? All men. Who owned the law? I asked myself. I was very angry now—at all those superior guardians of the law, at those brutal gangsters who flouted it, and particularly at my father whose life I had come here to save.

I excused myself and went down to the foyer where the ushers were still handing out prayer books and tallises for the men who had not brought them. I approached one of the ushers, a bent, elderly man with a face of gnarled and leathery skin.

"Excuse me, sir," I said, "but do you know Carl Greenstein?"

The usher peered into my face. "Carl Greenstein?" His eyebrows lifted and a kind smile spread across his thick lips. "What would a nice young lady like you want with Carl Greenstein?"

"Is he here today?"

"You know what curiosity did to the cat?"

"I have business with him."

"Today is *Shabbos*, Miss. No business. Have I seen you here before?"

"I'm from out of town and I have to talk to Mr. Greenstein."

The usher drew me to a corner of the foyer and leaned very close. His teeth were stained with tobacco and his breath was sour. "Let me give you a piece of advice, Miss. I wouldn't have anything to do with Carl Greenstein."

"It's a matter of life and death."

"It generally is with him."

The anger which had driven me from the balcony evaporated. Only fear remained. But I couldn't run away now. "If you would just point him out to me."

"Don't you have parents?"

"They sent me."

"With such parents, who needs enemies?"

"Please."

The usher stared into my eyes and then shrugged. "Well I can point, but that doesn't mean that you'll get close to him. He doesn't come to *schul* alone."

He led me inside the synagogue and pointed out a group of men seated in the left front section. There were empty seats around them. All the men, except one, kept looking about suspiciously. "Greenstein's in the middle, wearing a white yarmulke," said the usher. He turned away, handing a prayer book to a latecomer.

I lingered a moment and then walked quickly down the side aisle to the first row where I sat down. I grabbed up a prayer book and opened it, pretending to follow the service. After all, I told myself, they can't kill me right here in the middle of the synagogue. It took me some time before I had courage enough to peek around behind me. Now I recognized the man in the white yarmulke, Carl Greenstein, just as the usher had said, the same man who had sat next to us at Beechams. This morning his face looked calm, at peace as he concentrated upon his prayer book. With his curly black hair, dark brows, and dimpled chin, from certain angles he was almost handsome. But there was something odd about the shape of his head, emphasized by the smooth flesh around his bulging eyes and small mouth, and the alert, sudden movements of his head. He resembled one of those neat, upright dinosaurs in my schoolbooks—vegetarians, I thought, hopefully. Then he looked up.

For a moment, the gangster's eyes caught mine. His gaze was mild, reproachful—as if he wondered why I wanted to bother him. He seemed to enter my mind without my permission and examine the contents. I couldn't turn away. The gangster made a slight motion of his head and resumed his prayers. Two of his companions got up. I recognized onc of them, the very short, fat man who had raised such a commotion at Beechams about the reservation. The men moved toward me. I turned toward the altar and gazed at the red glow of the lamp. I gave myself up to that lamp and the scrolls over which it burned. The short, fat man seatcd himself directly between me and Carl Greenstein. The other man seated himself next to me.

"You got a problem, Miss?" muttered the man sitting next to me.

"I want to talk to Mr. Greenstein."

"Mr. Greenstein don't like to be disturbed when he's praying."

"Will you tell him that Henry Bearwald's wife and her daughter want to talk to him?"

"That's all you got to say? A lot of people want a lot of things."

Now I turned to the man, tears moving down my cheeks. "Tell him it's a . . . a plea, a plea for mercy."

The man, very pale and thin, with a pockmarked face, and a red scar running from one ear up his cheek, looked alarmed. "All right, all right, you don't have to cry about it. Just wait here, Miss, and don't make any sudden moves, please." The man leaned back and whispered to the short fat man, who turned and whispered to Carl Greenstein.

I waited. Soon a message came back. "Mr. Greenstein will be glad to talk to you and your mother. One o'clock at The Cream of Michigan on 12th Street. You know where that is?"

"I can find out."

"One o'clock! It's closed on the Sabbath, but the owner is a friend. Knock on the side door. And be on time. The boss gets very hungry after praying." The man got up, but then remembered something. He bent down, his mouth close to my ear, his whispered voice intimate, almost paternal. "And for Christ's sake, don't bring any weapons."

*

As we walked toward 12th Street, my mother scolded me for taking matters in my own hands. "Why didn't you wait for me?"

"You left it to me."

"Well, this time I'll do the talking."

"As long as you tell the truth."

I walked along, my arms clasped around myself as if I had a stomach ache. I kept looking around, expecting to see Carl Greenstein's thugs following us.

"Are you feeling sick?"

I did not answer. I regretted my whole plan of forcing Mother to confess. Now I had put her in danger too. But I was afraid to meet the gangsters alone.

In her diary, Mother stated that this interview was one of the most important acts she had ever undertaken. As she walked, she wondered just how she would approach Carl Greenstein. She did not believe he would harm her or Rebecca. Henry was his target. But even if she confessed her lies as her daughter demanded, even if Rebecca displayed Cleo's medical records, she doubted whether the gangster would believe her. Perplexed, her resentful thoughts turned once more toward her husband. How could an upright man like Henry commit adultery and call it "unfinished business"? What a peculiar thing to say. Especially after he had refused to make love to his own wife for months.

She noticed that I continued to clasp myself as we walked. "Please don't walk like that. You look like an invalid, or something. Let your arms free and breathe deeply." She put her arm around me, straightened her back, and marched us along the boulevard. If it was necessary, she decided, she would do battle with the dragon.

And then she thought that perhaps the gangster might want to bargain for her favors—like in a movie. She still had her looks. It was an old story: the virtuous wife gives up her honor to save her husband. Her body for Henry Bearwald's life. Carl Greenstein wasn't all that bad looking—in good shape, too—strong, self-assured, a talker, probably. If she wanted to save Henry, she might have to sacrifice herself—against her will, of course. Henry had committed adultery solely for his own pleasure. She, at least, had a higher purpose. It would serve Henry right. And, who knows, it might be interesting.

Twelfth Street was quite deserted because of the Sabbath. Mother knocked on the side door and we were let in by the short fat associate of Carl Greenstein. After looking through our purses to make sure we had no weapons, he threw out an arm in a gesture of command. "Come on ladies," he said, and led the way to his boss, sitting at a table set for three. Carl Greenstein rose and held out our chairs. He was not a tall man. His movements were economical, controlled, self-confident. His suit fit tightly over his body, displaying muscle and bone. His white, starched shirt gleamed; the gold rings on his fingers gleamed.

As I sat down I began to speak. "Mr. Greenstein, my father, Henry Bearwald—" I wanted to present our case and to leave as soon as possible. I reached into my purse to pull out the medical files on Cleo's illness.

"After lunch, young lady, after lunch." His yellow eyes glittered, holding me in their gaze. "I had no idea what a gorgeous mother you have."

Mother inclined her head at the compliment and beamed at him. "Actually," she said, "I remember you quite well, Carlie, when you played basketball with my brother."

After that Mother and the gangster spent the lunch recalling old times in the neighborhood. They seemed quite cheerful, as if they had been close chums in their childhood. I kept reminding myself that this was the man who had sunk our boat and almost killed my father and my sister.

Finally, when the lemon meringue pie and coffee arrived,

I could no longer contain myself. "Mother! Will you please explain about Daddy."

"It turns out that Bella and I knew each other at the old Hannah Schloss Center."

"Mr. Greenstein, you tried to kill my father."

"I'm afraid that's true, Carlie," said Mother, sighing sadly as if she regretted bringing up something that might distress him.

"The two of you got the wrong party. I wouldn't hurt a fly."

"Oh come on, Carl," said Mother.

"All right, then. We'll talk. But no accusations, please."

Greenstein, Mother, and I sat drinking coffee, politely discussing my father's supposed crimes against the Purple Gang. I explained the circumstances of Cleo's discovery of the boat at Running Shoal, her renovation of the boat, and our sale of the whiskey. I brought out Cleo's medical records and showed them to the gangster. I described her illness and her obstinacy.

"Your sister may be crazy," he said, "but that don't make your fairy tale true. There you were riding around in the boat, like you owned it—and selling our whiskey. I mean, Capone got very angry at us."

My mother's voice rose. "Henry had nothing to do with your goddamn whiskey or your goddamn boat. Anyway, the boat is gone, blown to pieces, and there's no more whiskey—my crazy daughter sold it."

"Quietly, Quietly, Bella. Just don't try to play me for a sucker. You were sitting there in that boat. And you told exactly why you were there to my wife, bragging all about your husband's lousy operations."

"She was lying, Mr. Greenstein. Tell him, Momma, tell him!"

Carl Greenstein and I looked at Mother. She turned away. She pressed her nails to her forehead and flung her head back. "I exaggerated."

"Momma!"

"I fibbed. I lied. I was bored with our life so I made up a story. I wanted Maureen and Sy to think my husband was enterprising, brave, smart, and fearless. The truth of the matter," she paused for some time, "Henry is just a small town storekeeper." Mother blushed and buried her face in her hands. "But he's a good man."

Carl Greenstein stared sternly at Mother. "Then you should have been satisfied with him."

This remark took my mother and me by surprise. She looked at Carl Greenstein and then at me. She was silent for a minute and then said, "Who's to say what people should feel?"

The gangster threw up his hands, summing everything up, "That's just like a wife." And that was the end of it. Carl Greenstein actually believed us.

THIRTY-FOUR

THE WEDDING TOOK PLACE in late September. The Warburgs insisted that our family spend the weekend before the ceremony at the estate. We had a second floor wing to ourselves. From one side of the suite we could see down a cleared alley to the lake; from the other we looked upon the kitchen garden and the graceful gatehouse—a long, narrow structure of timber and fieldstone.

I woke very early Saturday morning and watched the dawn break over the mist-shrouded gatehouse, its steeply pitched shake roof capped with an eight-sided dovecote thrusting toward the sky. At first I heard only the gentle, insistent cooing of the doves. Then, moment by moment, I began to make out the birds entering and leaving their tiny arched doorways. I must have fallen into a doze then. When I woke, sparkles of light shone from the dew-soaked lettuces, cabbages, and tomato vines in the kitchen garden. I shut my eyes and shook my head, expecting the unfamiliar landscape to disappear.

After all, the summer had ended. The resorters had departed. *White Lightning* no longer existed. Mother and I had settled matters with the Purple Gang. Once more we were the Bearwalds of Charlevoix, Michigan. It was time to resume our morning walks toward our daily work, Mother and Father in the lead, me lagging behind with Cleo clinging to my coat. As I sat at the window waiting for the day to begin, I tried to convince myself that the events of the spring and summer had been a dream from which we would suddenly awaken and take up our normal lives as shopkeepers in a small, northern farm and resort town. It was simply a matter of seeking reasonable goals, I argued, hoping to dispel the mystery that had dislodged us from our familiar life.

But it was no use. When I opened my eyes, the kitchen garden, the gatehouse, and the dovecote, bathed in the first light of the sun, looked even more solid. My family and I remained enchanted by those forces which had beset us this spring and summer. Our imagination had not created *White Lightning* or the Purple Gang or that absurd childish world of our summer visitors who lured all four of us into its traps. The summer colony of Charlevoix and the Purple Gang were not dreams—or even cinema creations as my father charged. Under the masks of wealth and crime lurked ordinary humans like us and our fellow townspeople. The crooks and the rich simply lived by different laws. Or perhaps they lived without laws. When we stumbled into their anarchic worlds, our lives had been overturned. We could not restore our old habits. We had changed—each of us. History does not double back.

At lunch on Saturday, my father announced that the Warburgs had agreed to help finance a branch of our store in Florida.

Mother looked at him in disbelief.

"It's no joke," said Father with a smile to the Warburgs. He then went on to explain. During his convalescence, the Warburgs, who ran their own enterprises as a couple, had been kind enough to show a great deal of interest in his business. When he mentioned my mother's idea of opening a branch of our store in Florida, Hortense Warburg adopted the idea with enthusiasm, insisting that the store specialize in exclusive Women's Wear.

"A specialty branch?"

"Women's apparel," declared our hostess, "only the very best, designer clothes. It's one of my pet dreams. I've always admired your taste, Arabella, and when Henry mentioned the venture—why Jack and I jumped at the opportunity."

"We've worked out the financial arrangements," said Father. "But you'll have to look them over."

"You want me to run an exclusive women's shop in Florida?"

The Warburgs nodded. Mother's eyes and mouth opened wide in amazement.

I was overjoyed. Now, at last, I thought, my parents would be reconciled. Mother would have achieved everything she wanted—and all because of my father.

But as I watched, I could see that she was not nearly as happy about the prospect as I thought she should be. My father, too, seemed somewhat restrained. The two of them excused themselves from the table and took a long walk through the grounds of the estate.

As the afternoon passed, I caught sight of them strolling about. Sometimes they stopped, standing very close to one another, looking into one another's eyes. I waited anxiously for them to embrace. At other times they drew away from one another to such a distance that I only saw one or the other through the trees. For once, I noticed, my mother was not the only one who talked. That gave me hope, for my father's silence had always been her chief complaint. If Father was talking today, they would surely renew their love for one another.

Toward five o'clock, I came upon them seated on opposite ends of a wooden slat settee by the tennis court, looking at the court although there was no one playing. Both of them sat back listlessly, slumped over as if they had just completed an exhausting task.

"Are you all right?" I asked.

They turned to one another. Mother nodded. Father took a deep breath. "Your mother and I have decided to lead separate lives." They both looked stricken. I sat down between them and took hold of their hands in each of mine. "Your mother will be moving to Florida to open the new store and to run it. I'll stay here in Charlevoix."

I let go of their hands and clasped mine together.

"It was a mutual decision," said my mother.

"We don't quite know how to tell Cleo," said my father.

We all sat there staring at the tennis court. Father finally stood up. "Shouldn't we go in and get dressed?"

Mother looked at me and then said, "We'll stay out here a little while."

Father bent over and kissed my forehead. He hesitated a moment, smiled uncertainly, and then went off toward the house.

"You look so miserable," said Mother, throwing an arm over my shoulder. "It's not all that bad."

"I—I thought—I thought that at last you'd be—"

"Satisfied. Right? Isn't that what Carl Greenstein said: that I should have been satisfied with your father and not try to make him into something else?"

"Well, hasn't he been wonderful? And now the new store? The Warburgs? Isn't that enough?"

Mother looked out at the empty court. "Carlie Greenstein was right," she said in a low, brooding voice. "But so was I. After all, feelings have no logic. Most marriages are simply accidents—they aren't sculpted in marble. If we made you stay in Charlevoix," she said, trying to explain her dissatisfaction, "instead of going to Ann Arbor—how would you have felt for the rest of your life? It's not so easy to lay your dreams to rest, is it?"

It took me some time to find a response. "I guess it's just been a bad year for us all."

"No, no, not just this year. Becky, my marriage to your father . . . I wasn't ever certain about it. Who knows what would have happened if Cleo—?" She was silent for some time and then spoke vehemently. "Still, I'll tell you this, I've never betrayed him. You may think otherwise after this summer, but that foolishness on the North Side was just silly socializing, flirtation. All

Charlie Kuhn ever did was to talk, talk, talk. And I can tell you I enjoyed hearing a man talk for once."

"Maybe you and Daddy—"

She put her fingertips on my lips.

We walked back toward the house, our arms about one another's waist.

I slept badly and woke feeling both hope and despair. Luckily, I was kept busy the whole morning with the caterer from Traverse City and the florist from Petoskey, neither of whom had serviced such a grand event. Mrs. Warburg, Mother, Cleo, and I had to help set the tables, prepare the hors d'oeuvres, and arrange the many floral arrangements. Mr. Warburg and my father dealt with the beverages which the stablehands would serve. Before we knew it, the automobiles were driving up the long circular drive past the tennis court and gatehouse and discharging their passengers. The wedding party had just time enough to slip upstairs to dress before the door knocker fell.

It was strange to hear the murmur of voices, laughter, and the tinkle of glasses as the grand house below filled with the people of our lives. Mother, Cleo, and I dressed together. Mother, afraid that Cleo would fall into one of her fits, kept losing things—her brush, one of her shoes, and then her purse. I was distracted too. It was Cleo who managed to get us ready and out onto the landing of the staircase in time for the first strains of the string quartet's music.

The wedding took place on the verandah overlooking Lake Charlevoix. It was a traditional Jewish wedding with a *chupah* arch composed of white orchids, a rabbi from Traverse City in a long black gown, and a cantor all the way from Cheboygan. The men of the wedding party wore striped trousers and morning coats. The women wore gowns of white organdy and lace in the Empire style. My father's family, the Bearwalds from Detroit, attended, as did Sonny Kuhn. When I saw my father greet Sonny, I realized that their dance together at Sonny's party early in the summer had been much more than an accidental meeting of old acquaintances. It was only in Paris that I came to know of his love for her. The Lefkowitzes appeared with Seymour's intended and Cynthia's fiancé. The town was well-represented: the Clovers and their children, the Weyriches, the Snows, the Morrises, the Tollivers, the Hayes family, the Nears, Patty Kelley, Mrs. Thrush, her sister Amelia, back from the Dordogne, and a number of my friends.

My mother, who marched down the aisle with the Warburgs, resembled a slender, urgent black swan between two tall, drab cranes. For the first time in many years, she appeared to be happy. Still, in her expression, in the tilt of her head, she had not lost that quality of restless yearning so essential to her beauty.

I don't know how I managed the stairs and the long aisle over the flagstones of the crowded terrace. During the entire march to the altar, I thought of my mother. I had come closer to her in the last two weeks than at any time in my life. As I approached the flower bower through which I could see the intense blue of my Lake Charlevoix, I realized that Mother and I would never again experience such intimacy. Within hours, the two of us would be launched into new and very separate lives. Seeing Mother standing there next to the Warburgs, her dark head held high, her olive skin glowing, I had the sense that the years she had spent in Charlevoix from the age of eighteen to forty had been a detour from her true destiny, an interlude. Her black eyes were fixed on me with pride, but already, I thought, with some detachment.

"Most marriages are simply accidents," she had said, "they aren't sculpted in marble." It was not a happy statement to recall as I faced the smiling, black-robed rabbi under the flowery *chupah*.

It seemed an eternity before Father appeared with Cleo on his arm. She floated down the aisle wearing the antique wedding gown which had been created by the most skillful hands of 19th century Bremen for the wedding of Mr. Warburg's grandmother. My father, mother, and I were astonished at the Warburg's joyful acceptance of Tony's decision to marry my strange sister. Their sophisticated understanding of their son's weaknesses and Cleo's strengths was my first glimpse of the power of true culture in forming a flexible imagination, unbound by hypocrisy or prejudice. When we all gathered to discuss the marriage, they stunned us by declaring that they considered Cleo a savior of their family and of its future. In fact, their vision proved to be true.

Cleo's dark head, framed in gauzy lace, her neck, her back, remained utterly erect while her long, graceful strides hidden under folds of silk carried her forward as if she were sailing over water. My father had to trot to keep pace with her. Her gaze was fixed on Tony with such intensity that I could see it took all of his will power to keep from rushing to meet her.

Once my father handed Cleo to Tony, they clung to one another, their dark eyes flashing with happiness. As the maid of honor I stood next to them and could sense the passion they felt for one another. In their black-and-white wedding costumes, they gleamed at the center of the ceremony like a flame. Perhaps, I thought, this was a marriage that would be sculpted in marble.

During the ceremony, I gazed down the long alley of hardwood trees to the lake. A cold spell had begun two days before and the leaves had turned brilliant reds, yellows, and oranges, framing the bright blue of Lake Charlevoix. I wanted to cry and to laugh, for today I would be leaving my beloved home.

EPILOGUE

From the moment of Cleo's first awakening in the hospital, she had understood that everything would turn out well. She had lain there, hovering in and out of consciousness. Dim figures in white came and went, bending over her, holding her wrist, gently thrusting pills into her mouth, propping her up, laying her down, turning her over, sticking needles into her arms and backside. She allowed everything to happen. The fury had receded, the explosions, the pain, the loss.

While the soft light from the windows brightened, darkened, and brightened again, Cleo dreamed of the buoyant white hull dancing over the waves, thrust forward by powerful twin screws. Until her discovery of that lamed craft in the shallows of the great lake, her life had passed in a kaleidoscope of images, laced together by fear. Every day in her life, Cleo had awakened in terror that all would be taken from her: the house, her father, her mother, her sister, the lakes, the sand, and the forest. But then she had rescued the craft and nursed it to health.

Most of all, Cleo responded to need. To exist, the world of sand and water and rock and leaf needed her sight, touch, smell. But people—one had to beware of their needs. They possessed malicious intentions which she felt and avoided. Machines had no intentions. They had a logic and organization that she could eventually master. Each machine had its own problems which she could feel, hear, smell—a friction, a short circuit, a worn bearing, all spoke to her. Machines didn't run wild for no reason at all. Machines could be relied upon.

Lying in the hospital bed, Cleo rehearsed each mechanical task in the restoration of White Lightning, *until its return to the water. Back in its element, her creature cavorted over the depths, sensitive to the wind and the waves and, most of all, to her controlling touch. Cleo's hands spread out, flexed, hovered in the air. In the tips of her fingers, she carried the texture of wood, steel, copper, and iron that made up the entire, magical boat. Cleo felt blessed by the craft that had ordered her life.*

The shattered fragments of Cleo's mind gathered and dissolved in wild patterns of memory. For a moment, the terror returned. Sweat started up out of her forehead; froth came to her open lips; her muscles tensed for the frenzy which was about to seize her. The black hull rose up and assaulted her craft with a crash. Her father and mother disappeared into the waters; her sister clung to the stanchion. Before her eyes the flames consumed her beached craft. As she lay cradled in her sister's protective embrace, the final, the expected explosion obliterated all.

In the dim hospital room, Cleo's normal breathing resumed, her body relaxed. The destruction of White Lightning *had fulfilled her worst expectations. Her joy had been too great. The wreck, no accident, came as expected punishment. When the nightmare of her daily terror had taken substance under the brilliantly colored sky, a flood of relief washed over her and she experienced an astonishing state of repose.*

A hand held Cleo's hand. A presence hovered by the side of the bed. Her eyes fluttered open to see the dark tousled hair, the dark brows, the deep black eyes, the flashing white teeth of that creature who had emerged from the depths, gleaming, wet—her fish. She narrowed her eyes, pretending to be asleep again. The needy young man waited for her to rise up and recognize him. She would keep him there a while longer. The boat was gone. Cleo knew that. In her bones and flesh, she had felt her handiwork fly to pieces. She didn't have to worry about it anymore. Her gleaming young man remained, waiting. He was waiting today, beside her under the bower of flowers.

She had felt the young man's need from the very first time they had danced in the garden. Her sister thought she needed Cleo. Her father and mother thought they needed Cleo too. She was fond of all those who clung to her. When she caught the needy creatures of the world, coherence settled down upon the chaos.

By today, the day of their wedding, this young man had become her fondest possession. His luster had not dimmed like fish when she caught them. On the beach where she had found the boat, she had felt his body burrowing into hers, his skin wet, his hair wet. The fish had landed and snaked its way deep into her. In relief the two had clung together to find contentment.

The young man needed Cleo more than any of the others now. She would salvage him as she had salvaged the boat. He would take Rebecca's place. He would cling to Cleo and confirm her existence. Perhaps she would lose him too. Sooner or later, she knew that she would lose all that she loved. But she had gained strength in that knowledge. Once she admitted loss, there would be order. There would always be lamed creations for her to revive. Her own power would simply grow.